FORTUNE

FORTUNE

STEEL BROTHERS SAGA
BOOK TWENTY-SIX
HELEN HARDT

WATERHOUSE PRESS

*To the woman—I wish I remembered your name—
who gave me my first tarot reading at a writers
convention fifteen years ago. You said some things
I needed to hear, and you sparked my interest in the
practice. I've never forgotten you!*

PROLOGUE

Brendan

Ava is in better spirits after a few hours of baking. She's helping us in the front now, taking orders, making sandwiches. It's nearly eleven, so I need to get home, clean up, and get ready to open the bar around noon.

I tap her on the shoulder.

"Yeah?"

"I have to go."

"Yeah, I'm surprised you stayed this long." She grabs my hand. "But thanks so much, Brendan. It was great having you here, and we needed the help today."

"I'm happy to do it."

"If you need help at the bar tonight, I'm your girl."

"I might take you up on that. That way we can spend the evening together, even if we're both working again."

"I'd love it, to tell you the truth. You can teach me how to mix drinks."

"Absolutely. Just show up whenever you feel like it."

"I will."

I give her a quick kiss on her lips and then I leave the bakery, but first I make sure to remove the apron and hairnet. Enough people saw me looking like that today. I'm not taking that look into public.

I walk a few buildings to my own place, and someone's waiting for me at the back door.

He looks vaguely familiar, but I can't place him. He's average height, nondescript brown hair, dark-blue eyes. Nice enough looking.

"Can I help you?" I ask.

"Yeah. My name's Pat. Pat Lamone."

I've heard about Pat Lamone. Some of the Steels have mentioned him in passing. Apparently he has a history with the Pike sisters, and it's not good.

"We're not opened yet, Pat."

"I'm not here to have a drink. I need to speak with you."

"What about?"

"About my grandmother. Her name is Sabrina Smith. That's the name she goes by, anyway."

"I'm afraid I don't know what you're talking about," I say.

"Her real name is Dyane Wingdam."

"Again, doesn't ring a bell."

Another figure approaches us.

"You have got to be kidding me," I mutter.

It's Ryan Steel. Ava's father.

Here, at the bar, with me.

"Ryan," I say, "what can I do for you?"

"You can let me in."

"I'm kind of in the middle of something here."

Ryan glances over at Pat. "I know who you are," he says.

"Yeah, I know who you are as well, Mr. Steel."

"So you think you're a Steel relative?" Ryan says.

"Yeah. That's what I hear, anyway."

"Okay," I say. "Clearly this has nothing to do with me, so if you'll both excuse me—"

"Actually, this *does* have something to do with you," Ryan says. "Could we go inside, please?"

"For God's sake." I unlock the door and hold it open. "After you."

Ryan Steel and Pat Lamone traipse into my bar via the back door.

What the hell could this be about? Pat Lamone, who thinks he is related to the Steels, and Ava's father. Both here, at my bar, wanting to talk to me.

Pat about his grandmother, who I don't know from Adam. And Ryan about… Well, I can only guess it has something more to do with those messages Ava and I received.

"All right. I've been helping Ava all morning at the bakery, and as you can see, I'm filthy. I need to take a shower so I can open this place by noon." I glance at the clock on the wall of the bar. "That gives the two of you about three minutes. What the hell do you want?"

CHAPTER ONE

Ava

By two o'clock, it's time to close the bakery. I leave Maya and Luke to clean up. I want to go upstairs, get a shower, and go over to the bar to help Brendan. As soon as I get back to my apartment, though, my gaze falls on the card still sitting on the table.

The tower.

Why haven't I put it back into the deck?

But I know why.

I've been waiting. I've been waiting, hoping I could get some kind of positive thought from it.

But nothing has worked.

Not kneading bread this morning.

Hell, not even sex with Brendan last night.

I'm still getting nothing but negative feelings from the damned card.

Mother.

My mother.

I haven't drawn *that* card—the empress—but why is my mom at the forefront of my thoughts?

Because the card sometimes can mean illness, and I'm so very afraid she'll get sick again.

Ill, and about to celebrate her twenty-fifth anniversary.

Plus, she hasn't gotten back to me with her interpretation of the message. She said she had apps that could help decode it. I certainly don't have access to the kind of software my private investigator mother has, but I can easily find apps that may help.

I head to the sink, wash the flour off my hands. Then I fire up my laptop and type *Darth Morgen*.

Nothing I haven't already seen.

My mother was thinking it might have a code embedded in the letters, with each of the letters standing for a different letter. I could start with R. It appears twice so it would be the same letter.

But what if it's not?

What if the code isn't letter per letter but based on something else?

Like perhaps, the letter that precedes it?

God, where to start?

I rise, grab a pad of paper and a pen from a drawer in the kitchen, and come back. I write the letters on the piece of paper.

Darth Morgen.

Then I start playing with them.

What if these letters were rearranged? What if it's one big word? Or several small words? An anagram?

I play with it for a little while, finding several three-letter words and writing them down, but then I laugh.

"What the hell are you doing?" I say out loud. "If you're looking for anagrams, find an anagram maker online."

I don't know why I didn't think of this before. I was so overwhelmed with my developing feelings for Brendan and with the cards that were telling me all kinds of horrible things.

Plus, I was depending on my mother. My ex-cop private-investigator mother who said she could decipher it.

But she kept putting me off.

I do a quick search, and I come up with something called *Dante's Anagram Maker.*

Good enough. I type in all the letters of *Darth Morgen.*

I close my eyes.

I'm not sure why, except something tells me that if I look, I'll be faced with even more of a mystery.

So I sit for a moment, eyes closed, and I inhale. Exhale. Inhale. Exhale.

I'm still waiting for some kind of positive feeling about the tower card still sitting on the table.

If I can get something—anything—that isn't a negative feeling...

Then I can open my eyes.

And I can begin to solve the mystery of Darth Morgen.

So I wait.

I continue breathing.

But it doesn't work.

Nothing works.

I open my eyes, and I glance at the screen.

And the word I see fills me with hope.

It's not my mother.

My mother's not ill. I feel that, and I know it in my heart, and I breathe a sigh of relief.

Because the first word on the list of anagrams for Darth Morgen is...

Grandmother.

Grandmother?

I wrinkle my forehead as I stare at the word.

I never knew my paternal grandmother. She died before I was born.

My maternal grandmother died when I was a little girl, but I do remember her. She had the worn and wrinkled face of a woman who was once a classic beauty before hardships had taken their toll. Diamond Lee Thornbush, who named her only daughter Ruby. My mother used to make fun of her mother's—and her own—gemstone name, but I always thought they were pretty.

Grandma Didi—what Gina and I called her—used to read to us in that raspy voice of hers. It wasn't until later that I learned her voice was the result of decades of smoking. She eventually quit, but the damage was done. She succumbed to lung cancer.

She gave me the pink silk scarf with the daisy pattern that I use to wrap my tarot deck. I glance at it on the side of the table. It helps me feel close to the feminine energy of my ancestors.

My ancestors on my mother's side, that is. But my other grandmother? Daphne Steel?

I never knew her, so it's impossible to feel any energy from her. Perhaps if I had more information about her, I could feel something, but my father doesn't talk about her, and neither do my aunts and uncles. At least not to me.

Dale, Donny, and Henry were all alive when she died, and so was Brad, although he was only a few months old. None of them ever met Daphne Steel, though. She was in the hospital, a mental health facility. She had broken away from reality years before.

Again . . . that's all I know. That's all any of us know.

It's odd, really. Mental illness. I've never understood it, which I suppose is a good thing. Like I said, my father doesn't talk about it. None of them do, but it must've gone through their minds at some point. Might they inherit the mental illness from which their mother suffered?

None of them have, thank goodness. Perhaps what she suffered from wasn't genetic.

I should ask Aunt Melanie. She's a retired psychiatrist and therapist, but already I know she won't go into any detail with me.

Daphne Steel is not someone our family talks about. Funny that it never occurred to me to wonder why.

She *is* my grandmother. She and Diamond Thornbush.

This message must be referring to one of them. Except that Brendan and his family got the same message.

An anvil settles in my gut.

This can't possibly mean . . .

I shake my head vehemently.

No. No way. We're *not* related to the Murphys. Not at all. The idea forces nausea up my throat. Brendan and I . . .

No.

Just no.

The message must have some different meaning. Or it refers to a person other than a grandmother.

I scan the list of words the anagram maker came up with, narrowing my eyes.

grandmother
arm thronged
armed throng

Darth monger
grander moth
grander Thom
mar thronged
marred thong
month regard

I stop. The list goes on for what seems like forever.

Most of the anagrams make no sense at all, but I can't help a slight giggle at *marred thong*. Grander moth? No. Darth Monger? Possibly a *Star Wars* reference. I could ask Dave, but already I know I won't.

It's got to mean *grandmother*.

When I saw the word, a feeling of relief settled in me—a relief that my own mother isn't ill. That was my fear—that Mom and Dad were acting strangely, keeping me at arm's distance, because Mom's breast cancer had recurred.

That fear dissipated instantly when I saw the word *grandmother*. My mom isn't ill. This message refers to a grandmother, and not my mother.

My grandmother?

Or Brendan's?

Or someone else's?

I know for a fact that both my grandmothers are dead, so it can't refer to my grandmother.

Or . . . perhaps *is alive*, as part of the message, is also part of the anagram.

I return to the anagram maker program and type in *Darth Morgen is alive*.

Again, hundreds of results.

The first is *alderamin oversight*.

I have no idea what *alderamin* means, and when I search the term, I find it's the name of the brightest star in the constellation Cepheus and an anime series.

No. My gut again. It's telling me that *is alive* means what it says. Darth Morgen is the puzzle ... and I figured it out.

It's *grandmother*.

But *whose* grandmother? Both of mine have been dead and buried for years. Decades, in the case of Daphne Steel.

What can it possibly mean?

And what does it mean in relationship to the tower card that I drew, which left me with goose bumps of fear dashing over me?

My mother isn't ill.

My grandmothers are dead.

I assume Brendan's are as well.

So *what* does this mean? And why did Brendan and his father get the same message?

I don't know.

But with everything that's going on? With my family keeping things from me and the rest of the cousins, and with the cards I've drawn ...

I'm frightened.

Very, very frightened.

CHAPTER TWO

Brendan

"I'd prefer to speak to you alone," Ryan says.

"So would I," Pat agrees.

"Fine. That gives you a minute and a half each." I shrug. "Which one of you wants to go first?"

"Since you're dating my daughter, I'm going first." Ryan walks to the other side of the bar.

"You got a problem with that?" I say to Pat.

"I suppose not. Would it matter if I did?"

"I don't fucking care what either of you has to talk to me about. Stay here. I'll be back in a minute and a half." I follow Ryan to where he has settled himself at a table near the pool tables in the back of the bar.

He sits, his hands clasped in front of him. I take the seat across from him, and he meets my gaze. His light-brown eyes seem troubled. I've seen the look. Every bartender has. Eyes slightly narrowed, a gaze that seems unfocused. It's the classic look of someone who's distressed about something. Could be anything. I've heard it all from across the bar. But Ryan Steel isn't troubled because of a work conflict, a bill he can't pay—he's a Steel after all—or a doomed relationship.

"Spill it," I say. "You're down to a minute and fifteen seconds. And if this is about your mandate that I take you to my safe-deposit box in Grand Junction for those documents, it's not happening. I don't take orders from anyone. Not even Ryan Steel."

In truth, the documents were in a safe at my parents' house, but I brought them to my place after Thanksgiving dinner. I lied to Ryan yesterday, but he's still not getting them. I expect an argument, especially since I laced the last part with sarcasm, so I brace myself.

"It's not about that."

No argument? Color me surprised.

"Good." I check my watch. "A minute and ten seconds."

"You may want to give me more time than that."

"I've got somebody else waiting to see me, and—"

"That guy waiting to see you is . . ." Ryan rubs a hand over his forehead, his knuckles white. "Fuck, this is so fucked up."

Tell me something I don't know.

I massage my temple. "Is it? Maybe you ought to tell me what's going on first, and I'll make my own assessment."

Ryan shakes his head, raking his fingers through his gray-speckled brown hair.

Ava doesn't look a lot like him. She looks more like her mother. But in his distressed expression, I see Ava. I see the same look Ava had as she was looking at those tarot cards after doing the reading for both of us.

Something is bothering Ryan Steel, and it concerns his daughter. Why else would he be here? The only link Ryan has to me is Ava.

"Is Ava all right?" I ask.

"Seems you would know better than I would."

Interesting choice of words for Ryan. Sure, Ava and I are dating, but she's very close to her family. Has she been avoiding them? Not from where I'm sitting. It's Ryan and Ruby who have been avoiding *her*.

"I just left her, and she's been..."

"Been what?"

I pause a moment, searching for the word I want. "Concerned," I finally say.

Concerned is too tame a word, but I owe Ava some discretion.

"God..." Ryan drums his fingers on the table.

I meet his gaze head on. "What is troubling her? She doesn't know, so how could you?"

"God... I can't even believe this is happening."

My patience is down to a nub. "What? *What* is happening?"

He lets out a heavy sigh. "My mother. My fucking mother."

"Daphne Steel?"

He doesn't say anything.

Sweat emerges from Ryan's brow. "I watched her die. I watched her fucking die, Brendan."

"I'm sorry."

"That's not what I mean."

It's not what he means? Then I'm done feeling sorry. "You're down to about thirty seconds, Ryan."

He rises. "How do you feel about my daughter?"

"I'm fond of her."

"Are you in love with her?"

I drop my jaw. Am I that obvious? Hell, I think I just admitted it to myself. I'm sure not going to tell her yet because she's not ready to hear it.

"What if I were?" I ask.

"Then I'd expect you to protect her. Protect her from everything."

Another odd comment. Of course I'll protect Ava. But isn't that his job as well? He's her father.

I clear my throat. "I'm happy to do that anyway."

Ryan wipes his forehead with the palm of his hand. "Why is this all happening now?"

"Since I don't know *what* is happening, I can't answer that question, Ryan."

He regards me with an expression I can't quite read. "Look. I need to speak with you privately. And I need more than ninety seconds. When can we talk?"

"I've got to get the bar open, and it's going to be a busy day. People are here for the holiday, and they're going to want to come into town to have a drink. Ava's going to come over to help me tonight after she closes the bakery."

"She is?"

"Yeah. I helped her this morning at the bakery, and she's going to return the favor this evening. And then tomorrow is your party."

Ryan sighs. "I know. That damned party."

Damned party? This is his twenty-fifth wedding anniversary. A milestone.

"It's your anniversary."

"I know. I love my wife, and she loves me. Twenty-five years. Twenty-five years we've been happy. And now..."

I narrow my eyes. "You're *not* happy?"

Ryan strokes his fingers over his upper lip. "No, we are."

"Is Ruby okay?"

"Yes. As much as she can be."

Uh-oh. My thoughts go to Ava, to her fear that her mother's cancer has returned. "Ava's concerned. She thinks her mother might be sick again."

Ryan shakes his head. "God, no. She's fine. She just had a mammogram a couple of months ago."

"Thank God. Ava drew some cards and—"

"The cards said her mother is sick?"

"The cards don't tell Ava anything. She uses them for—"

"Yes. For guidance. I know."

"Right. Anyway, she's worried about her family. That Ruby may be sick. You should go over to the bakery and tell her that Ruby's fine."

He shakes his head. "I can't. I can't face my daughter right now."

My nerves jump. "What are you *not* telling me, Ryan? What do you mean you can't face your daughter? There's a big party in your honor tomorrow night, and your daughter—both of your daughters—will be there. Ava's helping plan the party with Marjorie and Jade."

"I know that. God, I love my wife and my daughters more than anything."

"I don't think anyone has ever questioned that. I know Ava hasn't."

"Ava. Gina. They're *going* to question it. They're going to question both Ruby and me."

My nerves again. I can't stomach the idea of Ava in any kind of pain. "Why would they do that?"

"God..." He shakes his head again. "I've got to get out of here. But you and I do need to talk. Find an hour for me. Tomorrow morning. Got it?"

I want to resist. I hate taking orders. But this concerns Ava. "Fine. Tomorrow morning. How about ten o'clock here at the bar?"

"Good enough. I'll be here." He whisks out of the bar

through the back way.

Where Pat Lamone still stands, waiting to talk to me.

I sigh as I walk toward him.

CHAPTER THREE

Ava

I force myself to walk to my bathroom to take a shower. Once I'm clean and dressed, I sit back down at my table and stare at the tower card.

The tower. So solid and erect and unyielding, yet one strike of lightning brings it down.

Does that mean it's built on shaky ground?

Does that mean *I'm* built on shaky ground?

Is there some falsehood in my life that I've been ignorant to all this time?

A bolt of lightning can represent so many things.

Illumination.

Destruction.

Or a combination, which is what I fear.

Something illuminating and also destructive.

My skin goes cold, and I brush my hands over my upper arms, trying to ease the chill. It doesn't work.

I need to get my mind off the card and whatever it may represent, so I grab a jacket, wander outside, and walk around town. Most of the smaller shops are closed for the long Thanksgiving weekend, but the tattoo shop is open.

I walk in.

Cyrus Banks is alone in the shop. He's sitting behind the counter reading a magazine. For a tattoo artist, he only has a little ink himself—if you call both arms being sleeved with tribal designs a little ink. The rest that's visible is completely clean. He's wearing a black T-shirt, and his sandy hair is shoved inside a Colorado Rockies ball cap.

"Hey, Ava."

"Hi, Cy. Did you give Kiki the day off?"

Kiki is Cy's receptionist and a budding artist herself. Unlike Cy, she is covered in ink, and she's the only other woman in town who colors her hair pink—neon in her case, though. Not a soft honey pink like mine.

"Yeah. The whole long weekend, actually. She went to Grand Junction to be with her folks for Thanksgiving."

"What are you doing open?"

"I don't have any appointments today," he says. "But I had some paperwork. It's done, and I thought I'd hang for a while. You never know who might want some ink on a Friday, though I do need to close soon." He smiles.

"I've been thinking a long time about getting a tattoo. I love the ones you did for Brendan Murphy."

"Those were a while ago. Like ten years."

"That long ago?"

Ten years ago, Brendan was twenty-five years old. I was fourteen. Funny. The age thing doesn't bother me much anymore. Not at all, really. Brendan and I—we just seem to fit.

"You think you could design something for me?" I ask.

"That's what I'm here for. What do you have in mind?"

An image comes to me. Seriously, it just pops into my head as if by divine intervention.

"I always thought I'd want something related to the tarot," I say, "but I've changed my mind."

I close my eyes for a moment, visualize the tattoo on the back of Brendan's left shoulder.

A triquetra—the Celtic symbol for mind, body, and spirit. Balance.

The tower being struck by lightning.

Destruction.

Illumination.

I open my eyes. "I want a triquetra...being struck by a bolt of lightning."

Cyrus widens his eyes. "That's an interesting concept."

"The triquetra symbolizes balance," I say.

"Right. Which is why the lightning striking it is an interesting concept. Is the balance being disrupted in your life?"

Cy is a tattoo artist, not a therapist. Why is he asking me such a question? Still, I feel compelled to reply.

"I don't know. But I think I need to be reminded on a daily basis to expect the unexpected. Not to get too comfortable with the status quo. You know what I mean?"

I expect him to ask me more questions, but instead—

"That's a powerful image. Let me make some quick sketches for you and see if anything speaks to you."

I nod and take a seat in the waiting area. I grab one of his books and leaf through it. He's done some beautiful work.

He looks up from his sketch pad. "Where do you want the tattoo?"

"The middle of my upper back. Or the middle of my lower back. Or do you have a better suggestion?"

"Depends," he says. "If you want it to remind you of

something, it's better to put it in a place you can actually see. You can't see your lower back or your upper back without looking in a mirror."

"Interesting. That's a good point. Maybe the inside of my forearm."

"You'd certainly see it then, but so would everyone else when you're wearing short sleeves. Something to think about as well."

"I don't mind if other people see it."

"Just remember, if other people can readily see it, they will ask you about it."

I rub my chin, pondering. "You're thinking of things that I never considered."

"That's my job. You need to think about these things before you permanently ink yourself. If it's something just for you, put it in a place where only you can see it. If it's something for someone else, put it in a place where they can see it."

"Why would anyone tattoo themselves for someone else?"

"A lot of people do. For example, a man will get his wife's name tattooed somewhere on his body. That's something he wants her to see and others to see as well. Which is why you see it on an upper arm a lot."

Interesting. I've racked my brain for years trying to find the right image, only to have it come to me like an epiphany. But I never considered the almost more important aspect— where to put the ink and why.

"Sometimes, someone wants to tattoo something for others to see that they won't see. Those are the tattoos you see on the back."

"And what if only *I* want to see it? And I don't want others to? Where would you put it?"

"That's a tougher one. But a lot of women will put it on the top of one of their breasts. Or on their hip."

Hmm. I don't like the breast idea. Besides, if I wear something low-cut... Who am I kidding? I never wear anything *that* low-cut. Still...the hip seems like the better choice.

"I like the idea of my hip. Let's do that."

"Good. That way, no one will see it unless you're wearing a very low-cut bikini. But you'll see it every day when you get in and out of the shower."

"That sounds perfect."

"That gives me a good idea of the size you're looking for. Give me a few more minutes."

I nod and get back to leafing through his tattoo book. Such gorgeous work, and so colorful. A phoenix rising from the ashes, a raven with flaming wings, an American flag with starbursts all around it, and then...

Brendan's sea warrior, dated ten years ago. The colors are still as vibrant now. Cyrus is a true artist.

I continue leafing through the book, and then I grab another, peering out the window.

My jaw drops.

My father...

My father is walking by.

"Cy, I'll be right back." I exit the tattoo shop.

"Dad?"

He turns. His cheeks look...hollow almost, and his color is a little off. But those two things aren't what strikes me the most. It's his eyes. His gorgeous caramel-colored eyes are... unfocused. Distraught.

"Ava. Shouldn't you be baking?"

"I'm done for the day. What are you doing here in town?"

"I had an appointment."

"With whom?"

"With . . . no one you know."

I cock my head. "Dad, I know everyone in town. We all do."

"What are you doing in the tattoo shop?"

"Talking to Cy about getting a tattoo. Why didn't you answer *my* question?"

Dad clears his throat. "Ava, what I do is not always your business."

"You're my father," I say. "You look . . . Are you all right?"

He gazes down at the concrete sidewalk. "I'm fine, Ava."

"And Mom?"

He looks back up. "She's fine. She's not sick again."

"I know that. But how . . . Wait . . . How did you know I was worried about that?"

My father's cheeks are ruddy. Is it from the brisk fall day? Or have I embarrassed him?

"What's going on, Dad?"

"Nothing's going on, Ava. I've got to get back to the ranch. See you tomorrow for the big party." He continues down the street.

I want to run after him. Yank on his arm and force him to tell me what's going on.

But I don't. I don't because his anniversary party is tomorrow and I promised my family I would let everything go until after the celebration.

I won't ruin this milestone for my mother and father.

But already I know where my father was.

The only other person who knew I was worried about

my mother being ill again is Brendan. Why would my father be talking to Brendan? Why would Brendan be talking to my father?

I will find out.

I head back into the tattoo shop.

Cy hands me a piece of paper. "How do these look?"

I widen my eyes. "Wow. These are magnificent."

Three images. The first is a triquetra in basic black with a lightning bolt poised above it, also in black. In the third, the triquetra is completely cut in half by a jagged line, presumably representing the lightning.

But the second... The second is exactly what I had in mind. The triquetra is severed by the bolt diagonally. Perfect. Just as I saw it in my head.

"I recommend the second one for a tattoo on your hip. It's a little less intricate, and we can make it smaller."

"Yeah, I totally agree. All of them are beautiful, but the second image does stand out to me."

"I can do the triquetra in whatever colors you want. The lightning, of course, should be either black or yellow."

"I want the triquetra in plain black, with the lightning strike in yellow. I think that will be the most vibrant. The most... I can't think of the right word, but it's what I want."

He smiles. "That's what matters. Do you want to make an appointment?"

"Can you do it right now?"

"I wish I could, but I have to get home. Lavinia's making wild rice and turkey soup, and we're going to eat it this afternoon and watch football together."

"Okay. Why don't I stop by after the holiday, and we'll set up an appointment?"

"Sounds good. See you, Ava."

"See you, Cy."

I walk out of the tattoo shop and head straight for Murphy's bar.

Brendan owes me some answers.

CHAPTER FOUR

Brendan

"Can we do this another time?" I say to Pat. "I really have to go up and get showered so I can open the bar."

Pat shoves his hands in his jeans pockets. "I suppose so."

"Good, because honestly I don't know anything about your grandmother. I'm not sure why you're here, anyway."

"I'm here because I got this really weird email."

"Oh, God," I say.

"Yeah, and it said to ask the Murphys." He pulls a crumpled piece of paper out of his pocket and hands it to me.

I scan it quickly. It's the same cryptic message that came to me through Hardy's office.

When echoes navigate down yonder, many anchors destroy ideas generated about neglect.

Still clear as mud. "What address did this come from?" I ask.

"Nothing I recognized, and when I tried to email them back, it bounced."

I shrug. "I don't know what the hell this means. But I got the same email, and so did the Steels."

He raises his eyebrows. "The Steels?"

"Well, Ava Steel. And mine didn't come directly to me."

"What does that mean?"

"It came to the sheriff's office. Did this one come to you?"

He nods. "It came to one of my email addresses, but not the one I commonly use."

I cock my head, eyeing him. "Why would you have more than one email address?"

"I opened a few email accounts when I was researching my relationship to the Steel family."

"Again . . . why?"

He shrugs. "It seemed like a good idea at the time. I didn't want to bog down my regular email address with all this stuff."

He's lying, and I've lost all patience. "And for the third time . . . *Why*, Pat?"

He drops his gaze to the floor for a moment. "I don't know. Hell, I don't know which end is up these days. All I know is that the woman in the hospital is the only link I have to who I truly am. Her name is Dyane Wingdam, and my mother is her daughter, Lauren Wingdam."

"And where is she? The daughter? Er . . . your mother?"

"I don't know. I only recently found out her name. I haven't been able to track her down. She may be dead for all I know. But her mother, Dyane Wingdam, using the name Sabrina Smith, is alive. Alive and sedated and in the hospital."

"And you're sure this woman is related to you?"

"I'm sure."

He doesn't offer any more explanation, and I don't push. First, I don't have the time. Second, I'm not sure I care.

Except I *have* to care because Ava and I got the same message.

"Look, I feel for you. I really do. But I have to get moving. The bar is going to be hopping this afternoon."

Pat shakes his head. "Come on. You've got to know something. Why would they send me to you? What is your connection to the Steels?"

"Christ." I rub my forehead. "This isn't a secret, so go talk to my dad. The only connection we have to the Steel family"—other than my dating Ava, which I keep to myself. Hell, he may know already—"is that my great-uncle died at Bradford Steel's wedding fifty years ago."

Pat's eyes widen. "He did?"

"Yeah. He OD'd. But the guy never used drugs in his life, according to people long gone now. My dad always wondered why it happened, but he was never able to trace it to the Steels." I hand the hard copy of the email back to Pat.

He shoves it in his pocket. "All right. I'll talk to your dad. Where do I find him?"

"Didn't you used to live here? His name is Sean Murphy. He used to run this place, and he lives here in town. Now if you'll excuse me, I have to shower and get the bar open."

"Yeah, okay."

He shuffles out the back door, and I'm ready to lock it when—

"Brendan Murphy, what the hell is going on?"

Ava.

Right at the back door of the bar.

And damn, she's as beautiful as ever, all fiery and angry—about what, I have no idea.

So I smile, hoping my pearly whites can defuse whatever's got her going. "Hey, baby. What can I do for you?"

Her full lips are turned down into a frown. "Don't you 'hey, baby' me."

I raise my eyebrows. So much for the patented Brendan

Murphy smile. "What's wrong? I thought we left things great between us today."

"I thought we did too."

"What's going on, Ava?"

Man, is she pissed. If she were a volcano, she'd be spewing hot lava on me right about now.

"You tell me," she demands. "You're the only one I told about my fear that my mother was sick again, but I found my father walking along Main Street today, and I stopped him to talk to him. He told me point-blank that my mother's not ill."

Uh-oh.

But Ryan came to me. I didn't go to him.

"Ava..."

"I won't stand for secrets between us, Brendan. I like you. I like you a lot, and I like where this relationship is headed, but no secrets. I've got enough family members keeping secrets from me right now. I don't need my boyfriend keeping secrets."

She's so beautiful. So worked up. My cock is already reacting.

She's also right.

So I tell her that.

"You're right."

Her blue eyes go wide for a second. Is she surprised that I agree with her? But she goes back to her fiery stance in a flash.

"Good. Now spill it. Spill it all."

I may never get to the shower, but Ava's more important than anything else. "Okay. Your father asked me to keep this a secret—"

"What?" Her arms clamp across her chest. "My father asked *you* to keep a secret from me?"

"Just let me finish, Ava. Please."

She glares at me.

I sigh. "I take confidentiality seriously, but you mean much more to me than your dad does. Although . . . I don't want to get on *his* bad side either."

"Right now you're about to get on *my* bad side, Brendan."

"Ava. Baby." I take her hand, forcing her to uncross her arms, and then bring it to my lips and kiss the back of it. "Could we get through tomorrow night? Your parents' anniversary dinner? I promise after that I'll tell you everything."

She opens her mouth, and I brace for yelling, but—

"Why is everyone so concerned about this damned anniversary party?" she asks, this time in a normal tone.

I kiss her hand again, still reeling from the non-yelling. "I think because they want it to be a happy occasion. Twenty-five years is a long time, and your parents deserve this chance to celebrate."

"But they're keeping things from me. I feel . . ." She withdraws her hand, withdraws from me. "Something strange is going on."

I tip her chin. I can't leave her hanging. She deserves so much more. "I'll tell you this much, but you have to promise not to confront your parents about it until after the party."

She shakes her head. "I'm not going to make any promises, Brendan. I can't. I don't want to break a promise to you, so it's better if I don't make one."

There's that integrity that I love about her. "Fine. I won't make you promise. Your mother and father came to see me yesterday."

She drops her gorgeous lips into an O.

"They had a lot of questions," I continue. "About some information that I found under the floorboards of my apartment."

"You mean the birth certificate? And the lien?"

I nod. I told Ava about the lien her family trust holds on my property. I also told her about the birth certificate for William Elijah Steel.

But I didn't tell her about the deed, signed by Bradford Steel, transferring all real property to Ryan Steel, her father. I hate keeping that from her, but she's been so distraught lately over her family.

Fuck. I don't know what to do. "Will you trust me?"

She scoffs. "Trust you? After you've been keeping things from me? How the hell am I supposed to trust you?"

"I just figured it'd be best if I told you everything after the party."

"Brendan Murphy, you will tell me everything now, or I swear to God, I'll—"

I can't have this conversation. Not now. So I quiet her the only way I know how.

I grab her, pull her to me, and crush my mouth to hers.

Unsurprisingly, she keeps her lips clamped shut.

But I'm nothing if not persistent. I run my tongue along the seam of her lips, cup her cheeks, and within a few seconds, her lips part.

I kiss her with passion. With angry passion, but the anger is not directed at her. It's directed at her parents for keeping secrets from her. I'm not sure what those secrets are, but I know they're going to hurt Ava. For that I'm angry. So very angry.

She returns the kiss, melting into me, until—

She pushes at me, breaking the kiss with a loud smack.

"Damn it! Damn it, Brendan. I won't let you do that to me." She bites her lip, toys with her lip ring.

While my cock goes crazy.

"I thought you were different. But you're not. You're just like every other man out there. Out for one thing."

"Ava, I'm not." Though my dick begs to differ at the moment.

Ava's cheeks are pink. The kiss clearly affected her, but she swipes the back of her hand across her lips. "Right. I won't be kissed into shutting up, Brendan."

I feel like an idiot. What was I thinking? This is Ava Steel. "You're right. Kissing you was a mistake. I mean, it wasn't a mistake. I love kissing you, but you're right. I'm sorry."

She meets my gaze, and for a moment, I'm not sure which way this is going to go, until—

"Why didn't you just tell me?"

"Because…"

She sighs. "Brendan, come on."

"Because… I promised them I wouldn't. Plus, they said it might hurt you if I told you. And Ava, I would rather die than hurt you."

Ava's blue eyes change from angry to fearful in a flash, and she melts into my chest. "I'm scared, Brendan. So very scared that my family is in some kind of trouble. I don't understand why."

"I don't understand either, baby." I kiss the top of her pink head, inhale the woodsy peppermint scent. "But I swear to you, I will not let anything or anyone hurt you. I swear to you."

She gulps audibly as she looks up at me. "How? How can you make that promise? How, when the tower is falling?"

"The tower?"

"The card I drew earlier. I swear to God, I've never had such negative feelings from a card before, Brendan. I couldn't see anything good in it, and it scares me. It scares me so much."

I draw her into my arms. "What can I do for you?"

"I'm going to do something that goes against everything I believe in," she says. "I'm going to let you keep the secret until after my parents' party. Thank you for being willing to tell me at all, but it seems to be very important to everyone that this party be allowed to go on as planned. I've worked hard for it, and so have Aunt Marjorie and Aunt Jade. And I…" She chokes back a sob.

"It's okay, baby. Everything's going to be okay."

The words are automatic, and I want to believe them, but something nibbles at the back of my neck.

And I fear my words are a lie.

CHAPTER FIVE

Ava

With Brendan's strong arms around me, I almost believe his words are true.

I almost feel like the tower has no meaning.

I mean, what are tarot cards anyway? I don't believe they're the be-all and end-all of everything. Yet I do believe in my own intuition and the guidance of the cards.

And that feeling of foreboding... of impending doom...

It frightens me.

Grandmother...

What does it all mean?

Then the other message. The crazy one that makes no sense.

What does *that* mean?

Brendan kisses my forehead. "Baby, I wish I could stay here with you and help you through this, but I really do have to go shower and get the bar open."

I nod. "I understand. Can I come with you?"

"To take a shower?" He grins. "Absolutely."

Brendan takes my hand and leads me up the stairway to his apartment. His beautiful new apartment.

Paid for by Steel money.

Is it fair for me to ask him to violate a promise he made

when I'm keeping something from him? That my family paid for this new apartment?

God, none of this is right.

I will tell him. I'll tell him when he tells me everything after my parents' party.

Forty-eight hours. In forty-eight hours, we'll both level with each other.

And hope that our relationship survives.

"I saw Cy today at the tattoo shop," I hear myself saying.

"Did you? Did you finally decide on an image that works for you?"

"Yeah."

"Something from the tarot?"

I shake my head. "I chose a triquetra...with a lightning bolt going through it."

Brendan wrinkles his forehead. "A lightning strike through your balance? Why?"

"Because of the tower, Brendan. Because of the tower."

"The card you drew. Right. What does it have you thinking?"

I rub my hands over my arms. "You already know. It scared the hell out of me. Destruction. Hypocrisy. So much negativity. But that's not all."

"What else?"

"I think I cracked the Darth Morgen code. It's an anagram for *grandmother*."

He narrows his eyes. "My grandmothers are both dead. And aren't yours, as well?"

"They are. I don't have any idea what it means. I tried figuring it out several ways. But *grandmother* seems to be the solution."

"You sure?"

"Yes, I feel very sure. And I also know my mother is sure as well, and it means something to her. All it took was a simple anagram solver on the internet for me to figure it out. I was relying on my mother, so I didn't even think to do that until now. But surely it was the first thing that came up for her. In fact, she may have been able to read it when she first saw the message. That's how good she is. She will never ever convince me that she didn't have this figured out from the start."

"Sweetheart..."

"Why would she keep it from me? Is one of my grandmothers still out there? Still alive? Or does it refer to your grandmother? Is one of *them* still alive, maybe? And if that's the case, why is it such a horrible thing? It would be great if someone were still alive, right?"

"I suppose so. But I know both of my grandmothers are dead."

I sigh. "Yes. I know. Mine too."

"What about the other message?" he asks. "Apparently Pat Lamone got that one as well."

"Pat Lamone? That guy who thinks he's related to our family?"

"One and the same. He got that same message, that weird one about *down yonder.*"

"Do my parents know about that message?" I ask.

"They do. I showed it to them on Thanksgiving Day."

Part of what he promised not to tell me. But why? "And they didn't seem to know what it meant?"

"I think your mother knew. She got a strange look on her face. She tried to keep a poker face, but her eyes widened slightly. I believe she knows what it means."

"And my father?"

"I couldn't get a read on him. He seemed confused."

"But my mother's a detective..."

"Right."

"Did my father ask you about that message when he came by earlier?"

"No, he didn't. We didn't really talk about much. I think there was a lot he wanted to say, maybe questions he wanted to ask, but I was in a hurry. I told him I needed to go up and get a shower so I could get the bar open. Which I still need to do."

"Right. Of course. You helped me with my work today, and I'm going to help you with yours. So let's get that shower."

"I hope you're thinking about joining me."

"Absolutely." I trail my fingers over his arm. "Believe me, I need something to make me feel good right now. And you, Brendan, always make me feel good."

He takes my hand and leads me to his bathroom. He peels off his clothes and throws them in the hamper, and then he undresses me.

This isn't going to be one of those raw and feral sessions, though that's kind of what I need.

When I stand naked before him, he just stares at me.

"You're so damned beautiful, Ava. I'll never tire of looking at you."

I open my mouth to tell him I'm not beautiful. That Gina's beautiful. That Diana and Brianna are beautiful. My mother is beautiful. But I'm not.

But the look in his eyes silences me.

And now, with him staring at me, his gaze raking over me with love and passion in those blue eyes, I feel beautiful.

I, Ava Steel, feel as beautiful as Aunt Jade. As Aunt Melanie. As Gina.

He trails a finger down my cheek, over the top of my breasts, and then he tweaks one nipple.

I let out a soft gasp as the sensation travels to my pussy.

I gaze at him—at his amazing big cock.

And I think...

No, I know...

I'm in love.

I'm in love with this man. I'm in love for the first time in my life.

I want to tell him, but I freeze. I can't make my lips move.

He turns on the shower, and within a few seconds, steam fogs up the mirror. He takes my hand and leads me under the warm water.

He brushes his lips against mine, and then he lathers my hair for me and gently massages my scalp. Once I'm completely rinsed, I do the same for him. His long, gorgeous red hair tangles between my fingers, and I love the feel of it slick with shampoo.

After we're both thoroughly cleansed, he leans down and kisses me gently and smoothly.

I open for him this time. Because this time, he's not trying to keep me from talking about something.

This time, he's cherishing me.

He's—dare I think it?—*loving* me.

He may not be in love with me. I'll have to live with that if it's the case. But I am in love with him. In love with Brendan Murphy.

Because I can't say the words, I say it in this kiss. I pour all of myself into this meeting of our lips—my heart, my body, my soul.

And I hope he feels what I'm telling him. What I'm telling him with this kiss.

He lifts me in his arms then and slides me down onto his cock.

I'm so slick and wet that I take all of him easily.

He's so strong, and he grips my hips, moving me up and down as we continue to kiss.

So complete, so full am I. I love the sensation, and I wish for a moment that we could stay in the shower forever. That the hot water would never run out and our skin wouldn't wrinkle up like prunes.

That we could just stay here—the water like the sun's rays shining down on us and keeping us safe.

That's what this lovemaking is. Safety. Comfort. I'm not pushing for an orgasm, so I'm completely swept away when it creeps up on me as a beautiful surprise.

I groan into his mouth as the climax shatters me, pulses through me, ending in my pussy and clamping me around Brendan's big cock.

He returns my groan, and he moves forward until my back hits the tile wall.

His thrusts become more urgent. More urgent, urgent, urgent, until—

"Fuck, yeah," he growls into my mouth.

As my orgasm subsides, I enjoy the feel of his, as he pulses inside my now sensitive core.

I love you, I say inside my head.

I love you so much, Brendan.

CHAPTER SIX

Brendan

As expected, the bar is hopping from about four o'clock on. Ava's an excellent bartending student, and within an hour, she's making our most popular drinks without any guidance at all.

Working alongside her makes me happy. I warm all over.

By six o'clock, we're both starving, so Ava goes up to my apartment to make us some burgers. She brings mine down with a smile on her face.

"I love that George Foreman grill," she says.

"It's a lifesaver for me." I bite into my juicy burger.

The evening goes on, and it only gets busier.

At around eight, Ava's sister, Gina, enters, along with the rest of the awesome foursome, Brianna Steel and Angie and Sage Simpson.

"Ava!" Gina shouts. "What are you doing behind the bar?"

Ava's right about her sister. Gina Steel is gorgeous—Ryan Steel in female form, with a lean but curvy body, simmering amber eyes, and long black eyelashes. Her dark hair falls nearly to her waistline.

Ava smiles. "Hey, G. The usual?"

"You can make my usual?"

"I can make almost anything. I've taken the Brendan

Murphy quickie bartender course this evening."

Gina lets out a laugh. "Maybe I should take it. I'm always up for a quickie."

Ava forces a look of amusement, though she's clearly not amused, and I'd bet Gina knows it.

"What's her usual, Ava?" I ask in an attempt to defuse the situation.

"You don't know?" Gina bats her eyes at me.

Ava's look of faux amusement dissipates at her sister's obvious flirtation. Actually, I do know her usual. Gina, along with the rest of the awesome foursome, always orders a cosmopolitan.

"I do," I say, taking care not to respond to Gina's flirting even in a platonic way. "Just wondering if Ava does."

"Cosmos, for four," Ava says. "And I know how to make them. Grey Goose okay?"

"Tito's for me," Gina says. "Grey Goose for the twins, and Ketel One for Bree."

Ava stares at her with one eyebrow raised.

Gina erupts into laughter. "I'm just kidding. Whatever vodka you have is fine."

"Grey Goose is the house brand," Ava says.

"Grey Goose is great."

"Okay."

I can't tell whether Ava's amused or angry—I'd say a mixture of both—but she makes the drinks in quick order.

"Put those on my tab," Gina says.

"Will do."

Gina and the rest of the awesome foursome take their drinks and head toward the back where the pool tables are. That's usually where they end up, especially when Jesse Pike and his bandmates are here playing pool—which they are. The decor in the pool area hasn't changed since my father purchased the place decades ago and put up posters of sixties and seventies rock bands.

"Looks like your sister has eyes for the band," I say to Ava.

"My sister's a big flirt, as you well know. She's never serious about any guy."

"Brianna is all over Jesse," I say, scanning the back area.

"Is she? That's an age difference for sure."

"Yeah, well, whoever she likes, Donny and Dale won't be happy about it."

"Why wouldn't Donny be happy about Jesse? He's marrying Jesse's sister."

"Surely you know that your cousin and Jesse Pike have a rivalry that goes all the way back to high school. Plus, guys are just guys, Ava." I laugh. "They don't like older men hanging around their little sisters. Which makes me very glad you don't have a brother."

"I have cousins who treat me like a sister. And yeah, I know about Donny and Jesse, but Callie told me she made them get over it."

"That's good," I say, "because Brianna looks pretty intent on nabbing Jesse's attention this evening. And I know about those cousins who treat you like a sister. I'm pretty sure Brock and Dave will be watching us like a hawk at your parents' party tomorrow evening."

"They can mind their own business."

"Sure they can. But they won't." I give her a chaste kiss on her rosy cheek. "That's just how they are. Overprotective, and it seems the Steels are even more so than most."

Ava smiles. "I'm kind of pissed off at Brock myself right

now. And Dale and Donny for that matter. And my father. And uncle. Hell, let's just put all the Steel men in that category. Whatever secrets they're keeping? I'm so done."

"Hey..." I finger a lock of pink hair. "I'm going to level with you about everything I know. You're the one who decided to wait until after the party."

Ava wipes the bar with a damp rag. "True enough. The party. But after that? It's open season."

I don't reply. I don't blame her. She's angry and she's frightened and she feels her family may not be who they say they are.

Speaking of family, the bell on the door jingles, and in walks my father.

I wave to him. "Hey, Dad."

He takes the one open seat at the bar. "Can you take a break? I need to talk to you."

"Not really." I gesture. "Look at this place."

"Tell you what. I'll stay and help you and Ava. Where are Laney and Marianne? Johnny?"

"Marianne went out of town for the holiday. Johnny's unstocking. Laney's waiting tables. She's back by the pool tables."

"Okay." He darts his gaze around and then lowers his voice. "Seriously. I need a few minutes of your time."

Something in his voice sends a chill through me. "All right. Hey, Ava?"

Ava walks up to us. "Hi, Mr. Murphy."

"Hi, Ava. Call me Sean."

"Okay. Hi, Sean."

I lay a hand on Ava's shoulder. "My dad needs to talk to me for a few minutes. You think you can handle the bar? I can grab Laney to help you."

Ava furrows her brow.

I can't blame her. She's sick to hell of all the secrets, and frankly so am I.

"Please?" I whisper in her ear. "He says it's important."

She shrugs. "I suppose I could take orders if Laney tends bar. There might be something that I don't know how to make."

"Good enough. I'll go get Laney."

I walk out from behind the bar to the back where Laney Dooley is taking an order from Jesse Pike and his friends.

"Hey, Lane, I need you behind the bar. Ava's going to take care of the tables because my dad needs to talk to me for a few minutes."

"Okay, no problem." She scribbles on her pad. "I'll get this order in for you guys, and Ava will bring it back when it's done."

Laney follows me, and Ava takes her place waiting tables.

"Okay, Dad," I say to my father. "I'm all yours."

"Let's go back to the office."

The office—which is the size of a small walk-in closet—is behind the bar in the kitchen, which isn't usually staffed. I do my paperwork upstairs in my place, so the office is pretty much storage right now—overflow from the stockroom where Johnny's unloading cases of liquor.

"What is it?" I ask.

"Why did you give that guy my address?"

"What guy?"

"Pat something. Lamone."

"I didn't. I said you were in the book. It's not exactly private information in a small town."

"Yeah, whatever. He came by to see me this afternoon."

"So?"

"He was a damned pain in the ass, Brendan."

"Why?"

"He kept asking me about some woman named Dyane Wingdam. I've never heard of her. And then he showed me the same message that you and I got through Hardy's office. The one that didn't make any sense."

"Wait a minute." My mind races. "This woman he's talking about is his grandmother, right?"

"That's what he says. He says he has DNA proof."

"The first message. The one about Darth Morgen. It's an anagram for *grandmother*."

Dad raises his eyebrows.

"Ava figured it out. It took her all of two seconds once she plugged it into an anagram maker on the computer."

"And her mother couldn't figure that out?"

"That's the point. Ryan and Ruby are keeping something from Ava. We asked Ruby for help with this over a week ago, and she just kept putting it off."

"Ruby Steel's a bright woman. No way she didn't know what was going on here."

"Right? I think the same thing . . . and so does Ava."

"That must be upsetting her."

"It totally is. She's not sure why her mother wouldn't help her solve these riddles."

"So Ruby probably knows what this other puzzle means too."

I nod. "I'm pretty sure she does."

"So the question is," Dad says, "why did this Pat Lamone fellow get the same message?"

"He thinks he's related to the Steels."

Dad cocks his head. "And is he?"

"Hell if I know. I believe he went to school here. He's around Callie Pike's age. Maybe Rory's."

Dad clears his throat. "So you would have graduated long before he did."

"Yeah. I don't remember him from Adam. I don't think he graduated anyway. They moved before or during his senior year. I might be wrong. I'd have to check with the Pikes. They'd remember."

Dad rubs his jawline. "So he might be related to the Steels. He has this grandmother of his in the hospital. And he got the same message that we and the Steels got."

"Right. The grandmother may be the key. Maybe this is referring to Pat Lamone's grandmother. The woman in the hospital."

"Maybe it is, but how does that have anything to do with us?"

"Dad, I just don't know."

"All right. You don't have any more answers than I do, I guess. Let me give your mom a call and let her know I'll be helping you at the bar tonight."

"I appreciate it, Dad. Thanks."

I head back out to the bar, and a few minutes later, Dad joins me.

"You know? It's good to be back behind a bar." He grabs a towel and wipes up some condensation on the counter.

"You want to take over?" I laugh.

"Are you kidding me? You're so busy here, I'm surprised you didn't call me before. Don't you have people on standby for when you get nights like this?"

"I have Ava now. She picked up things like you couldn't believe. She's smart as a whip, that one. Obviously gets it from her mother."

"You saying Ryan Steel's a dummy?"

"No, that's not what I meant. But Ruby has that puzzle-solving intelligence, and that's what Ava has. It's amazing how she can read those cards the way she does."

"Yeah, the cards. Your mom likes those cards." Dad's expression remains noncommittal.

"I know she's been to Ava for some readings. But Ava wouldn't talk about it."

"She shouldn't. It's probably very confidential."

Very confidential.

Absolutely right, and Ava has a lot of integrity. I'd like to think I do as well. I did promise Ryan Steel I wouldn't speak to Ava about what he and I talked about. But . . . some promises have to be broken. They have to be broken when the woman you love is at stake.

"How is Mom, by the way?" I ask.

"She's good." And again . . . Dad seems noncommittal.

"She hasn't . . . talked to you about maybe *not* researching your uncle again?"

He laughs, finally. "Oh, she has."

"That happened so long ago. I can't believe what's happening now could possibly be related."

Dad fills two pilsner glasses with beer from the keg. "It's a long shot, but I feel like it's connected somehow."

I open a bottle of Fat Tire and hand it to a customer. "It seems to be the only way we could possibly be connected to the Steels, for sure. But it was so long ago."

"Think about this, Brendan. If Ava's solution to the puzzle is correct, and it's telling her that a grandmother is alive, perhaps it *does* go back that far."

"But whose grandmother? Your mother and Mom's

mother are both gone. And Ava's grandmothers are also both gone."

"Which means maybe it's referring to this Pat Lamone's grandmother. I mean, why else would he have come to see you, and then me, about her?"

"He came because the email told him to. But I have no idea what any of that means or why we're even involved."

"Which is why I think it must have something to do with my uncle and his death at the wedding of Brad and Daphne Steel. That's our only connection to the Steels, son. The only one."

CHAPTER SEVEN

Ava

Watching my sister play pool is like watching a romantic comedy. Guys flock to her, and she gives them just enough attention so that they want her, and then she eases away.

She's never serious.

She likes to pick up men, have some sex, and then move on. It's her way. I sure didn't like her coy flirting with Brendan at the bar. That won't happen again on my watch.

I distribute the drinks and then dart my gaze to Jesse Pike, Cage Ramsey, and Dragon Locke.

The band.

Has my sister been with any of them?

They're all in their early thirties, and Gina's only twenty-two, so probably not. But I'm sure she'd gladly add them to the notches on her bedpost.

They're all incredibly good-looking, of course—especially Dragon, in a completely unique and dark way. I've never really been attracted to him—or any of them—in a sexual way, though. Not like I am to Brendan.

I can't believe I'm in love.

Gina and the rest of the awesome foursome are like Brock, Dave, and me. All the same age, so they were treated more as siblings than cousins.

Funny—they got the moniker the awesome foursome, while the three of us got Huey, Dewey, and Louie.

Of course, they *are* awesome.

All of them are tall, beautiful, and built. And all smart as anything as well. Gina is the artist of the group, Brianna's the rancher, and Angie and Sage are both interested in the culinary arts, like their mother, Aunt Marjorie.

They both look like Dave in female form except Sage's eyes are brown, like her mother's.

Angie is the quieter of the two, and Sage is just like Gina—a complete and total flirt. She and Gina are hanging all over Cage Ramsey and Dragon Locke.

So I'm not surprised when Angie walks up to me, her brown hair swept into a high ponytail, which somehow makes her eyes look bluer.

"Hey, Ava."

"What's up, Ang? Do you need a refill?"

Angie lifts her pink cosmo, which is still half full. "Not yet. When did you become a bartender?"

"This afternoon. Brendan came over and helped me at the bakery this morning, so I offered to help him tonight." I dart my gaze around the bar. "And he sure needs it. This place is packed."

"Friday nights are usually packed, but you're never here."

"The bar's not really my scene. But Brendan and I . . ." My cheeks warm.

"So I've heard." Angie smiles. "I have to admit, I didn't see that one coming."

"I didn't either, to tell the truth. But it's nice. It's really nice."

Angie looks toward the bar, where Brendan and his father

are working. "He's a lot older than you, Ava."

"I know, and it kind of freaked me out at first, but honestly? When I'm with him? There don't seem to be any years between us. It's so easy. And believe it or not, we have a lot in common."

Angie raises her finely lined brows. "Really? You and Brendan Murphy?"

"Yeah, actually." I feel myself getting a little bit defensive.

She shrugs with a smile. "Well, if you're happy, cuz, so am I."

I glance again at the other three of the foursome, who are flirting up a storm with the band. "What's going on with you guys?"

"Just enjoying our senior year. I've been dating a guy at school, but it's nothing serious."

"Oh?"

"Yeah, it's pretty casual. But it's more than Gina and Sage are doing. You know them, hopping from one guy to the next."

"Yeah, I know. What about Brianna?"

"She has eyes for one man and one man only." Angie gestures to Jesse Pike.

Jesse Pike, rocker extraordinaire.

"Yeah, I noticed that earlier. Or rather Brendan did. That's an age difference."

"Right? He's thirty-two and she's twenty-two. But that's still one year less than you and Brendan."

I can't help a laugh. "I guess you've got me there. I just don't see the two of them together. Jesse's a rocker. And Bree? A hundred percent cowgirl. She'll never leave the ranch."

"No, she won't. Besides, none of us has the heart to tell her that Jesse Pike has never once glanced in her direction."

"He seems to be glancing now."

"He's being nice to her, Ava. He always is. He's a good guy. But I think he sees her as a little sister."

"Yeah, probably because she's the same age as Maddie." I look over my shoulder, scanning the area. "Where is Maddie, anyway?"

"I don't know. I assume one of the girls invited her to come. She's kind of an honorary fifth member of the awesome foursome."

"Maybe she's doing something with her family."

Although, once I say that, I realize it can't be true, because Brock, Rory, Donny, and Callie have just walked into the bar, and trailing behind them is Maddie. Maddie, the youngest Pike sister, who looks a lot like Rory, with rich dark hair and dewy brown eyes. Maybe not quite as classically beautiful, but a close second.

She glances toward Gina and Sage at the pool table, and her lips turn down to a frown.

"Maddie just walked in," I say to Angie.

Angie looks toward the door. "Oh. Hey, Mads!" She gestures.

"I think she feels left out a lot with you guys," I say.

"I know." Angie's shoulders slump as a look of guilt mars her pretty face. "But the four of us are family. It's different."

"Yeah, I suppose so."

"Maybe you don't get it, Ava. You know, since you left the family fold and all."

"I didn't leave the family fold."

"Yeah, you did. You live in town, and you don't take money from your trust fund."

I dig my feet into the hardwood floor, feeling defensive. "I'm still a member of the family, and I love them all just as much as you do, Ang."

"I don't think anyone's questioning that. But you know . . . You're . . ."

"Different?" I give her the word. "I've always been different, even when I was *in* the family fold, as you like to say."

"Aves, I didn't mean to start a fight or anything."

I let out a sigh. "Sorry. I'm just a little defensive. Things are . . ."

"What? Things are what?"

I can't say any more to my cousin. The awesome foursome are the youngest of our family, the ones who are always kept in the dark. Everyone is way overprotective of them. I hold back a scoff. I'm only two years older than they are, and I'm so damned sick of the elders keeping things from me. Now I'm keeping something from Angie. It's all so ridiculous.

I sigh. "I'd better get back to the bar. I'll make my rounds in about fifteen minutes to see if you guys need new drinks."

Angie waves as I amble back toward the bar, where Brendan and his father are talking.

"Hey," I say. "What do you need me to do?"

"Just what you're doing, Ava," Brendan says. "Take orders from the tables when you need to, and when you're not busy, help me behind the bar."

I smile. "I'm actually having a really good time, Brendan."

"Are you?"

"Yeah. It kind of . . . forces me to get out and talk to people."

Sean, Brendan's dad, lets out a guffaw. "That's tending bar for you. You have to talk to people because they talk to you. We're honorary counselors. Therapists."

"Yeah, I see what you mean now. I think I've talked to more people today than I have the last month."

"You should talk more, baby," Brendan says. "You have a lot to say."

He doesn't know the half of it. Plus, he's got something to say to me ... after that damned party for my parents tomorrow night.

So much to say ... and so much to hear.

But not now. Not before the party. The sacred party.

Aunt Marjorie and Aunt Melanie both told me I need to talk to my parents, confront them.

But not yet.

Not until the anniversary party is over.

I've never been very good at compartmentalizing. But I'm determined to let this all go ... At least until Sunday.

Mom and Dad can have their party. It's important to them, and it's important to Aunt Marj and Aunt Jade, who have spent so much time planning it.

I paste on my smile, and I take the next drink order.

CHAPTER EIGHT

Brendan

The last customer finally leaves at the wee hour of three o'clock in the morning. Ava is still going strong. I'm not sure where she got that second wind, after getting up so early to start baking. But she can sleep in tomorrow. Rather...today. But not for too long, because she has to finish baking for the party, then head over to help her aunts prepare the main house, where Talon and Jade live.

A giant yawn splits her pretty face.

I smile. Everything she does makes me smile.

"What is it, about twenty-two hours that you've been awake now?"

Ava rubs her eyes. "Twenty-one if we're being accurate. And yeah, I'm definitely ready for bed."

"I'd ask you to sleep over, but you won't get any sleep if you stay with me."

"No kidding. And I'd invite you home with me... except..."

"The same thing," I say.

She nods and yawns again.

"Let me walk you home, then."

She nods again, and after she puts on her light jacket, I walk her out the back way and then three doors down to her bakery. I stay with her as she unlocks the door to the bakery, and then I walk in with her just to make sure no one's hiding inside. Once I determine that she's safe, I give her a searing kiss and then listen as her deadbolt clicks shut.

Then I return to the bar, lock up for the night, head up to my apartment, and flop down on my bed without even taking off my clothes.

★ ★ ★

I jerk upward in bed.

What time is it anyway?

The sun has already risen, and its rays stream through my window.

Why am I awake?

Then I hear it. The buzzing of my cell phone. It's on the kitchen table.

I rise, yawning and stretching, and get to the phone. It's not a number I recognize.

"Hello?" I say into the phone.

"Brendan. It's Ryan Steel."

Crap. I forgot I'm supposed to meet him at the bar at ten this morning. I still don't know what time it is.

"What can I do for you?" I ask.

"Tell me what Pat Lamone wanted."

I yawn and wipe sleep out of my eyes. May as well be honest with the man. "Can't this wait until we meet later?"

"It is later, Brendan. That's why I'm calling. I'm outside the bar."

Fuck. I stare at my phone. It's a little after ten. "I'll be right down, but just so you know, Ryan, before we go any further, I'm going to tell Ava everything."

"You can't." His voice sounds desperate.

"I can, and I will. I haven't told her this yet, but I'm in love with your daughter. I don't want to keep secrets from her."

A pause. Then, "These things could hurt her, Brendan."

"I know that, and that's why I agreed to this in the first place. But if I want a relationship with Ava, I can't keep things from her. I know what that does to relationships."

"God..."

"She knows I'm going to tell her. But...she agreed that we wouldn't talk to each other about this until after your party tonight."

"Brendan, I love my wife. The twenty-five years with her have been the best of my life, but right now, this party is making me insane."

"Why is that?"

"Why don't you tell me? What did you talk to Pat Lamone about?"

"Nothing. I referred him to my father because, quite frankly, neither of us were able to figure out why he got the same message that we all got."

"Which message did he get?"

"The really strange one. When echoes navigate down yonder, many anchors destroy ideas generated about neglect."

Silence on the other end of the line.

"Ryan?"

"Yeah?"

"What does that message mean?"

"I don't know."

"That's bull, and we both know it. Your wife figured it out when she first saw it."

"You're imagining things."

"I'm not. I've been tending bar since I turned twenty-one. I know how to read people, and I saw a flicker of recognition in her eyes. And by the way, the first message—the one about Darth Morgen. It's an anagram for *grandmother*. But you already know that, don't you?"

Again...silence.

"Both of my grandmothers are dead," I continue. "As are both of Ava's. So I can only surmise that it has something to do with Pat Lamone's grandmother, the one in the hospital in the mental ward."

Silence once more.

"I know you're not going to tell me anything. But I'm willing to bet Ruby had all of this figured out after she first talked to Ava and me in the bakery that day. Then she kept putting Ava off when Ava asked her if she had figured things out."

Ryan sighs through the phone. "I can't believe this is happening. Again."

"*What* is happening again? I don't know what you're talking about, Ryan."

"I saw her die. I saw her fucking die."

My heart thumps. "Who? *Who* did you see die?"

"I can't discuss this any more." Ryan's tone has become darker. "Could you please just tell me what your father talked to Pat Lamone about?"

"Sure I can, Ryan. After your party. Sunday. And only if Ava is involved in the discussion."

"You would put my daughter through that? You would put her through the pain of..."

"The pain of what? That's what none of us are getting. The pain of what?"

The line goes dead.

Apparently I won't be talking to Ryan Steel any more today. If he was truly outside the bar, waiting for me, he's gone now. Certainly not tonight, either, when he and Ruby are the center of attention at the party.

A feeling of dread settles in my gut.

My phone already in my hand, I do a quick search. The tower card—the card that sent Ava into a tailspin.

I don't know much about the tarot, and I never put any stock in it before. But Ava believes in it, and I believe in Ava.

Hundreds of pages come up about the tower card. I've learned never to click on the first or second response. Instead, I go down ten or eleven links, and then I click.

I don't like what I find.

Chaos.

Destruction.

Unexpected change.

Revelation.

Loss.

The spike of dread inside me worsens. No wonder Ava is freaked out.

I move to another entry.

Same old same old, until—

The tower may seem to be showing impending doom, but this is not always the case. Will there be change? Yes. Will it be difficult? Perhaps. But with change also comes liberation. And with liberation comes awakening.

I exit the page.

The tower.

Damn, Ava.

What the hell are your parents keeping from you?

CHAPTER NINE

Ava

Pita bread is remarkably simple to make.

Sugar, flour, olive oil, and yes, yeast.

Pita is generally considered a flatbread, but you still need yeast because the dough must rise a bit to create the pocket.

Gentle handling of the dough is imperative while rolling. Otherwise the air bubbles will be deflated. After rolling, the dough has to rest for fifteen minutes to recover so it will puff slightly before it goes into the oven. I used to make pita this way.

I don't anymore. Instead of rolling it out, I like to form the dough into balls, and then push my knuckles into it until it creates the right-sized disk. This makes those dimples that all pita is supposed to have.

Some bakers use a baking steel for pita, but I prefer a baking stone. It gives the bread a more even bake, and if you preheat the stone, which I do, it quickly transfers heat to the dough, which causes it to spring almost instantly.

I don't normally sell pita in the bakery, but I imagine after this party, I'll get requests. Why? Because if I do say so myself, I make a damned good pita.

So simple, and as I form the dough and push my knuckles into its sponginess, I meditate. Allow the Zen to flow through me as I knead, poke, bake.

Soon the wondrous aroma of golden-brown pita fills my bakery.

Once I'm finished, I pull out the Kalamata olive loaves that I started yesterday, and I pack them up to take over to Aunt Marjorie's, where they will finish their bake as we need them. Dave comes by in one of his trucks, packs a good portion of pita, bread, and baklava, and then salutes as he drives out of town toward the ranch.

I clean up and head up to my apartment, where I shower and dress for the party.

I choose one of my flowing bohemian dresses—this one in brown paisley—and my brown army boots with woolen socks. I pull my pink hair back into a ponytail because I'll be helping at first and don't want a pink hair in any of the food. I'll be comfortable as I help prepare for the party and then comfortable during the party.

I pack up my truck with the rest of the bread, and as I'm doing so, Brendan meets me in the alley.

"Hey," he says. "How's my favorite lady today?"

"I'm all right." I smile. "Something about baking pita bread puts me in a good place. The simplicity of it."

He inhales. "Smells amazing."

"Doesn't it?"

"It totally does. I could smell it all the way over at my place. Mornings are the greatest. I can always smell what you're baking. It's great to wake up to."

"You didn't wake up to it today. I didn't start until later."

"No, I woke up to a phone call."

"Oh?"

"Your father called me, Ava."

I widen my eyes. "He did?"

"He did. He wanted to meet with me today at ten, and I forgot. Anyway, I told him. I told him that after the party, you and I were going to tell each other everything."

I bite my lip, play with my lip ring a little. "How did he react to that?"

"He's not happy about it."

My skin tightens, as if someone has wrapped me in plastic wrap. "I've got to say, Brendan. I don't think I understand my mom and dad anymore."

"I know you don't, baby. Everything's going to be all right. That much I can promise you."

"How can you make such a promise?"

"Easy. I'll *will* it to be if I have to." He trails his finger to my cheek. "Don't you know that I would do anything for you?"

I can't help a smile and a soft sigh. "I wish I could tell you how much that means to me."

"You don't have to. I can see it in your beautiful blue eyes." He brushes his lips over mine.

"You want to come with me? Instead of meeting me later?"

"I wish I could, but I have to mind the bar until five. Then I'll be headed over your way."

"You realize a lot of your bar patrons will be at our party," I say.

"I know. But Johnny's not coming in to take over until five, so I need to be there."

"Good enough." I head back into the bakery.

Brendan follows me. "I can, however, help you load up."

"Thanks. That's a huge help. Dave already took a bunch, but I still have some more to do. Maya and Luke aren't coming in today at all, so it's all on me to take over the rest of it."

With Brendan helping me, we finish in half the time, and I'm ready to head over to Aunt Jade's with the rest of my bounty.

Brendan pulls me into an embrace. "I'll see you soon, baby."

"Yeah. Soon," I say into his chest.

Then I step into the truck, start the engine, and begin the half-hour drive to Aunt Jade and Uncle Talon's.

★ ★ ★

Aunt Jade and Aunt Marj hired extra help for the party, but there's still plenty for me to do to get the pita and olive bread ready. I keep busy, and I don't have a chance to think about things I don't want to think about. A nice respite, actually.

Aunt Jade's kitchen is mammoth-size, but with everything the staff is setting up and all the extra help involved, it's suddenly not large enough. Her granite countertops are crowded with large stainless-steel catering pans, white porcelain plates, and, of course, sterling flatware. She and Aunt Marj have chosen paper over cloth napkins. Perhaps because this will be a plated dinner rather than a buffet. Already it's more work than usual, so using paper alleviates a little of the fuss.

I take a glance outside to where the staff is setting the tables. Each table is covered in a disposable burgundy-hued cloth and sports a centerpiece of a candle in one of my father's wine bottles, surrounded by a wreath of grape leaves. Really gorgeous.

No one asks me about how things are going with Brendan because we're all too busy. I don't ask anyone about what may be going on with my parents because we're all too busy. Just as well, as I promised I wouldn't say anything...until after the party, that is.

Time flies, and at six o'clock sharp, people begin arriving.

Oddly, I haven't seen my parents.

Aunt Jade, Aunt Marjorie, and I leave the kitchen to the staff then and join the party ourselves. *Come as you are* is always the dress code for a Steel party. Some, like me, dress more casually. The guys mostly wear jeans, but the women go from super casual to semiformal.

Brendan arrives—jeans that accentuate his gorgeous ass, a light-blue button-down that brings out his gorgeous eyes, and brown leather loafers that pull it all together nicely—and he takes my hand. Together we go out to the backyard, which is kept warm on the brisk November night with large heaters.

It's a beautiful clear Colorado night, and here on the Western slope, we can see the stars so much better than in a big city like Denver. This is what I liked about growing up on a ranch. The big sky. The sheer beauty of nature.

Even living in town, I appreciate the splendor. Snow Creek is a small municipality, and at night, I can still see the beauty of the stars.

"Where are your mom and dad?" Brendan asks.

"I don't know. Let's go ask Gina."

My sister stands by the stage, where Jesse Pike and his band are setting up for their performance later. She looks like a runway model in her velvet leggings and silk tunic, complete with thigh-high leather boots. While I dress down, Gina always dresses up.

"Gina," I say.

She turns from her conversation with Jesse's cousin, Cage Ramsey. "Oh, hey, Ava. Brendan."

Good. She's focused on Cage, so she doesn't try that eye batting thing with Brendan.

"Do you know where Mom and Dad are?" I ask.

"I don't. They actually left the house before I did. They should be here. Aren't they?" She glances at her Rolex.

"Not that I've seen," I say.

"I'm sure they're around somewhere," Brendan says.

I know what he's doing. He doesn't want Gina to worry. He already knows I'm worried. My sister is completely naïve to what's going on with our family, and she still has one semester left of college before graduation. I want her to focus on that, not on some family drama that I can't even put into words—other than *grandmother*. Gina will find out soon enough that our parents, aunts, and uncles have been keeping secrets, and she'll be as pissed as I am. She can be blissfully ignorant for one more semester.

"Let us know if you see them," I say as nonchalantly as I can, and then I pull Brendan aside. "I don't like this."

"They're going to be here, sweetie. This party is for them, after all."

"I have no doubt that they'll show up. But they were late to Thanksgiving."

"They were late to Thanksgiving because they were talking to me. They're not talking to me this time, obviously."

I glance around the backyard. "But your parents... They're not here yet."

Brendan raises his eyebrows. "You think your parents might be talking to *my* parents?"

"I don't know. I'd believe anything at this point. Maybe—" I grab his arm as his parents arrive. "I guess not. Your parents just walked in."

He takes my hand and leads me over to them. "Hey, Mom. Dad."

"Hello, honey." Lori Murphy looks casual but elegant in midcalf boots, a black skirt, and a white angora sweater. "And hello, Ava. You look beautiful."

"Thank you," I murmur. "So do you."

"You haven't by any chance seen Ryan and Ruby, have you?" Brendan asks.

"No, we just got here." Sean smiles. He's wearing the usual for men. Jeans and a button-down, his in canary yellow. Interesting choice with his graying auburn hair, but it works for him.

Easy to tell the ranchers from the townies. Brendan and his father wear semicasual shoes. My cousins and uncles wear cowboy boots.

"Okay. I'm sure they're here somewhere." Brendan takes my arm, and we walk away from his parents. "Can I help you with anything?" he asks me.

"No. The staff is handling things for the rest of the evening. Aunt Jade, Aunt Marj, and I are officially off duty."

Where the hell are my parents?

Surely they wouldn't blow off their own twenty-fifth anniversary party.

What's going on? And what does it all have to do with a grandmother?

I try desperately to wipe the thoughts from my mind. I worked hard for this party, and so did Aunt Jade and Aunt Marj.

But I'm losing patience. I want to know what's going on.

And come tomorrow?

My parents will answer every one of my questions. I will

use every tactic, both fair and unfair, to get the information out of them. I'm done waiting.

If the tower is going to fall, I will be ready.

CHAPTER TEN

Brendan

Ryan and Ruby Steel finally show up a half hour later, and the party officially begins.

Ava is clearly distraught. Her cheeks lack their usual gorgeous flush, and she's biting nonstop on her lip ring.

"First Thanksgiving and now this? My parents are never late to any family gathering." She rubs her hands over her arms, as if easing a chill. "The tower. The damned tower."

I want to ease her mind, but she knows much more about the tarot than I do, and she trusts it for guidance.

"I looked up the tower card online," I say.

"Why?"

"Because you've been so disturbed by it. But you know, it doesn't have to be a bad thing."

"I know that, but I depend on my intuition, Brendan. I didn't get any positive feelings at all from that card. Not from the situation, not from the card."

"What about liberation? Revelation?"

"Maybe I don't want anything to be revealed. Maybe I want to live in the world that I've lived in for twenty-four years. The Steel universe as it is."

"I'm sorry." I drape my arm over her shoulder. "I should've known I couldn't find anything to make you feel any better."

"I appreciate that you tried, Brendan." She leans forward onto her toes and brushes her lips lightly over mine. "Really, I do. But looking up a card online isn't the same as having studied and practiced the tarot for as long as I have. The tarot isn't something you can learn overnight. It requires dedication, practice, intuition, emotion. All I can tell you is how I'm feeling about that card."

"It's still sitting on your kitchen table, isn't it?"

"It is."

"Why haven't you put it back in the deck?"

"I don't know. I feel like it's glued to the table."

"But without it, you won't be able to do any more readings."

She drops her gaze to the ground. "I know. I've thought of that. I thought of it today, even when I got home early this morning. I thought about drawing a card, but I couldn't bring myself to replace the tower in the deck."

"I wish there were something I could do."

"I know you do. I appreciate you trying. I really do. But looking up cards online isn't going to help me, Brendan."

"What *will* help you?"

"Just knowing you're here. Knowing that whatever this is between us isn't some fleeting thing."

"It's not," I say. "Not on my end, anyway."

Her cheeks redden. Finally that gorgeous flush. She looks up and meets my gaze. "Not on my end either, Brendan." She takes one of my hands. "I wasn't looking for this. I certainly wasn't expecting it. But I'm so glad we have it. Whatever it is."

"I think"—I push a stray hair that's come loose from her ponytail behind her ear—"it might be love, Ava."

She tongues her lip ring, which makes me crazy, of course.

"I was afraid to hope."

"Afraid to hope what?"

"That you might . . ." She blushes further. "That you might feel it too."

I warm all over, and my cock responds in my jeans. Bad timing, in front of the whole damned town. "I do feel it. I love you, Ava. And I honestly didn't mean to tell you that in the middle of a Steel party."

She smiles, fiddling with her lip ring again. "I'm glad you did. I think I needed to hear it right now. I think your timing is perfect, and I love you too, Brendan. I love you too."

Now my dick is about ready to explode. How I wish I could take her inside the house, find a secluded alcove, and we could celebrate our love physically.

But that isn't going to happen.

Not until tonight, at least.

"Are you hungry?" she asks me.

"Hungry for you." I discreetly pat her on the backside.

"Yeah, me too. I can't believe this is happening."

"Believe it, baby. I've known for a while that you're the one for me."

Her eyes widen. "Really?"

"I think I've made that pretty obvious, haven't I?"

"You made your attraction obvious to me. I had no idea your emotions ran deep."

"They do, sweetheart. They do."

She blushes adorably. "They do for me too, Brendan."

With Ava blocking me from the crowd, I adjust the bulge in my jeans. "That said, since we can't go make love somewhere, yes, I will settle for some food. The magnificent Greek food, and some magnificent bread made by my love."

She takes my hand and leads me to a seat. It's the table of

honor, where her parents are seated.

Ryan and Ruby are smiling, though it seems kind of forced from both of them.

"Hello, Brendan." Ryan stands and shakes my hand. "So you're Ava's date tonight."

"I am, sir."

I'm not sure where the *sir* came from, but I'm seeing him now as Ava's father and not the man who's keeping secrets.

"We're happy to have you join us at our table." He gestures. "Have a seat."

I hold out a chair for Ava.

"You look lovely this evening, sweetie," Ruby says.

"Thanks, Mom."

It doesn't escape my notice that Ava does not meet her mother's gaze.

Gina arrives then, taking the seat next to her father. She gives him a kiss on the cheek. "Hi, Daddy."

"Hi, sweet pea."

"You look gorgeous, Mom."

Ruby smiles again. "Thank you, G."

I've been to many Steel parties during the past ten years. Sometimes there's a sit-down dinner like tonight, served in their vast backyard. Other times it's a buffet setup, like it was for Talon Steel's welcome home party after he was shot.

Another unsolved Steel mystery. Who shot Talon Steel? So much going on with this family. Is it possible that these messages have anything to do with his shooting?

Servers appear and slide plates of food in front of Ryan and Ruby.

They wait politely until Ava says, "Go ahead and eat, Mom and Dad. You don't want your food to get cold. No need to wait for the rest of us."

"Don't be silly," Ruby says. "We'll wait."

Turns out they don't have to wait long. Within another minute, the rest of the people at the table have been served, and it looks delectable. I slide my paper napkin onto my lap and inhale the spicy aroma. Then I turn to Ava. "I don't know anything about Greek food. What do we have here?"

"That is a stuffed grape leaf." Ava points to the dark-green bundle at the top of my plate. "It's a Greek dinner, so Aunt Marj and I decided we had to have stuffed grape leaves. But they're tiny, and you may not like it."

I pick it up and take a bite. It's surprisingly good, in an acidic sort of way. "I will eat whatever you put in front of me. This is good. What's inside?"

"Rice and ground beef, seasoned with parsley, dill, and mint, plus some salt and pepper, of course. I'm surprised you like it."

"Why wouldn't I? It's delicious. What else do we have?"

She smiles. "The thing that looks like lasagna is moussaka. It's made with eggplant and béchamel sauce. And then of course this is a kebab with basmati rice seasoned with saffron. On the kebab is beef marinated in gyro spices—mostly garlic, cumin, and thyme—along with onion and red pepper. Then we have some tabbouleh—a wheat salad—and some tzatziki sauce made with yogurt and cucumber."

"It all looks amazing. I'm not sure I've ever had any of these things, other than a kebab, of course."

"I hope you love them all."

She grabs the breadbasket from the table. "And I know you don't want to miss my pita and my olive bread. But save room for dessert. I made fresh baklava, and Aunt Marj made one of her famous cakes."

Ryan and Ruby don't say much during dinner, but that's not all that unusual. The Steels always serve a ton of food, and people eat heartily here.

I clean my plate quickly, and the server comes by and asks if I want seconds, but I shake my head. "No, thank you. I need to save room for my lovely lady's baklava."

Only then do I notice that neither Ryan nor Ruby ate much. Both their plates are nearly full when the server takes them away. Very unusual for a Steel—or anyone at a Steel party, as the food is always delicious and plentiful.

Ava interrupts my thoughts. "Did you like everything?"

"I cleaned my plate, didn't I?"

"You did. I'm noticing a lot of plates going back to the kitchen with the stuffed grape leaf intact."

She's frowning, but I can't tell if she noticed her parents' plates.

"I can't say it was my favorite thing on the menu," I reply, "but I enjoyed it. I love trying new foods."

"I do too. We do have a lot in common, don't we, Brendan?"

I squeeze her hand. "I always knew we would."

That's no lie. For some reason, I felt a connection to Ava Steel when she first opened her bakery in town. It took me a while to act on it, given the age difference, but something about her called to me. Now I know why. Because she's the love of my life.

Once the plates are cleared, Talon Steel walks up onto the stage where the band will play later. Dale Steel and his wife, Ashley, are busy pouring glasses of bubbly and distributing them.

Right. The time for the infamous Steel toast. They'll eventually pull Ryan and Ruby onto the stage, where the two of them will act like everything's fine. A tiny part of me feels kind of sorry for them. But the other part of me—everything *but* that tiny part—doesn't feel the least bit bad. Something's happening. Something that may hurt Ava.

And that does *not* make me happy.

"Hey, everyone," Talon says over the microphone. "Thank you all for coming to celebrate my little brother's twenty-fiftieth anniversary of his marriage to the love of his life. We are so grateful to all of you for being here."

Thundering applause.

"I'm going to get Ryan and Ruby up here to say something, but first I want to talk a little bit about their wedding and what it meant to all of us here in the Steel family."

He clears his throat, and for a moment, I think he may choke up.

"Twenty-five years ago today, my little brother and his wife stood in this very yard and promised to love each other forever. Standing next to me that day were my two sons, Dale and Donny. They weren't legally my sons at that time, but Jade and I had taken them in, given them a home, and begun adoption proceedings. That's how I remember this beautiful day. Because it was not only the beginning of a life of love and family for Ryan and Ruby, but it was Dale and Donny's introduction into the Steel family. Ryan and Ruby played a huge role in bringing my sons into this family, and they've both always been close to my brother and sister-in-law, especially Dale, who shares Ryan's love of and talent for wine. So I think it's only fitting to bring Dale and Donny up here to do the toast to their Uncle Ryan and Aunt Ruby."

More applause.

Dale and Donny walk up to the stage, and Donny takes the microphone from Talon.

"I'm going to let Dale—with his gift of gab—"

Laughter permeates the crowd, and Donny joins in.

"Right, though Dale does talk a lot more now that he's married to his lovely wife, Ashley. I'll let him do the majority of the talking, because he's the resident wine guru and Uncle Ryan's protégé, but before I hand him the reins, let me just say that I remember when Uncle Ryan and Aunt Ruby got married. We stood up for them that day, next to our father, wearing little gray suits, which were the most uncomfortable thing in the world for little boys to wear. We had just recently lost our birth mother. But we were welcomed into the Steel family that day, and it's been the best thing that ever happened to both of us. Well, the second-best thing, next to Ashley and Callie."

Laughter and applause.

"Thank you, Uncle Ryan and Aunt Ruby, for letting us be part of your day twenty-five years ago." He slaps his forehead. "Damn, twenty-five years! It doesn't seem possible, but I look in the mirror, and I see a little gray in my blond hair. I'll be celebrating my own wedding soon to the lovely Callie Pike"— he blows a kiss to Callie, who's seated with Brock and Rory at the table next to ours—"and none of that would've been possible without all of you welcoming us into the family the day Ryan and Ruby got married. So thank you, Aunt Ruby and Uncle Ryan, thank you, Mom and Dad, Uncle Joe and Aunt Melanie, Uncle Bryce and Aunt Marjorie, and all the people here who were around that day and welcomed Dale and me into the community. Thank you."

More applause as he hands the microphone to Dale.

I've known Dale Steel since he came to Snow Creek. He was a quiet and frightened little boy of ten, and we were the same age and in the same grade at school.

Now he stands tall and proud, and he still wears his hair long like I do. He brings his wife, Ashley, to stand next to him. I've never heard him say more than about ten words at a time, and even from our table, I can see his eyes are glistening a bit.

It's clear that Ryan and Ruby mean a lot to him.

"Hey, everyone," Dale begins, and then he clears his throat.

A few seconds pass until he starts speaking again.

"I may be a man of few words, as you all know, and that's okay right now, because I don't think there are words in the English language to describe exactly what Aunt Ruby and Uncle Ryan mean to me. I agree with everything Donny said. Your wedding twenty-five years ago was when Donny and I realized we were actually part of this amazing family. Still, it took a while for me to come out of my shell. I suppose a lot of you would say I never really did. But I did. I did when I began working with Uncle Ryan at the winery. Who would've thought an interest in wine would be my saving grace?" Dale's voice cracks a little, and he clears his throat again. "Turns out I have kind of a knack for it. Uncle Ryan saw that in me. He saw it, and he nurtured it, and he allowed me to go at my own pace. There were days when we'd work together and neither one of us said a word. He didn't force me to talk when I didn't feel like talking, and when I did feel like talking? He listened. He gave me sage advice. He helped me realize that every member of this family was on my side. He's been a second father to me, and that's meant everything."

Ashley slips her hand into his, while I consider his words. *Every member of this family was on my side.* Dale truly believes that, but I'm forced to wonder . . . Are the Steels on Ava's side? How could they be if they're keeping secrets?

After a few seconds, Dale speaks again.

"And then there's Aunt Ruby. Aunt Ruby, who let me tag along on an investigation twenty-five years ago. I found a polished rock. That may sound silly to you, but we were looking for clues—any kind of clues—and I found a polished rock outside on the ground. I handed it to Aunt Ruby, and I told her it didn't belong there."

Laughter trickles through the audience.

"She told me I was right, and that polished rock ended up being a significant clue in her investigation. You gave me a voice that day, Aunt Ruby, and I'll never forget that."

Soft murmurs through the group.

Dale sniffs. "I could say more, but I'm already getting misty up here. Just suffice it to say the two people we're celebrating today mean as much to me as my own parents do. Uncle Ryan and Aunt Ruby, you both gave me what I needed at a time when I didn't know *what* I needed. So here's to your twenty-five years, and we will all be here to join you when you celebrate the next twenty-five." He holds up his glass of sparkling wine. "To Ryan and Ruby, and twenty-five years of happiness!"

The rest of us hold up our glasses. "To Ryan and Ruby," I chorus with all the others.

Ryan and Ruby walk onto the stage, and though they should be radiating happiness, I'm not getting that feeling at all.

Dale hands the microphone to Ryan, but he gestures to Ruby.

Ruby smiles at him and takes the microphone.

"I think Ryan's a little choked up. That was a wonderful tribute from you guys." She nods to Dale and Donny. "There's a lot of love in this family, and Ryan and I have been so lucky to share in that love for the last twenty-five years. Dale talks about coming out of his shell. I was a mousy detective when Ryan and I met, and he certainly helped me come out of my shell as well. Everyone welcomed me into the Steel family, especially my best friend in the world, Melanie—"

Melanie waves and smiles from her table.

"And I've had a life I never thought I'd have because of this wonderful family. So thank you so much for being here, all of you. And thank you to my wonderful husband, Ryan Steel, for giving me this incredible life. I love you so much, babe."

She nods, smiles, and hands him the microphone while applause echoes through the yard.

Ryan doesn't bring the microphone to his lips. Instead, he lets it hang at his side as the applause dies down.

Finally he brings it upward. "I wish I knew what to say. To my brothers and sister, my sisters-in-law and brother-in-law, my beautiful daughters, Ava and Gina, and all my amazing nieces and nephews, thank you all for being here. And to all of you in the community who came out to celebrate with us tonight, thank you.

"Ruby and I have had an amazing life together, and I can only hope that . . ."

Ruby touches his forearm.

Ryan looks out into the crowd, but he seems to be seeing something else. "My brothers stood beside me in the backyard of this very house. I wore a black suit, no tie, and Talon and Joe both wore blue-gray. The weather cooperated beautifully for November. The orange and gold colors of fall surrounded us, and the temperature was a balmy sixty-two. Ground had already been broken for Ruby's and my house. It was

Thanksgiving Day, and Ruby and I thought it was a perfect day to exchange our vows and begin our life as husband and wife. We had so much to be thankful for. Then Dale and Donny..." He trails off for a moment, and Ruby grabs his hand.

"They had put on a little weight and wore suits matching Talon's and Joe's—which I didn't realize were so uncomfortable, Don."

Laughter.

"Melanie was pregnant with Brad, and Jade had just found out she was pregnant with Diana. Ruby's mother, Diamond, was there, wearing a soft-pink dress. A string quartet played. Marjorie wore light blue, Jade a shade darker, and Melanie darker yet. Melanie, my wife's best friend and her matron of honor. And I'll never forget"—he gazes at his wife—"the sight of you as you walked toward me in dark-blue silk." He smiles. "I expected white, but you surprised me that day. Your skirt billowed in the soft breeze. Your hair was darker then, and you wore it swept up. And your arm sparkled. You wore the sapphire bracelet—"

The microphone drops to the ground with a thud that reverberates from the sound system.

Ruby tugs on his arm. "Ryan, are you all right?"

Ryan says something, but I can't hear what it is.

Ava rises and runs up to the stage. I follow her.

Talon and Joe are at Ryan's side. Another few seconds pass, and they're helping him off his feet.

"Daddy," Ava says, her voice catching, "what's the matter? Are you all right?"

Then Ryan finally speaks.

"Hospital," he rasps. "I need to go to the hospital."

CHAPTER ELEVEN

Ava

"I don't understand," my sister whines. "He's not even sixty years old. And he's in perfect health. What's going on?"

I gasp in a breath. "I don't know. I just don't know."

Brendan sits next to me in the emergency room waiting area, holding my hand. "I'm sure we'll have news soon," he says. "Your mom is back there with him."

The rest of the family stayed at Uncle Talon and Aunt Jade's home to see to our guests. Only Mom, Gina, Brendan, and I came to the hospital with Dad. Brendan, God love him, drove us all in Dad's truck. Mom, Gina, and I were in no condition to drive, and we knew that waiting for an ambulance would take longer than if we just drove into Grand Junction ourselves.

All that time I was so scared my mother was ill. It was my father. My father is ill, and somehow I feel I should've known.

He's fifty-eight years old, my father, and he doesn't look a day over forty. He eats a lot of beef, of course, but it's grass-fed Steel beef, which is lower in saturated fat. He drinks wine, but never to excess. Plus he takes care of himself. He works out, stays lean. In fact, his body hasn't changed in the twenty-four years I've been alive. No beer belly on Ryan Steel. Only hard and solid muscle.

I wish I had my tarot deck. I need some guidance now. All I can see in my mind is that damned tower card. Is this what it was warning me of?

Perhaps. But my intuition says no. My intuition says this isn't related.

But how can it not be? For the first time since I began practicing the tarot, I doubt my interpretation and intuitive skills.

How could I have missed this?

The tower.

This was its warning. My father is ill.

Perhaps Darth Morgen doesn't mean *grandmother*. Perhaps it's something else that I haven't figured out yet.

I need to ask my mother. I promised everyone I would wait until after the party, but now the party has been ruined.

And honestly? I don't give a rat's ass about the party. I don't give a rat's ass about those messages. I don't give a rat's ass about anything except my father right now.

I can't lose my father.

I need him. I need his strength, and I need his compassion.

Brendan squeezes my hand. "It's going to be okay, baby."

I don't reply. I appreciate his optimism, but I don't share it. I've known something devastating was coming. Something involving my family.

I just didn't expect it to take my father with it.

An hour has passed.

And nothing. Nothing from any doctors or nurses or even my mother.

Finally I rise, disengaging my hand from Brendan's. "I can't stand this. I'm going to go see what's going on."

"Honey," Brendan says, "they'll tell us when they know anything."

I curl my hands into fists. "Damn it, Brendan. That's not good enough. I want to know what's going on. Now."

Gina rises then. "Me too. He's our father, for God's sake!"

"All right, all right." Brendan rises. "You two sit down. I'll see if I can find anything out."

I plunk my ass back down, and so does Gina.

Fine. Brendan will find out.

But he returns a moment later. "There's nothing new, and even if there were, they wouldn't tell me anyway. I'm not a family member."

"Fine." I rise again. "I'll find out."

I walk briskly to reception. "I'm Ava Steel. My father, Ryan Steel, has been back there for over an hour. I'd like an update, please."

"I just told your friend that I don't have an update," the receptionist says. "I'm sorry, but that's the best I can do. When there's news, someone will be out to tell you."

I tap my foot on the tile floor, my army boot making a clomping noise. "I want to talk to my mother. She's back there with him."

"We can only allow one person back in the ER with the patient. I'm sorry, but that's all I can tell you."

"Damn it." I bring my fist down on the counter. "That's just not good enough."

Brendan is beside me then, his arms around my shoulders. "Come on, baby. She's just doing her job."

"I don't care. Doesn't anyone understand that this is my *father*? This is my father, who's celebrating his twenty-fifth anniversary today. My father!" Tears well in my eyes.

"Baby," Brendan soothes, "come on. We all know how much he means to you. I'm sure there will be news soon. But until then, you need to keep a positive attitude."

"There's nothing positive about any of this. Ever since I drew that tower card, I've known this was coming. I just didn't expect it to be my father."

He takes my hand again, rubs his fingers into my palm.

I know what he's doing.

He's placating me. He doesn't believe in the tarot. He's trying to relax me so that I'll forget about that card.

I jerk my hand away from him. "I know what you're thinking, Brendan."

His eyebrows rise. "You do?"

"Yes. You're thinking I need to forget about that stupid card. You're just like everyone else."

"Ava, I never said—"

I jerk away from him and walk out of the waiting room. I'm sick to death of it, anyway. Uncomfortable chairs. People coughing. Magazines from last year. I have no idea where I'm going, but I know I can't stay with people who don't take me seriously.

I have my cell phone. Gina or Brendan will call me if they find out anything about my father. I can no longer sit here. Sit like my feet are rooted to the ground. I need to *do* something.

If only I had my tarot deck with me. Brendan, Gina, and the rest of the free world may think it's ridiculous, but it means something to me. It soothes me when I need soothing.

But that card . . .

The tower . . .

It did not soothe me.

And even now, when I'm trying to find a positive spin on everything happening, all I can see is that card, pulsing out at me, moving with my own heartbeat.

I walk. I have no idea where I'm going, and within a few minutes, I find myself in the main part of the hospital.

"May I help you?" a volunteer asks me.

I ignore her and keep walking.

When I come to the elevators, I read the list. Cardiac wing, gastrointestinal, mental health.

Mental health. I sigh. Am I going insane? Insane like my grandmother Daphne Steel?

None of the rest of the people in my family, all of whom are descended from her, show any signs of mental illness. But it has to surface somewhere, doesn't it?

At this moment, I feel anything *but* mentally healthy.

I'm a woman who rejects her family's money. I'm a woman who colors her hair pink. I'm a woman who believes in the wisdom and guidance of the tarot cards.

And I'm a woman who...

I'm a woman who's doubting her sanity at this moment.

I pull out my cell phone and dial Aunt Melanie.

"Ava?" she gasps. "Do you have news?"

I back against the wall of the alcove where the elevators are, and I slide into a sitting position. "No, Aunt Mel. I don't have any news. Not yet."

"Well, he's going to be fine. We just all have to keep believing that."

"I'm trying, Aunt Mel. But I..."

"What is it, honey?"

"I'm frightened. I think I may be going...crazy."

"Oh, honey. You're not. You're fine. Just worried about your father."

"That's not it. I just don't seem to know myself anymore. No one will tell me anything. No one, not even my mother, and she's deciphered those messages I received. I'm sure of it. But now? How can I ask her about any of that? I love my mother and my father so much. I can't lose them. I just...feel like something horrible is coming, Aunt Melanie."

"Ava..."

"What?"

"Pause a moment. I want you to take a few deep breaths. Breathe with me right now, okay?"

"Okay," I choke out.

"Breathe in deeply through your nose. I want to hear you do it."

I obey, sucking in as much air as I can through my nose.

"And out through your mouth," Aunt Melanie says.

I obey again, letting my breath flow out of me.

"All right, Ava. Two more times. With me."

Inhale.

Exhale.

Inhale.

Exhale.

"Now," Aunt Melanie says. "Have you come down a bit?"

Have I? I don't feel like I'm losing it. At least not as much. But my father... The secrets... All of it...

"Not really."

"Actually, you have. I can hear it in your voice. Now listen to me. Right now, we need to focus on your father. Focus on him, and—"

"No one will tell me anything."

"That's because there's nothing to tell you."

Aunt Melanie thinks I'm talking about my father's condition, and I am. But deep down, I mean everything else the family has been keeping from me.

"Ava, do you want his doctors focused on him? Or do you want them focused on you?"

I let out a sigh. "I'm not trying to be self-absorbed, Aunt Melanie."

"I know that, dear. And I know you're in a horribly difficult situation. We're all worried about Ryan right now. Just know that he's getting the best care possible, and when the doctors have something to say, they will come out and let you know."

"I know that. It's just all so frustrating."

"I know it is, honey. Let's just concentrate on your dad right now. None of the rest of this stuff matters at this moment."

"I know."

"And Ava," she says, her tone loving but firm, "you're mentally healthy. You just have a little anxiety right now. It's perfectly normal given the circumstances. I don't want you questioning your mental health."

"But my grandmother."

"Look at your aunt, at your uncles. They're all fine. All their children are fine. No one inherited your grandmother's mental illness."

My heart has slowed down. A little. "All right. Thank you for saying that."

"Are you going to be okay? Do you want me to stay on the phone with you?"

"Are you still at Uncle Talon's?"

"Yes. All the guests have gone home, but the family is waiting here to hear about Ryan."

"Is anyone coming to the hospital?"

"I just spoke to Ruby on her cell phone."

"You spoke to my mom? And there's no news about my dad?"

"Not yet, sweetheart. But she did tell us that she wants us to stay here in Snow Creek. At least until we know more."

"All right. Just as well. There's nothing any of us can do anyway."

"You can pray. You can send positive thoughts. You can try to be optimistic, Ava. That's the best thing you can do for your father and for yourself right now."

Still, that tower card pulses in my mind.

"I'll try, Aunt Melanie."

"Do I need to pull a Yoda on you?"

I can't help an eye roll. "Don't tell me you're a *Star Wars* geek too."

"Of course not. I leave that to Brock and Dave. But Yoda did say something that is worthy of repeating. He said, 'Do or do not. There is no try.'"

"Yeah? Well, he's a Muppet."

Aunt Melanie laughs. "True. But he's a very wise Muppet."

"So you're saying I shouldn't try to be optimistic. I should just *be* optimistic."

"That's what I'm saying, Ava. And you knew that the whole time, didn't you?"

I sigh again. "I did."

"All right. As I said, I promise you there's nothing wrong with your mental health other than a little anxiety, which is totally understandable. Just remember, when you feel like you can't handle things, those three deep breaths in through your nose and out through your mouth will do a lot of good. If you need more than that, a brisk walk will help. We're all in your corner, Ava. We're all in your father's corner."

"I know. Thank you, Aunt Melanie."

After ending the call, I consider Aunt Melanie's words.

Look at your aunt, at your uncles. They're all fine. All their children are fine. No one inherited your grandmother's mental illness.

And I realize...

She mentioned Uncle Joe, Uncle Talon, Aunt Marjorie...

She didn't mention my father.

CHAPTER TWELVE

Brendan

I rise when Ava returns.

She walks into my arms and murmurs, "I'm sorry."

"It's okay." I kiss the top of her head. "I understand. You're just worried."

She nods against my chest.

"No one's been out to talk to us yet, and Gina went to get a Coke. I guess we just wait—"

She looks up. "What?"

I gesture toward the door. "Here comes your mom."

"Oh, God," she says.

"She doesn't look too bad. Let's just hear her out. If it were something really bad, a doctor would come out."

Ruby comes toward us, a bit haggard and pale, but she's not crying. "Where's your sister?" she asks Ava.

"She'll be back in a minute. How's Dad?"

Ruby lets out a heavy sigh and hugs Ava. "He's going to be fine."

"Was it his heart? A stroke?"

"Neither. They suspected a mild heart attack, but they couldn't find any blockage or any cardiac damage. His heart rhythm is good now, and his EKG is perfect."

"Then what was it?"

"The doctor thinks it was a panic attack."

"A panic attack?" Ava gasps, her eyes wide. "Dad doesn't get panic attacks."

"That's what I told the doctors. He's never had one before. At least not as long as I've known him."

"Panic attacks are common," I offer. "My mother has had a few."

"I know they're common," Ruby says. "Just a first for Ryan."

"A panic attack in the middle of his anniversary party?" Ava shakes her head.

"Yes. Your father doesn't have great timing, does he?" From Ruby.

Gina returns to the waiting area, holding a bottle of Diet Coke. "Mom! Is Dad okay?"

Ruby nods, hugging Gina and then Ava once more. "Yes, he's going to be fine."

"Oh, thank God!" Gina bursts into tears.

Ruby kisses her daughter's forehead. "Just like you. You never cry until it's good news."

"I just . . . I couldn't . . ." Gina sniffles.

"We're all happy that he's going to be fine."

But there's an edge to Ruby's voice. An edge that perhaps only I hear.

And I get the feeling that she's not sure everything's going to be fine.

"Will we be taking him home?" I ask.

"Not until tomorrow," Ruby says. "They've given him some medication, and they want to keep an eye on him for the night, make sure there's nothing they missed."

"Would they do that for just anyone?" Ava asks. "Or is it because he's a Steel?"

Ruby sighs. "Does it really matter, Ava? Your father's getting the best care."

Part of me expects Ava to fight her mother, but instead she says, "That's all I want. For him to get the best care."

"He is. This is the best hospital in Grand Junction, and it's one of the best in the nation. So he's in good hands."

"What should we do?" Gina asks. "We all came in the truck."

"You all can go on home," Ruby says. "Uncle Talon and Uncle Joe will come pick Dad and me up in the morning."

"Are you sure we should go?" Gina asks.

"I'm sure. If you want, you can get a room at the Carlton, but your dad isn't in any danger, so there's no reason why you shouldn't be sleeping in your own beds."

"If you're sure," Ava says.

"I'm sure."

"Can we at least see Dad?" Gina asks.

Ruby bites her lip lightly. "He's a little out of it right now. But yeah, if you'd like to see him. I'm sure he'd like to see you both. I got permission to bring you back, but only for a minute."

Ava and Gina go with their mother back into the ER, while I stay in the waiting area.

A panic attack.

Ryan Steel had a panic attack at his anniversary party.

Ryan Steel, who's never had a panic attack in his life.

Whatever they're keeping from Ava has got to be the source.

And I swear to God, I will make sure it does not harm Ava in any way.

CHAPTER THIRTEEN

Ava

My handsome father is pale, and he's wearing a green-and-white hospital gown. His eyes are closed, and an IV is attached to his left hand. Why an IV? He must be dehydrated.

Mom kisses his forehead. "Ryan, the girls want to see you."

He opens his eyes and smiles—sort of. "Hey. How are my lovelies?"

"Scared to death," Gina says.

"I'm so sorry." Dad clears his throat. "I'm pretty embarrassed about the whole thing."

"Don't be embarrassed," I say. "We're just glad you're okay."

"I'm better than okay at the moment." He gives a goofy grin. "They've pumped me full of something that's got me feeling pretty good."

"Good. Not that I want to see my father stoned, but…" I chuckle.

Dad's eyes are heavy lidded, and a yawn splits his face. "I'm not sure I've ever been *this* stoned."

Gina jumps on that. "You mean you've *been* stoned?"

"Of course not," Mom says.

Dad just chuckles.

"Is there anything we can do for you, Dad?" I ask.

"Just let it go," he says. "Let it all go."

"Let *what* go?" Gina asks.

"Ryan, the drugs are talking." Mom smooths Dad's hair.

"I just don't understand it, Ruby. Why this? Why now?" Dad furrows his brow but doesn't go rigid. Probably the drugs. Just a second ago he wanted to let everything go.

"Ryan . . ."

"Whatever is bothering you, Daddy, just forget about it," Gina says. "It doesn't matter."

"Right. It doesn't matter," I echo.

And still the tower pulses in my brain.

The tower.

The fucking tower.

"Girls, your father needs his rest," Mom says.

"Okay." I squeeze Dad's right hand. "I'm so glad you're going to be okay."

"Me too, Daddy." Gina kisses the top of his head.

"Let us know if you need anything, Mom," I say.

"I will. I don't want you girls to worry. Dad is fine, and we'll be home tomorrow."

"Let it go . . ." From Dad, his eyes now closed. "Just let it all go . . ."

I give my mom a quick hug, and I feel like . . .

I don't know what I feel.

Like she's holding something back in her hug, which doesn't make sense. My mother's a very loving mother.

Gina hugs her, and then the two of us walk back out to the waiting area where Brendan is.

"Everything okay?" he asks.

"Yeah," Gina says.

I simply nod.

Because everything is *not* okay.

I'm trying to push that to the side and concentrate on what really matters, which is my father's health. He's not in danger.

But my strong and robust father, who has no history of panic attacks, had his first at his twenty-fifth anniversary party?

I don't question his and my mother's love for each other. So why would he have a panic attack at their party?

And inside I know.

It's what Aunt Melanie told me I need to ask my parents about, and it's what Aunt Marjorie told me to wait until after the party to bring up.

My father knows it's coming.

And it has him panicked.

He may be stoned, but he will *not* let this go.

★ ★ ★

It's after eleven by the time Brendan and I get back to town after dropping Gina off at Mom and Dad's house and then heading back to Uncle Talon's to turn in the truck and get both Brendan's car and my truck.

Brendan walks me to the back door of the bakery and kisses me on the lips. "I love you. You okay?"

Apprehension races through me. "You're not leaving, are you?"

"I didn't want to be presumptuous."

I brush my arms against the chill. "I need you tonight, Brendan. This is all such a mess."

"I need to go over to the bar and just check things out. But

I'll be right back, okay?"

"All right. But I don't want to be alone. I'll come with you to the bar."

He nods, and we walk the three buildings down and enter the bar through the alleyway. It's hopping, and we get pounced on.

"Ava, how is Ryan?" comes at me from dozens of voices.

This wasn't the best idea. I should've gone up, gotten into bed, and waited for Brendan. But I didn't want to leave him. I wanted him with me. I needed his strength and his presence.

"Shit, I'm sorry," Brendan says in my ear. He pushes a key into my hand. "Go up to my place and wait for me there. I'll take care of all this."

"You're a lifesaver." I head up to his apartment, unlock the door, and go in.

I inhale the aroma of Brendan. It's only been a few days that he's been living in his refurbished apartment—paid for by my family, unbeknownst to him—and already it smells like him. That aromatic mixture of warmth and spice and man.

I inhale, letting it give me some peace, and then I walk to his bed and sit down. Even though it's late and I didn't get much sleep last night, I can't relax.

I rise, pace around the apartment for a few moments, until my gaze lands on his bookshelf.

Only a few books grace it—books he either was able to save after his apartment got trashed or that he bought new. A couple of bartending manuals, a couple of commercial novels, and a couple of classics.

The Adventures of Tom Sawyer.

I haven't read that since I was a kid, so I grab it. It falls open, revealing some folded white pages.

I open one, and my jaw drops.

It's a quitclaim deed, transferring all Steel real property to my father, Ryan Steel. The signature at the bottom reads *Bradford Steel.*

My grandfather, who I never met.

My fingers lose hold of the paper, and it flutters to the ground.

I pick it up and stare at it again.

I don't understand any of this. Why would my grandfather want to transfer all his property to only *one* of his children?

It doesn't make any sense. Since my grandfather's death, Dad, Uncle Joe, Uncle Talon, and Aunt Marj have all owned the property in equal shares.

This document would change that.

Is my father supposed to be the sole owner of all the Steel land and real property?

I'm still staring at the paper when Brendan walks in.

"Ava?"

"What the hell is this?" I shove the paper at him.

"Were you snooping?"

"Not on purpose. I thought I'd read to try to relax."

"Fuck." He grabs the paper from me and glances at it. "I just put those in there."

"Those?" A couple of papers are still left in the book. I pull them out and hand them to him. "Could you explain all this, please? Is my father supposed to be the sole owner of all the Steel land?"

"No, I don't think so. The deed has to be recorded to be valid, and this one hasn't been."

I take the paper from him . . . not gently. "But it's dated . . . My God, it's dated like fifty years ago."

"Right. And he didn't die until about twenty-five years ago."

"How did everything transfer?"

"I don't know, Ava. That's something you have to ask your dad and your uncles. It either transferred through probate or through a different deed. Possibly through a trust benefitting your dad and his siblings."

My pulse is rising. "Why do you even have this?"

"That's a long story."

"Well, I'm not going anywhere until I hear the whole thing."

Brendan takes his hair out of his low ponytail and threads his fingers through it until he looks like a wild man. "No more secrets. We promised, right?"

"We did."

"All right, then." He sighs. "These are the copies of documents that I found under the floorboards of this place a couple of months ago. I told you about the lien and about the birth certificate."

"Why were they here?"

"If I knew the answer to that question, I would gladly tell you, but I don't."

I walk back to his bed and sit down. "I'm so confused. There's some connection here that we're not seeing. Some reason why your family and mine are getting the same messages. And the tower, Brendan. The tower."

"This doesn't have to be a bad thing. Nothing is changing in your life."

"But this all has to do with my family." I gulp back tears. "My family is my foundation. My rock. How can you say that nothing is changing?"

"I can say it because you, Ava Steel, are who you are." He firmly places his hands on my shoulders. "That will never change. And we don't even know what these documents mean."

My heart is racing, and my breath, I . . .

"Brendan, I . . ."

He releases my shoulders, sits next to me, takes me in his arms. "Relax, baby. It's just panic. Just like what happened to your father."

He's right. I'm twenty-four years old and in excellent health. I'm way too young to be having a heart attack. Still, the squeezing in my chest, the shortness of breath . . .

I try.

I try to hold on.

I try . . .

But . . . darkness falls before my eyes.

CHAPTER FOURTEEN

Brendan

"Ava?" I kiss the top of her head.

She doesn't respond.

"Ava? Ava, are you all right?"

Her eyes open. "Brendan... Please..."

"Baby, tell me what it is. What do you need? What can I do for you?"

"Don't... Feel... Good..."

I don't think. I only react. I scoop her into my arms, head down the back way, managing to dodge the bar patrons, and put her into my car.

Then I race back to the hospital.

As I drive through the night roads, I keep one eye on Ava. Her eyes open and close, but she does not react.

When we come screaming into the emergency room parking lot, I take her hand, but when she doesn't move, I scoop her into my arms again and carry her in.

"Sir?" the receptionist says. "Weren't you just here? Is she all right?"

"I don't know. She seems to be responsive. Sometimes."

"All right. Let's get her back."

A nurse comes out with a wheelchair.

I place Ava in the chair. "You okay, baby?"

Her eyes are glassy, and she doesn't reply.

"Fix this," I say to the nurse. "You've got to fix this."

"Are you her husband?"

I shake my head.

"Then we'll need to call her next of kin."

"Her next of kin is ... He's already here. Ryan Steel."

"This is Ryan Steel's daughter?"

"Yes. Ava Steel."

Things go better after that. She's whisked back to the ER, and I follow her.

No one says a word to me. Just as well, as I'm liable to pummel anyone who tries to keep me from Ava.

Several orderlies help get her onto an exam table, and then she turns her head and looks at me.

Thank God.

"Brendan?" she ekes out.

"Everything's okay, baby. You're at the hospital. We're going to take care of you."

"I'm all right."

"Ava, you're not all right. You weren't responsive for over half an hour."

"I just didn't know how to respond, Brendan. I was afraid. My heart was beating so fast. For a moment, I couldn't get my breath, so the only thing I was able to do was turn my mind off."

I kiss her forehead. "Whatever you had to do doesn't matter. We're at the hospital now, and we're going to figure out what's going on."

She closes her eyes. "I think I just ... panicked."

"Like your father did?"

"Yes. My chest hurt so bad, my breath got shallow. And I was so scared, so I closed my eyes ... I just wanted to escape into oblivion. For a moment, I think I did."

"Did you lose consciousness?"

"I don't know." She closes her eyes for a few seconds and then reopens them. "I don't know, Brendan. Just . . . stay with me. Okay?"

"I will never leave your side."

A technician comes in with a machine. "I'm going to do an EKG," he says. "You need to remove your shirt." Then he glances at me.

"I've seen it before," I say dryly.

I help Ava get out of her shirt, and the technician puts the magnetic pads on her chest and stomach. Then the EKG starts.

"How does it look?" I ask him.

"The doctor will discuss the results with you." He prints out a portion of Ava's EKG, and then he unhooks her.

"That's it?" I say.

"Yeah. Getting prepped for an EKG takes longer than the test itself."

I have no idea what the lines on the EKG mean, but the technician didn't look alarmed. Of course they're probably trained not to look alarmed.

Next, another tech comes in. "I'm going to draw some blood, Ms. Steel."

Ava simply nods, and the tech wraps the rubber band around her upper arm and pats the veins in the crease of her elbow.

"You have good veins," she says.

"Thanks . . . I guess . . ." Ava murmurs.

"Why are you drawing blood?" I say.

"Just some routine lab tests ordered by the ER doc."

"We haven't even seen the ER doc."

"You haven't?" The tech scans the clipboard. "Well, he's seen the chart, and he ordered these lab tests. I'm sure he'll be in soon."

I sit on the ER bed, holding Ava's hand. Moments tick by, until—

Someone opens the curtain harshly. A young man in green scrubs enters. "Ms. Steel? I'm Dr. Tonaki. Your EKG looks great. Now we just have to wait and see if your blood tests indicate any reason for your symptoms."

"Okay."

Dr. Tonaki takes a stethoscope and listens to Ava's heart and then to her lungs. "Let me check your airway. Open up."

Ava complies, and then the doctor feels her neck.

"No swollen lymph nodes in the neck. Heart and lungs sound great. EKG looks good."

"So what happened, then?" I ask.

"Given the symptoms, which seem to have resolved, I'd say you had a panic attack, Ms. Steel."

Ava sighs. "Just like my father."

"Yes, I understand your father, Ryan Steel, is currently a patient here. I just came on duty an hour ago, but my colleague, Dr. Amos, probably saw your father."

"Ava," I say, "do you want me to find your mother and father? Tell them you're here?"

She shakes her head. "They've had enough to deal with tonight. And I won't be spending the night here."

"I don't think you'll have to," Dr. Tonaki says, "but I do want to wait until we have the lab results before I discharge you."

"Do I have to?" Ava asks. "I really just want to go home."

"Baby, you need to listen to the doctor. I think you're

probably fine, but we need to make sure."

Dr. Tonaki makes a few notes on the chart. "Your panic attack was mild, so I'm not overly concerned. I'll be back to check on you in a bit." He leaves, closing the curtain behind him.

"Mild?" Ava says.

"It was a lot milder than the one we witnessed your father have," I say. "The doctor knows what he's talking about."

"This is ridiculous. My father has never had a panic attack in his life, and neither have I."

"If I had to wager a guess," I tell her, "I'd say your panic attack was caused not just by the documents you found in my book but also because of worry for your father. For your family. And..."

"The tower," she says.

"Yes. The tower."

"I need to talk to Aunt Melanie."

"Do you want me to call her?"

"It's after midnight, Brendan. No, I don't want you to call her. I already talked to her earlier this evening when we brought my dad in. I was freaking out a bit." She wrinkles her nose. "Okay, make that a lot."

"A panic attack isn't anything to be concerned about," I say. "You heard the doctor. A lot of people have them."

"I don't know. They drugged my dad pretty well earlier."

"They did, but your dad's symptoms were a lot worse than yours."

"True."

I hand her the remote control. "Do you want to watch some TV while we wait?"

"No, I think I just want to close my eyes. I don't want any

drugs, but part of me wishes I could have whatever they dosed my dad up with."

"It was probably Valium."

"Yeah, probably."

She sets the remote control back down. "I want to try to sleep."

"All right. I'll be right here. I'm not going anywhere."

CHAPTER FIFTEEN

Ava

I'm running . . .

Running from the falling rubble as the tower burns in the background.

My heart races as I run . . .

Run, run, run . . .

Until—

"Ava."

My eyes pop open.

For a moment, I don't know where I am, until I remember the panic attack, the ER, the hospital.

"The doctor's back. He has your blood test results."

Right. The doctor. The young man with brown hair and brown eyes and wearing green scrubs.

"Excellent news, Ms. Steel. All your labs look great. There's no reason for you to stay here. But if you do have another panic attack, I want you to see your primary care physician. He or she will be able to help you."

"I've never had a panic attack before," I say. "I don't plan to have any more of them."

"That's a great attitude," Dr. Tonaki says, "and chances are, this will be your one and only panic attack. But just in case it's not, please do seek medical treatment. I'm not necessarily talking about medication. Therapy is often very helpful with anxiety."

I open my mouth but then close it.

I really don't have anything to say.

I don't think I'll have another panic attack, but if I do, I will speak to Aunt Melanie.

"Are we free to go, then?" Brendan asks.

"You are." Dr. Tonaki signs some documents and then leaves the room.

Brendan helps me get dressed, and then we head out to the car. It's early Sunday morning, and he has to open the bar the next day. At least the bakery will be closed, so I don't need to work until Monday.

I'm silent during the drive home, but I don't sleep.

I don't want the nightmare of running from the tower again.

But I can't run from sleep forever. I have to accept the fact that my life may be changing. I can do that. I'm a strong person. I've always been a strong person.

And I have Brendan. I'm not the kind of woman who ever thought she needed a man for strength, but it's nice to have him anyway. Having someone to lean on is never a bad thing.

Brendan parks in the alley behind the bar and then walks me to my place.

"I thought you might like to sleep in your own bed tonight."

"I would, but I would like you lying next to me."

"All right. But I want you to sleep. Nothing else."

"Brendan, I'm so exhausted right now, I can't even think about anything else."

★ ★ ★

My eyes open to the sun streaming through my window. We get over three hundred days of sunshine per year in Colorado. This year we had a little bit of snow in mid-October, but so far that's it. The weather reverted to an Indian summer, and I'm enjoying it immensely.

I reach toward Brendan, but—

I sit up in bed. "Brendan?"

He walks into the bedroom. "I'm here. Just making some coffee. You want some breakfast?"

Do I? After everything that went on, how can I possibly eat?

"Do I even have anything in the refrigerator?"

"A few eggs. And of course some bread." He smiles.

"Eggs and toast. Sounds good. I'll make it." I pull my covers back.

"No, baby. You stay right there. I'll make it."

I rise from bed anyway and pad toward the bathroom. "I'm not the kind of person to stay in bed, even after the kind of night we had. I'm sorry to put you through that, Brendan."

"Sweetheart, you didn't put me through anything. I am here for you, no matter what happens. Anyone in your situation would've reacted the same way."

"Yeah, true. But I know it won't happen again. Dr. Tonaki doesn't have to worry about me. That was my first and last panic attack."

"I hope you're right." He smiles. "I'll get breakfast ready."

After I go to the bathroom, I throw my robe on and walk to the kitchen.

On the table . . .

The card...

The tower...

The tower has been my whole problem since I drew the damned card.

I pick it up, replace it in the deck, shuffle. Then I wrap the deck in my grandmother's scarf and place it back in the wooden box.

I wait then. I wait for the sensation of relief that I'm expecting once the card is gone.

It doesn't come.

I inhale deeply. *Let it go. Just let it all go.*

Perhaps my father had a point, stoned though he was. Maybe I need to let it go. The tower doesn't have to take me over. So I didn't feel a sense of relief. I'll let it go anyway.

Brendan brings me a plate of eggs and toast and a cup of coffee. "So you finally put it away."

"Yeah. I think that card was my whole problem, Brendan."

"Oh?"

"Yeah. Not the fact that I drew it but the fact that I couldn't put it away. That I let it consume me. It doesn't have to consume me."

"Absolutely," he says. "It does not have to consume you. Nothing has to consume you. Except me, of course." He gives me a corny wink.

"I think maybe it's time to draw another card. After breakfast."

"Yeah. Maybe you should draw one for both of us."

"I'd be happy to. What time do you need to get over to the bar?"

"By noon. It's ten thirty now."

"Okay." I sigh. "The whole town is probably talking about

my father. And about me."

"They're not talking about you, baby. I made sure I got you out of the bar without anyone seeing."

"How in the world did you accomplish that?"

"I'm Houdini." He winks again.

"Seriously…"

"There's another staircase from my apartment that leads to the storeroom. It comes to the back of my closet. It used to be boarded up, but when I had my apartment redone, I told the contractor to make it accessible. Now I know why."

"To sneak your girlfriend out when she's having a panic attack?"

"I just thought it might come in handy, and it did. No one saw us leave. And once we got to the hospital, I texted Laney to let her know I wouldn't be back in for the rest of the night."

"You're something else, Brendan Murphy."

"Like I said… Houdini."

I take a bite of eggs, and I'm surprised at how good they taste. I ate surprisingly little of that beautiful Greek dinner that Aunt Marjorie prepared, and I didn't get any of my baklava. No one did, as my father had his attack before dessert was served. Did Aunt Jade and Aunt Marjorie serve the dessert after that? Probably not. So we have a giant cake and baklava for two hundred sitting at Aunt Jade's house.

Oh, well. Food never goes to waste when the Steels are around.

I finish my breakfast, Brendan finishes his, and then I take a sip of my coffee.

"Brendan?"

"Yeah?"

"Would you mind if I didn't draw a card for you and me?"

"Why would I mind?"

"I think I need to draw a card for my father. A three-card spread. Maybe it will give me some insight into what's going on, why he had such a bad panic attack."

"You know those documents you found last night?"

"Yes."

"Those are why—well, part of the reason—your father and your mother came to see me on Thanksgiving Day."

I raise my eyebrows.

"The other reason," he continues, "is because of the messages that you and I have received."

"You and I and Pat Lamone, apparently."

"Yes."

"So it's all connected."

"Whether it is or not, I don't know, but I get the feeling your parents think so."

I rise from the table, head to the kitchen, and wash my hands, drying them on the dish towel. Then I grab the mahogany box containing my cards.

"How can you draw for your father when he's not here to hold the cards and give them his energy?"

"I can do it. I've done it before, with family matters. I have my father's energy inside me. My body comes from his body."

"I see."

I chuckle. "You don't see it at all, but that's okay. Thank you for trying to understand anyway."

"No, I do understand, Ava." He squeezes my hand. "I won't pretend to put the faith in the tarot that you do, but I respect the fact that you do, and from what I've seen from the readings you've shared with me, you do have good insight and good intuition when it comes to the cards you draw."

"That means a lot to me." I take the cards out of the box, unwrap the scarf, and hold on to them for a moment.

Somewhere in this deck are the tower and the hierophant—the two cards that have caused me the most consternation over the past several days. Already I know I won't draw either of those in this reading. I'm not sure how I know, but I'm utterly confident.

I shuffle the deck once, twice, three times, and then I hold it to my heart, imagining my father—his strength, his intelligence, his creative force, and the love he has for his family.

Then I cut the deck.

The three-card spread.

Mind, body, spirit. Past, present, future.

I close my eyes, breathe in deeply, and then I draw the first card.

The two of cups.

And it's not reversed, thank God.

My parents' marriage is strong. Not that I believed otherwise, but seeing it in the card helps a lot. Two lovers stare into each other's eyes.

But...

There *is* a downside to the card.

The lovers sometimes create such a bond that it excludes others. My parents never excluded Gina and me from their love. To the contrary, we were cherished by both Mom and Dad.

That's not the feeling I'm getting here.

No. I'm getting a more sinister feeling... as if my parents have excluded us from information that we need to know.

That we have the *right* to know.

I gulp.

"You okay?" Brendan asks.

I nod. I won't panic. Already I know this. I will face whatever comes.

"Tell me about the card," he says.

"It's the two of cups. A card of romance, attraction."

"Makes sense, I guess," he says, "since your parents just had their twenty-fifth anniversary."

"Right. Except it was supposed to be a happy occasion. A warm occasion. But all I felt last night—and the feeling is the same as I look at this card—is that they're excluding Gina and me from something. Something big."

"I'd say they know what the documents mean," Brendan says. "And maybe the odd messages too."

"That's definitely what I'm feeling here."

"You said the first card in the three-card spread represents the mind or the past."

I can't help a smile. Brendan is taking me seriously, remembering what I tell him about the tarot and my use of the cards.

"Usually. Nothing is set in stone, Brendan."

But it occurs to me that I'm saying that for myself. Obviously, my mother and father were happy together in the past. For the past twenty-five years, for sure.

But now?

God, I hate feeling this way.

I inhale a deep breath.

I stave away the panic.

I won't have another attack. I know this in my soul.

I breathe in again as I draw the second card.

The ten of pentacles.

HELEN HARDT

Oh, God.

Family. That's the word that shoves itself into my mind when I see this card. Sometimes finances... and I wonder...

Finances...

The deed transferring everything to my father.

Why?

"What do you see, Ava?" Brendan asks.

Family. Affluence. Riches.

Something's about to happen. Something with regard to my family. Both my family as a whole—the extended Steels—and my nuclear family. Mom, Dad, Gina, and me.

I regard the two cards together. The two of cups and the ten of pentacles.

Marriage and family. Changes in the family dynamic.

The past, my parents, and their happy marriage.

The present, something wavering, becoming unthreaded or unraveled.

"The ten of pentacles," I tell Brendan. "Sometimes called the ten of coins. It's usually associated with family matters."

"That seems interesting," Brendan says, "given the focus on your family lately."

"Yes, but it may indicate financial matters, affluence, or riches."

"Your family already has that in abundance."

"I know. I'm getting the feeling of a change here. This card represents the present or the body. And..." I shake my head. "Something's changing, Brendan."

"You've known that for a while. Not just because of the cards you've drawn previously but because of the conversations you've had with your family members."

"I know. In the back of my mind, I was just hoping..." I

play with my hair absently. "I was hoping I would draw some cards that might give me some peace. That might solidify my family. But I seem to be doing the opposite."

"You can't control the cards you draw," he says.

"I know. But I believe in fate and fortune and destiny. I believe I draw the cards that I am meant to draw. I still believe that, Brendan, even though I don't like what my cards have been telling me."

"There are no guarantees in life—or the tarot—that you are going to get the results you want."

I nod. "Tell me about it."

"So, one more card?"

I nod again, draw in a deep breath, and choose my third card.

The empress.

The card representing the mother.

My mother.

But then I cock my head.

Not *my* mother. I'm doing this drawing for my *father*. So this card represents not my mother but *his*.

And it represents the future.

"This doesn't make sense," I say.

"Tell me what you see."

"The card is the empress, which is mostly associated with the mother. But I'm doing this drawing for my father."

"Which means . . ."

"I feel very strongly that this card represents *his* mother."

"But his mother is dead."

"I know. But this card represents the future. And I'm not getting any feelings that this card has anything to do with a dead person." Invisible insects gnaw at my neck. "In fact . . . I almost feel like . . ."

"Like what?"

I search for words as I search for meaning.

But the words don't come even as the meaning does.

Chills skitter over my flesh. "I'm not sure. Is it possible my grandmother *isn't* dead?"

"How old was your grandmother when she had Joe?"

"Really young. Nineteen, I think."

"And Joe is how old? Sixty-three?"

"Yes."

"So that would make your grandmother eighty-two if she were alive. Many people live to be eighty-two."

"I know, but she's *not* alive. I don't feel her. And that's the strangest thing. I don't feel her at all."

"But you never knew her."

"No, I didn't. But as I was drawing these cards for the reading, I felt my connection to my father."

"Of course. He's your father. You know him."

I bite my lip, fiddle with my lip ring. "I'm not explaining this very well. What I mean is, I could feel his blood in my veins. I don't feel that with my grandmother."

"I think you're maybe reading too much into this, Ava." Brendan places his hand on my forearm. "It's difficult to feel someone when you've never met her. When she died before you were born."

"I know you don't believe in the kind of divination that I practice, but I believe that we get a lot of our power—our energy—from our ancestors. That they live through us, and not just in our physical characteristics and genetics. But in our souls. In transferred memories."

"I'm afraid you've lost me."

"It's not something I talk about a lot, but I've always

believed that our ancestors continue to live through us, more than just in our memories."

"But you can't have any memories of someone you never knew."

"That's precisely my point, Brendan. I never *knew* my grandmother, but I should be able to feel some connection. I don't feel her at all."

He wrinkles his brow. "Do you feel your grandfather? Her husband?"

"I do. And it's nothing I can put into words, but I know he's in me."

"What about your mother's parents?"

"That's something I've suppressed, for my grandfather, I mean."

"Why?"

"I knew my grandmother, and I feel her very strongly. But my grandfather ... I haven't thought of this since I was a little girl."

"What, baby?"

"I had a dream once about my grandfather. I dreamed that he came after me with a knife."

Brendan's jaw drops.

"My mother came and comforted me that night, and I told her about the dark-haired and dark-eyed man who chased me in my dreams, telling me he was my grandpa."

"What did your mother tell you?"

"She said it was a nightmare. That I needed to go back to sleep and that I was perfectly safe in our house. I believed her. I never had that nightmare again. But I did feel a connection to him—a dark connection. I didn't like the feeling, so I suppressed it."

"So you never knew your grandfather on your mother's side?"

"No, he also died before I was born. The only thing my mother has ever said about him is that he was Greek. Other than that, she doesn't talk about him, and because we always had such a happy life, neither Gina nor I ever insisted that she elaborate. After that nightmare, I preferred to forget about him anyway."

Brendan traces his finger over my forearm.

"But I'm getting ahead of myself," I say. "This reading is about my father, about what's happening *now*. Not about my mother and her ancestors."

"Family is family," Brendan says.

"True, but I was thinking specifically of my father when I drew these cards, so that's what I must concentrate on to make sense of them as a whole."

"All right. So what are you getting as a whole, then?"

"I don't know. I feel that my parents' marriage was strong. It *is* strong. I don't think that's the issue at all. What I feel more than anything is that they've excluded Gina and me from something. Whatever it is, it has to do with our family and our fortune and my father's mother. But still... I can't *feel* the woman. And if this card is referring to my father's mother, I should be able to feel her."

"Think about your father's mother," Brendan says. "Don't think of her as Daphne Steel. Think of her as an extension of you and of your father. Maybe you'll feel her then."

I regard Brendan, his raw masculinity, my sea warrior. He has more intuition than he gives himself credit for. Then I suppress a chuckle. He gives himself a lot of credit for intuition. He would say it's what bartenders do.

I close my eyes, concentrate on the cards, and I concentrate on my father and his mother.

I feel maternal instinct. I feel my maternity very strongly, but I have to ease past that, into my paternity, and look for maternity from there.

My father's love surrounds me, envelops me. He would do anything for Gina and me. He's a loving father, a kind father, a father who will protect us at all costs, and...

He has a mother who feels the same way about him.

I jerk my eyes open.

CHAPTER SIXTEEN

Brendan

Ava's eyes are wide, and there's a look of almost—is it terror?—on her face.

I squeeze her forearm. "Baby?"

"I felt her. I felt my grandmother. My father's mother."

"Good."

"I felt like... My God, Brendan. It was like a dark cloud. Maternal love, yes, but a dark cloud."

"I'm trying to understand, Ava."

Her lips tremble slightly, and her cheeks lose some of their rosiness. "I'm not sure I can explain it any better."

"It's okay. It's okay. Just don't let it consume you."

She nods. "I won't. I learned my lesson earlier. No more panic for me. But I'm glad I made myself aware of that, because if I hadn't, I'd be panicking now."

"Why?"

"Because... This woman. This woman I'm feeling. I have no idea who she is, but there's one thing I'm sure of."

"What's that?"

"She's not dead, Brendan. She's very much alive."

"Daphne Steel?"

"Yes. My father's mother is alive."

"All right." He rises. "We need to talk to your father."

"I can't do that. He just got home from the hospital. The man just had a panic attack at his anniversary party. I don't want to add to his stress."

"Where else can we get answers?" I ask.

She shakes her head. "I don't know. Maybe Aunt Melanie."

"But didn't Melanie and Marjorie both say that you needed to talk to your parents?"

"They did. But… My God, Brendan. I truly don't know what to do. I just don't."

She rises then, grabs the journal from the bureau where she keeps her cards, brings it back to the table, and jots down some notes.

"All the cards I've drawn since I got that message," she says. "The first message about Darth Morgen. *Grandmother*. My father's mother. That's who it refers to."

"So Daphne Steel is alive."

"So it would seem." She shakes her head. "That was my initial thought. But I don't feel *her*, Brendan."

"But you just said—"

"No, I said I felt my father's mother. But I didn't feel Daphne Steel."

"That doesn't make any sense."

"I know. It makes no sense at all. But maybe it does. Maybe there's something I don't know. My God, is it possible I'm not a Steel?"

"No, that's not possible. Bradford Steel was your grandfather."

"Yes. That's true. He was. I feel that very strongly."

"But you don't feel Daphne."

"No. I never have, but I never gave it much importance. I figured, as you said, that I never met her, and some ancestral ties are stronger than others."

Ava's beliefs astound me. I can't say that I agree with all of them, but I respect how powerful they are to her.

"I love you, baby, but I have to get over to the bar."

She nods. "I understand, Brendan. Will I see you tonight?"

"I'm afraid I'll be tending bar until late."

"I could come help you again."

"Are you sure you want to do that when you have to open the bakery early tomorrow morning? We're back on a regular schedule."

"Maybe not until the wee hours of the morning, but I can help for a few hours after dinner."

"And what are you going to do in the meantime?"

"I'll drive to the ranch. I don't want to bother my father and mother about this, but I'll visit them. See how Dad is doing. If he seems strong enough—mentally alert enough—I'll ask some questions. Some hard questions."

I give her a kiss on the lips. "All right. You call me if you need anything, okay?"

"Thank you, Brendan. I will. I love you."

"I love you too, baby."

★ ★ ★

After a shower and some quick inventory at the bar, I open. My father used to close the bar on Sundays, but I changed that, and it's done well. The townies especially like their last hurrah before going back to work on Monday.

Two employees specifically help me on Sundays—Darby and Shaw Peterson. They're a husband and wife who run a small liquor store in town, which is closed on Sundays. They like to make some extra income by working at the bar on their one day off, and it allows me to give my other employees Sundays off no matter what.

I get the bar stocked and am wiping down the counters when Darby and Shaw walk through the front door.

They're a middle-aged couple, but they stay young with exercise and a good diet. Neither of them drink, which I always found interesting since they own a liquor store and spend their one day off working for me in a bar.

"Brendan." Shaw removes his cowboy hat.

"Good afternoon," I call to them.

"Do you have any news on Ryan Steel?" Darby removes her jacket and sets it behind the bar.

"He's supposed to be coming home today. I'm sure you heard that it wasn't a heart attack after all."

"Actually, we haven't heard that," Shaw says.

"Yeah. He's going to be fine."

I specifically don't mention a panic attack. I'm not sure if the Steel family wants that known, although I'm not sure how they can keep it quiet. Gossip runs rampant in a small town like Snow Creek, and God knows I've been the subject of it myself more than once. But no one inspires gossip like the Steel family.

"I heard he has cancer," Darby says.

"And that's so sad, after Ruby just had breast cancer three years ago." Shaw frowns.

"You're dating Ava, Brendan," Darby says. "What's really going on?"

"I'm afraid I don't have any more information than you do, but I haven't heard anything about cancer." I begin to slice a lemon, purposefully not meeting their gazes.

Darby and Shaw continue to chatter—mostly Darby—as they don their aprons and get ready for the bar opening.

I turn the sign to *Open* at two p.m.

And customers arrive.

We're decently busy, which means Darby and Shaw are busy and they're not peppering me with questions. Good.

At five o'clock, I leave the bar in their capable hands and run up to my apartment to make myself a sandwich. The papers Ava found hidden in my copy of *Tom Sawyer* still sit on my small table. I take a quick look at them. The lien on the bar property held by the Steel Trust. The deed transferring the bar from Jeremy Madigan to my father, Sean Murphy the second. And the birth certificate of William Elijah Steel.

I pull out my copy of *The Adventures of Huckleberry Finn*, where I keep the printouts of the emails we received at Hardy's office.

Darth Morgen is alive.

Grandmother is alive.

Ava's grandmother.

Her grandmother on her father's side.

Daphne Steel.

I adore Ava, and I believe she has amazing intuition, but . . . I believe she's wrong here. Daphne Steel is *not* alive. And Ava's feeling that she has no connection to Daphne? I believe she's wrong there as well. I respect her convictions for sure, but how can you *feel* an ancestor you've never met?

I look at the other paper.

When echoes navigate down yonder, many anchors destroy ideas generated about neglect.

What in the hell could this possibly mean?

There's no doubt in my mind, though, that Ryan and Ruby Steel know what it means. There's also no doubt in my mind that Ruby already knew that Darth Morgen unscrambled to *grandmother*.

Why would they keep this information from Ava?

Perhaps Ava is finding out at this very moment.

I grab my laptop. Darth Morgen was an anagram. Maybe the long message is one as well, but man, it will take forever to figure it out. I don't have a lot of time, but I search for an anagram maker online and plug in the message.

And I wait.

The anagram generator is taking forever, so I stop, reload with Darth Morgen, and—of course—the first word is *grandmother*. Clearly the second message is too long to be an anagram, but it's some kind of puzzle.

But what kind?

Each letter could refer to another letter. I search for a codebreaker online, but I end up frazzled. I'm no cryptanalyst. That's for sure. There has to be a simpler solution.

If only I were a detective, like Ruby. She knows what this means. Damn it. I know she knows.

I regard the first word, *When*. Then I widen my eyes. I saw a detective show once where a kidnapping victim was forced to write a note telling everyone she was fine, and she managed to begin each line with a letter that—if read vertically—spelled out *Help*.

This message was typed, and it only takes up two lines, so that's not the case here . . . but—

It could be an acrostic.

I grab a pen and a piece of paper from my junk drawer.

Time to write out the message vertically.

When
echoes
navigate
down
yonder,
many
anchors
destroy
ideas
generated
about
neglect.

W E

We
Now I'm getting somewhere.
But *ND* isn't the beginning to any word I know, so the first word is not *We.*
Best to simply write it all out.

WENDYMADIGAN

But the comma could indicate a break in the words.

WENDY MADIGAN

I remember the name from when Dad and I first found the documents and did some research. She's Jeremy Madigan's niece. Who had an affair with Bradford Steel.
Which resulted in a child.
Fucking goddamn.

CHAPTER SEVENTEEN

Ava

I walk into my parents' house, only to see Gina's duffel bag sitting by the door. I find her in the kitchen, having a snack of tortilla chips with Mom's homemade salsa. Her long hair is up in a messy bun, and she's wearing faded jeans, a Mesa sweatshirt, and roughed-up cowboy boots, and still she looks better put together than I ever do.

"You going back to school?"

"School's over for the semester, but I'm heading back to the sorority house. We have a big party planned next weekend." Gina dips a chip into the salsa and brings it to her mouth. A drop of salsa slides down her chin.

She still looks perfect, even when eating messy chips and salsa. She makes a mess charming.

"Oh," I finally say. Sororities were never my thing, but Gina is the quintessential sorority girl. "How is Dad doing?"

"He's upstairs, with Mom."

"Everything okay?"

"Yeah, they say everything's fine. Dad looks good. His color is back." She wipes her mouth with a napkin and then lowers her voice. "But they're not *acting* fine, Ava. They're acting kind of strange, and I almost feel like I should stay."

"And miss the big sorority bash?" I resist an eye roll.

"I know this kind of stuff means nothing to you, but it's a big thing for me. And for Bree, Angie, and Sage. Our sorority has been a huge part of our college years."

"I know, sis. I don't get it, but I respect that it's important to you."

"Thanks, Aves."

"Tell you what. I'll keep an eye on Mom and Dad. You go ahead and go back to Grand Junction. Have your party, but then you'll be home next Sunday, right?"

"Yep. I'll be home from then until after the first of the year, when I start my last semester."

"Yup, you and the awesome foursome."

"You mean the gleesome threesome."

I raise my eyebrows. "That's a new term."

Gina shrugs. "Didn't Brianna tell you? She's graduating. She'll come back and walk with us in May for commencement, but she's done. After the big sorority party, she's coming home. For good."

"I had no idea. Good for her."

"She'll miss her last semester, but she doesn't seem to care about that. She's kind of all in with some new project. I'm not sure what it is. She's being really secretive about it."

"Ha. I'm sure she'll let us know when she's ready."

"Yeah." Gina puts away the chips and salsa, washes her hands at the kitchen sink, and then turns back to me. "I'm going to go say goodbye to Mom and Dad, and then I need to pick up Angie and Sage for the drive back."

"What about Bree?"

"She's driving by herself. Since she'll be coming home for good, she wants to stay a few extra days to wrap things up."

"Got it."

Gina leaves the kitchen, and I hear her clomping down the hallway to Mom and Dad's master bedroom.

I'll give them a few moments. I'll let them talk to Gina, and once she's gone, I'll go in.

I'll go in, assess the situation, and if all looks good, I'll shower them with the questions that I have.

I don't have any more time to waste. I need to know what's going on, and I kept my promises to Aunt Melanie and Aunt Marj. I waited until after the anniversary party.

But apparently Dad himself couldn't wait until after the anniversary party.

Something has him stressed, on edge. Enough on edge to have a panic attack when he has no history of panic attacks whatsoever.

I mean to find out what's going on.

About fifteen minutes later, Gina emerges from Mom and Dad's bedroom. She whisks by me, giving me a quick hug. "See you in a week, Aves."

"Okay, G. Drive safe."

"Will do."

Once Gina is out of the house, I head toward my parents' bedroom.

The door is usually closed, but it's cracked open. I'm not sure if they've noticed it, because they're speaking, and I can hear them quite well.

"It was bound to happen sooner or later," Mom says.

"You always thought that, Ruby?"

"Part of me did, yeah. I know you want to forget the past forever, but is that fair to our children?"

"She was supposed to be dead."

"Yeah? Well, people in your family have a tendency not to *stay* dead."

"That's only my father."

"Apparently your father's not the only one," Mom says.

What the hell are they talking about? Someone—a woman—isn't dead. Daphne Steel? My grandmother? Is this what the cards are trying to tell me?

"I've got my best investigators on it," Dad says. "Though she's always been able to elude investigators in the past. She's fucking brilliant, and she has resources."

A sigh then, so heavy I hear it through the door.

"Have you told your brothers?"

"No. Not yet. And I don't have any plan to. I'm pissed enough at them for keeping those other documents from me."

"Pissed?" Mom's voice goes higher, almost a hiss. "Your brother was shot, for God's sake. You're forgetting who's in danger if she *is* alive, and it's not you. You need your family right now."

"Sometimes I don't feel like they *are* my family."

"You got over that long ago. You know none of it matters to any of them."

"Right. And it never mattered to me either. But it does now."

"It doesn't have to."

"How can she still be alive? She's in her fucking eighties."

"Lots of people live into their eighties and beyond," Mom says.

"It was bad enough that the trafficking ring resurfaced and that whoever was behind it was trying to implicate our family. Thank God Joe and Bryce got that taken care of, but who knows what else is going on? Someone left those documents at Brendan's place."

"Yes, but they were hidden under the floorboards. I don't

think Brendan was ever meant to find them."

"Yeah. God only knows how long they've been there."

"My guess is," Mom says, "they were hidden there when the building was built. Probably by its original owner, Jeremy Madigan."

"Good old Uncle Jeremy." Dad scoffs.

Uncle Jeremy? What the hell is that supposed to mean?

"Did you ever meet him?"

"Hell no. I never met any of them. Only her. And I hardly remember that. I mean, I remember meeting her later, when I was thirty-two years old. She gave me that sapphire necklace."

"Bracelet, you mean."

"Right. My mind is a fucking mess, Ruby."

"I know, babe. It will be fine. And the bracelet is gorgeous. I loved it then, and I love it now."

"I never should've given it to you. It's tainted."

"It's a piece of jewelry, Ryan."

"It always seemed like it was meant for you. It matches your eyes. I told myself it was meant for you. That it was never hers. But I was wrong. It's a tainted piece of jewelry. Tainted with her evil."

I swallow, lean against the wall for support.

Evil?

"You and Ava," Mom says. "You put too much emphasis on things that have no basis in fact."

"Ava had to get it from somewhere. You're a cop. You deal in facts, evidence. But damn it, you'll never convince me that the woman isn't evil."

"*Isn't* . . . You're using the present tense, Ryan."

"She's still alive. I know she is. You and I both know she is because we know what those messages mean."

I push my palms flatly against the wall.

I shouldn't be eavesdropping, but they're about to drop some kind of bomb, and I need to be here to hear it.

But my phone buzzes in my back pocket.

Damn it.

Mom comes rushing out. "Ava?"

"Yeah. I'm here." I glance at the phone. It's Brendan. "Excuse me for a minute, okay?"

"Hi," I say into the phone.

"Ava, I just realized something."

"What's that?"

"The second message. The one that makes no sense. It's an acrostic."

"An acrostic?"

"Yeah. The first letters of each word form a message."

"What does it say?"

"Wendy Madigan."

"Who's Wendy Madigan?" I ask.

Mom's eyes dart into circles.

"Jeremy Madigan's niece," Brendan says.

But he's not telling me everything. His voice is slightly higher than normal.

My mother's staring at me intently. "Brendan, I have to go. I'll call you as soon as I can." I end the call quickly.

"Mom," I say. "Who the hell is Wendy Madigan?"

CHAPTER EIGHTEEN

Brendan

Though I hate to do it, I leave the bar in the capable hands of Darby and Shaw and drive out to the ranch, to Ryan and Ruby's house.

I don't want Ava going through this alone.

She's there, and she's going to ask her parents some hard questions.

I don't know what the relevant answers are, but I can guess, given what Ava truly believes about the cards she's drawn, her world could be upended.

I need to be there for her.

I gun it, hitting a hundred miles per hour as I thunder through the rural roads.

CHAPTER NINETEEN

Ava

"Were you listening to your father's and my conversation?" Mom asks.

"Would it matter if I was?"

Mom narrows her eyes. "None of that was meant for your ears."

"You haven't answered my question, Mom. Who was—or is—Wendy Madigan?"

She doesn't reply.

"You and I both know that you're the best private investigator out there. You and I both know that you figured out that Darth Morgen refers to grandmother. It's an anagram. And that other bizarre message? It's an acrostic, and it refers to Wendy Madigan. If I hadn't been waiting a week for your expertise, I could have figured it out myself. Who the hell is Wendy Madigan?"

"Jeremy Madigan was Wendy Madigan's uncle," Mom says.

I know that much. Brendan told me. "And that is relevant...how?"

Except...

I drop my jaw open. My father just referred to him as "Uncle Jeremy."

"Ava..."

I stand tall, determined, in the face of my mother, who I respect but who I'm also determined to get answers from. "Someone sent me these messages, Mom. Someone wants me to know about Wendy Madigan, and someone wants me to know something about my grandmother. They can't be referring to *your* mother. I remember when she died, and I remember when we buried her. But I don't know anything about Dad's mother. Only that she was mentally ill, and she passed away in her sleep at the facility where she lived."

Mom sighs. "She did."

"So why is someone telling me that my grandmother is alive? If it doesn't refer to your mother and doesn't refer to Dad's mother—"

Mom bites her lip.

Yes, my mother—the cop with nerves of steel—is biting her freaking lip.

Ruby Steel doesn't get nervous.

Ruby Steel doesn't bite her fucking lip. That's an Ava Steel thing.

"Damn it," I say. "What the hell is going on?"

"Language, Ava."

I draw in a long, deep breath, trying but failing to control my temper. "I don't give a flying fuck about language right now, Mom. Something's going on. I've known it for a while. Ever since I got that bizarre message about Darth Morgen and I drew a card. The hierophant. The fucking hierophant. I don't know who I am anymore, Mom, and I need you to tell me why that is."

My mother's features soften. "Nothing will ever change who you are, Ava."

I crunch my hands into fists. "Damn it! I'm so tired of cryptic answers. You were a police detective, Mom. A private investigator. You don't do cryptic."

"Ava, we need to let your father rest."

"Fine. Let him rest. You and I can talk now. You look pretty darned healthy except for that incessant lip biting, which I've never seen you do."

Mom bites her lip again but quickly stops. "This isn't my story. It's your father's."

"Then let's go on in and he can tell me."

My mother positions herself between me and the door to her bedroom where my father is. "No, Ava. Not now. Not while he's still weak."

"Gina says he looks fine."

"Gina sees what she wants to see. She paints her own pictures. She's an artist."

I shake my head. "That's BS, and we both know it. Dad is fine. He had a panic attack, Mom. A hardy and healthy middle-aged man, with no history of anxiety, had a panic attack at your damned anniversary party. Why? What the fuck is going on?"

"Ava . . ."

I grip my mother's shoulders. "You can move, Mom, or I'll move you."

Mom doesn't even wince. "I'm still your mother. I'm still a trained police officer."

"Yeah? I'm your daughter. I'm taller than you, and I'm damned strong myself."

"Don't underestimate me, Ava."

I let go of her shoulders and move away from her so that I meet her gaze head on. "Really? Is this really where you want to go, Mom? You want to get into a fistfight with your daughter?

Because I'll do it. I'm that frustrated. I'm that pissed."

"Your father loves you."

"Have I questioned that?"

"He loves all of us, his brothers, his sister. He loves this family."

"Again, not the issue."

"There are things... Things you don't know about that we all chose to keep from you kids."

"Yeah, yeah, yeah. Brock told me. He told me what happened to Dale and Donny, what happened to Uncle Talon. It's horrible. It made me throw up, Mom. But I'm an adult, and I can handle anything you toss at me."

"Ava, I—"

We both jerk at a pounding on the front door. The dogs are outside or they'd be going crazy.

"See who that is, please," Mom says.

Damn.

Who the hell is interrupting this now? She's going to go lock herself in the bedroom, and I'll never find out what's going on.

"I think I'll stay here," I say.

"Go see who it is, Ava."

"I stopped taking orders from you years ago, Mom."

The pounding gets harder, stronger.

"Ava..."

Then—

"Ava! Are you in there?"

Fuck.

Brendan.

"Sounds like it's for you," Mom says.

I love the man, but why now? I turn and walk down the

hallway toward the pounding. I open the door to find Brendan standing there, still wearing his bar apron.

"Your timing is impeccable," I say dryly.

"You okay?"

"I'm fine. Did you find out anything else about Wendy Madigan?"

"No. I came straight here. Let's go talk to your mother. Together."

"She's in her bedroom with my dad. My guess is the door's locked."

"Why?"

"I overheard them talking. It's a long story." I pour out what I can remember of the conversation.

"Family," he says. "The cards didn't steer you wrong, Ava. This all has something to do with your family dynamic and how you see yourself."

"It would appear to."

"Just remember who you are. You are Ava Steel, you're a baker, and you're beautiful and intelligent and hardworking. Talented and inspiring. You stand on your own two feet, and nothing you find out about your family will ever change that."

"What if my father's supposed to own everything?"

"So what if he is? You know your father. Would he really take away his siblings' inheritance?"

I shake my head. "No, he wouldn't do that."

"So there you have it. Nothing is going to change, Ava."

"Right. Nothing is going to change."

The words leave my lips. I hear them. I even see them as if they're typewritten in my head.

The only problem is?

I don't believe them.

Not for a moment.

CHAPTER TWENTY

Brendan

Something's brewing. Something big, and part of me already knows what it is.

I take Ava's hand and lead her out onto the back deck. It's a brisk day, but the sun is shining, and it warms our faces. The dogs come up to us to get their requisite pets, and then they go back to their play.

I hold Ava's hand in mine, rubbing it against the cool air. "Do you want me to make you a pot of tea or something?"

She shakes her head. "No."

"Some spiced cider?"

"I don't even know what my mom has in the kitchen. The housekeeper is off on Sundays, and I—" She buries her head in her hands, choking back a sob.

"Cry, baby." I rub the back of her neck, massaging her.

"I'm not crying."

And she's not. She choked it back.

"Your mother and father love you."

She raises her head. "I know that, Brendan. I've never questioned it. But I'm looking at the big picture now. Not just what's going on with my own family, but what's going on with the extended family as well. The things they've kept hidden from us all these years."

"For your own protection. So you could have an idyllic childhood."

"And we did. We all had amazing childhoods—even Dale and Donny, after the horror they had been through. But was everything built on a lie?"

"Of course it wasn't."

"I wish I could be as certain as you are," she says.

"I can't be certain that there haven't been lies involved," I tell her. "But what I *am* certain of is that your family loves you. They love Gina. They love all their nieces and nephews. Love is the most solid foundation there is, Ava. It's hard as granite, and nothing can break it."

She looks up at me then, her blue eyes glistening. "Truly, Brendan?"

I squeeze her hand, lean forward, and kiss her cold lips. "Truly."

The French doors open then, and Ruby peeks out. "You two need to come inside. It's getting too chilly out here."

"We're fine, Ruby," I say.

"Please. Your father wants to talk to you."

Ava jerks into a standing position so quickly that she almost knocks her Adirondack chair over. "Good. Come on, Brendan."

"He wants to talk to you alone," Ruby says.

"He had that chance. Brendan is here now, and I want him with me."

"Ava…"

"Baby," I say, following Ruby through the French doors and into the kitchen. "It's not necessary. I can sit here with your mom."

She shrugs. "Fine." She walks inside, leaves Ruby and me

in the kitchen, and disappears down the hallway.

"Come on, Brendan," Ruby says. "I'll make you a sandwich or something."

"I'm fine. I had a sandwich at my place before I came over."

"Who's taking care of the bar?"

"Darby and Shaw can handle it. I need to be here for Ava."

Ruby gives me a wistful smile. "You care very much for my daughter, don't you?"

"To be frank? I'm in love with her, Ruby."

Ruby clears her throat. "Does she feel the same way?"

"She says she does."

"Ava's very young."

"She's twenty-four. She's old enough to know if she's in love or not."

"Yes. I believe she is. She's an old soul, you know?"

"An old soul?"

"It's something my mother used to talk about. She and I were so different. She said that she was an old soul but that I was brand-new." Ruby shakes her head, chuckling. "I used to consider it an insult, but my mother wasn't a mean person. She didn't hurl around insults for no reason. So I grew to take it at face value. She believed in some things that I didn't, but as soon as Ava was born, and after the first time my mother held her, she looked up at me and said, 'Ruby, this one's an old soul.'"

"I think I kind of get it."

"Yeah, now that Ava's grown up, I get it too. Her fascination with the tarot. Her amazing intuition. Her desire to leave the family fold and make it on her own. That kind of confidence can only come from an old soul." She smiles. "If you believe in that kind of thing."

"I can't say I did before I met Ava, but I'm pretty sure I do now."

"My mother didn't have an easy life. She and I were separated when I was a teen."

I lift my eyebrows.

"It's a long story and not important right now. But if my mother were here, she would tell me to trust Ava. To trust my daughter. She can handle anything we throw at her." Ruby shakes her head. "But *I'm* not certain of that, Brendan. If you love her, she's going to need you. She's going to need you more than ever after this talk with her father."

I nod.

I'll be there for Ava.

Because if what's coming is what I think it is?

She's going to understand those cards she's drawn. More than ever.

CHAPTER TWENTY-ONE

Ava

My father is sitting in his brown leather recliner in the sitting room next to his master bedroom. My mother's recliner sits on his other side, a reading table between them. The sunshine streams in through a bay window and casts its rays on the brown-and-gold Turkish rug covering the hardwood floor.

"Ava." Dad nods to my mother's chair.

I take a seat and absentmindedly grab the crocheted afghan that sits on the arm of the chair and spread it over my legs.

I feel chilly, as if all the heat has been sucked out of the room.

The color is back in Dad's cheeks, but his eyes are sunken and sad.

"You're looking good, Daddy." It's not a lie. Not really.

"Thank you. I'm very sorry that I scared everyone last night."

"It's okay."

"No, Ava, it's not okay. The Steels have always prided ourselves on remaining strong and stoic in the worst of circumstances. God knows, we've known the worst of circumstances. But I let something get to me. Something I thought I'd put behind me long ago. But, as seems to be the norm in this family, it's creeping back up on me."

"Wendy Madigan?" I ask.

He widens his eyes slightly. "Where did you hear that name?"

"Brendan figured out the second puzzle. It's an acrostic, and it refers to Wendy Madigan."

"Yes. Wendy Madigan."

"So she's Jeremy Madigan's niece. Jeremy, who Brendan's father bought the bar from, right?"

"Yes. Jeremy was her uncle. Her father's brother."

"What's that got to do with the rest of the puzzle?" I ask. "What does it have to do with my grandmother?"

"Ava"—my father clears his throat—"Wendy Madigan *is* your grandmother."

My jaw drops, and my skin chills further. If I thought the room was cold before, now I'm covered in icicles, and they're poking me in the back of my neck.

"I don't understand." I gulp. "Am I not your child? Was I adopted, like Dale and Donny?"

The thought had occurred to me over the years because I'm so different from most of the Steels. But I didn't take it seriously. I felt the connection to my mother and my father so strongly.

"No, Ava. You're not adopted. You are the biological child of your mother and me."

A heavy sigh of relief pushes out of my mouth.

"Not that it would make a difference," Dad says. "You know we all love Dale, Donny, and Henry just as much as we love our own flesh and blood."

"Yes, I know. It's just… Dad, I've been questioning the foundation of this family, and my place within it, for a while now. I've been drawing cards—"

"Ava..."

"Just let me finish, Dad. I know you don't take the tarot seriously—"

"To the contrary, Ava. I take it quite seriously because I take *you* seriously."

"But anyway, I—" I gasp as something finally dawns on me. "Wait a minute. If I'm your biological child—yours and Mom's—how can Wendy Madigan be my grandmother?"

"Because, Ava"—Dad clears his throat again—"Wendy Madigan is *my* mother. My biological mother."

Chills again. I rub my arms to warm them away, but still, they permeate me, prickle me like icy pine needles.

The empress. My father's mother.

"My father, Bradford Steel, had an affair with Wendy Madigan. I'm the result."

"I..." My stomach clenches.

"I know this will be hard for you to digest, Ava. But you are still a Steel. Bradford Steel is my biological father, your biological grandfather. None of this changes who *you* are."

I drop my jaw as images flash before me. All the cards I've drawn, and then the thoughts...

How I've never been able to feel Daphne Steel as an ancestor, but I felt another presence—a grandmother.

"I'm shivering," I say through chattering teeth.

"I'm sorry to lay this on you, Ava, but clearly someone out there wants you to know. That's why you've been getting these messages."

"So she's alive? This Wendy Madigan?"

"That's what I've got our investigators looking into. Your mother and I didn't figure this out until Thanksgiving Day, when we saw that second message that you and Brendan received. We figured the first one referred to a grandmother of some sort, but we didn't understand the significance until the second. If she is alive, I will find out. I will find proof. Because you see, Ava, I saw her die twenty-five years ago. And your mother pulled the trigger."

A cannonball plummets into my stomach.

"She was a cop," I say, trying to make sense of this. "She . . . She did what she had to do."

"She had left the force by then." Dad sighs. "It's a long story, but her father saved her life that day."

"The father she never talks about." The grandfather I once dreamed about . . . in a black cloud of evil.

"Yes."

"Why doesn't she talk about him, Dad?"

"That's for her to tell you."

"Oh my God. That's what she told me about *this*. That it was for you to tell me."

"And she was correct. Wendy Madigan is *my* mother, not hers."

"If Mom shot her . . . Mom doesn't miss, Dad."

"No, she doesn't. And she didn't. But I also saw my own father shot that day as well—also by someone who doesn't miss—and he turned out to be very much alive."

I shake my head, trying desperately to make sense of what I'm hearing. "How? How do you cheat death like that? How do you fake your own death?"

"My father did it twice. He was well versed in it. When you have that kind of money lying around, you can do anything."

"But how?"

"None of us know the logistics, Ava. Bulletproof garments.

Blood pellets. Or most likely something more elaborate. To be honest, I don't want to know any more than that. I would never do that to my children."

My mind whirls. What have I walked into? What have I been *forced* into?

"You'd better not," I tell him forcefully.

"I won't, but I have some fears."

I gasp. "Are you in danger, Dad?"

He shakes his head. "No. I can tell you for certain that I'm not in any danger. Nor is your mother, nor are you and Gina."

"Then what are you afraid of?"

"If Wendy Madigan—my mother—is alive, your aunt and uncles—and all your cousins—could potentially be in danger." He rubs his hand over his face. "She could be behind Talon's shooting. Joe thought he was the target, but Wendy—she's gone after Talon before. When he was just a child."

More chills. More icicles. More pine needle pricks to the back of my neck. "Why? Why would she do that?"

"When Talon was a child, it was to hurt my father, to punish him for choosing Daphne over her. My mother was obsessed with my father. They had known each other since they were very young, in high school, and they were an on-again, off-again couple until my father met my mother—er... Daphne."

"So you always thought of Daphne as your mother?"

"I did, and she treated me as her son. No differently than Talon or Joe. In fact, I was the youngest for a long time until Marjorie came along. I was her baby, and she spoiled me rotten."

"So she considered you her own."

"She did, and later we found out why."

"Oh?"

"Yes. Daphne suffered from dissociative identity disorder. She dissociated during the time Wendy was pregnant with me, probably because the pain of her husband's infidelity was too much to bear. Once I came along, as far as she knew, I was hers."

"When did you find out?"

"Not until twenty-five years ago. It shattered my world, Ava. And for a while, I questioned who I was, just as I'm sure you will now. But be firm. Be confident in who you are. You are a Steel. You are my daughter, and you are the granddaughter of Bradford Steel. But more than any of that, you are Ava. My beautiful daughter of whom I'm extraordinarily proud."

"I don't know what to say to any of this. But it's all making sense now..." I close my eyes, pondering. "The cards I've drawn... The messages I've received... But who? Who is sending these messages?"

"I don't know exactly who's sending them," he says, "but I know Wendy is probably behind them. Why she's resurfacing now, I have no idea. But she is, and it's something we're going to have to deal with."

"But she's an old woman."

"She is. But I don't know what the hell she's been up to for the last twenty-five years, and we need to find out."

"Why do we need to find out, Daddy?"

"Because, sweetheart, you, your mother, your sister, and I may not be in any danger, but Uncle Talon was shot. And I don't want anyone else to be next."

CHAPTER TWENTY-TWO

Brendan

I sit with Ruby in the kitchen, drinking a pumpkin spice latte that she made from her Italian cappuccino machine. It's surprisingly good, especially given the fact that my taste buds are on hiatus.

"I should be going." I wipe the foam off my upper lip with a napkin. "I should see how things are going at the bar."

"Please, wait for Ava. She'll need you."

"Of course, I'll do anything for Ava. But I'm not sure she'll need me, Ruby. I think maybe she'll need you. Her mother. What she needs now are answers. She doesn't need me to protect her. She doesn't need you and her father to protect her. She needs, simply, to know what's going on."

"I'm not sure she's ready to hear all the answers," Ruby says.

"Ava is a strong woman."

"I'm not suggesting that she isn't, but there are things... Things about our family..."

"I know. Believe me, I've heard the rumors my whole life that the Steels own this town. Then when I found those documents hidden in my place, it seemed the rumors may be true."

"There are things even Ryan and I don't know about his

father," Ruby says. "Things we will never know. Things that died with him all those years ago."

"But you're not just talking about Ryan's father, are you?"

Ruby looks down at her latte cup, swishes the contents around a little. Then she looks up and meets my gaze. "No, I'm not."

"Ava says you never talk about your own father."

"No, I don't."

"I won't ask you to tell me anything," I say. "But I hope you'll tell Ava. She's feeling in flux right now, like she doesn't know exactly who she is. The cards she's drawn have got her pretty freaked."

"I've always wished she wouldn't take the tarot so seriously."

"But she does, and I respect that."

"I respect it too," Ruby says. "I have the utmost respect for my older daughter. She's an amazing young woman, and she's accomplished everything without the help of her family's money. That's something I'm very proud of. But I'm a detective, an investigator. We work on facts, on evidence. Not on intuition and emotion."

"I doubt that's wholly the case, Ruby. I would bet, as a detective, your intuition serves you well."

"Absolutely. I've followed my gut many times, and it led me to facts. But intuition alone is nothing without the facts to back it up."

"When you're a private investigator."

"Yes. When you're a private investigator." She chuckles lightly, but then her face regains its gravity. "But you have to understand, Brendan. That's my mind-set."

"I do understand. Probably better than Ava does."

"Ava has always had her own way of looking at things," Ruby says. "Even when she was a little girl, I knew she was different. She was so in tune with nature, with the animals on the ranch. Quite frankly, I was surprised she didn't stay on the ranch, take more interest in Joe's or Talon's professions."

"Interesting. She never told me any of that."

"This ranch is a beautiful place," Ruby says. "And I think she considered staying. She loves all nature, but I think, in the end, she couldn't stay *because* of her love for animals."

"I see."

"I've always been surprised that she still eats meat. When she was nine years old, she stopped going out to the north and northwest quadrants, where the cattle graze. She couldn't bear the thought of..." Ruby shakes her head.

"So she cut herself off from it."

"Yes, that's exactly what she did. But it was okay, because she got close to Marjorie, and she learned to cook, to bake. That became her new passion."

"Still, it's apparent, in her love for the tarot and what it represents, that she still puts a lot of stock in nature and the universe."

"She does. And she found a way to exercise those loves in a way that didn't torment her."

"Did she ever get close to any of the animals?"

"When she was a little girl, yes, she did. I remember one time, a calf was born, and she and Brock and David—our own Huey, Dewey, and Louie—were present at the birth with Joe and Bryce. She fell in love with that little calf. She named him Buster. But Buster grew up, Brendan. And he wasn't good enough quality, by Joe's estimation, to stable as a bull to impregnate the breeding stock. So of course, that meant..."

"That meant he became a steer. And we know what happens to steers on a beef ranch."

"Exactly."

"Jesus."

"Ava took it better than I expected. But she never went up to the quadrants again, never went to see the animals that she loved. She started getting close to the horses on the ranch and, of course, all the dogs. She loves dogs. I'm surprised she doesn't have one of her own, except that it would be difficult in that tiny apartment where she lives."

"Her family means a lot to her," I say.

"I know that. So this is going to be difficult for her. That's why I want you to stay and wait for her."

"I will." I grab my phone. "I just need to make a few quick calls."

CHAPTER TWENTY-THREE

Ava

I gulp as icy chills poke at me. "Why would the rest of the family be in danger?"

"Wendy Madigan, at least from the little I know about her, was an evil genius."

"Dad, this isn't a Scooby-Doo cartoon."

"No, it isn't," he says, his expression serious. "I'm not being hyperbolic. She had a genius level IQ, and she was inherently evil."

"Do you really believe people can be inherently evil?"

"I never did. Until Wendy Madigan."

I swallow again. "There are no absolutes in this world, Daddy. That's what you always taught me."

"I did, and I believe that. There was some good in Wendy Madigan. Her love for me transcended everything. Her love for my father. But it was an obsessive love. Not a nurturing, kind love."

"I don't understand. I don't understand how any of this happened. Why would your father . . ."

"Like I said, most of the answers died with him. I'll never understand the hold that Wendy had on him. It was strong, but the bond he and my mother shared was ultimately stronger."

"And she was mentally ill."

"She was. But so was Wendy. Or so *is* Wendy, I guess I should say, if she is truly alive."

"You said you watched her die."

"I did. Or thought I did." He closes his eyes and shakes his head. "That day, Ava. That day was one of the most horrific of my life."

"I'm so sorry. Can you tell me about it? Or is that asking too much? Especially after the panic attack?"

He nods. "I don't see how I *can't* tell you about it now. Wendy, if she is indeed alive—and at this point I'd bet my life that she is—has reached out to you. She's had someone else reach out to you through these bizarre messages you've been receiving. So I'll tell you the truth. Brace yourself."

I bite my lip, tug on my lip ring. Then grasp the arms of the recliner, my knuckles white. I breathe in deeply through my nose and out through my mouth three times, just like Aunt Melanie advised.

When I feel relaxed, or as relaxed as I'm going to get, I turn to my father. "Tell me, Daddy. Tell me about that day."

He begins, and I find my eyes closing, images forming as my father speaks.

★ ★ ★

Something was wrong. I was living in the guesthouse behind Talon's house at the time, and Ruby was with me. I went running from the bedroom clad only in boxer briefs.

"Ruby, are you all right?"

Then I saw my mother standing in the entryway to the kitchen. She was supposed to be locked up in a psychiatric ward.

"What the fuck?"

"Watch your language, Ryan. And for goodness' sake, put some clothes on. You're clearly just like your father." Wendy nodded to Ruby. "You too. It's the middle of the day."

"Spare me any information about my father's sex life, please. What are you doing out of psych?" I demanded.

"Really? You think they can hold me there? I could have gotten out long ago, but it suited my purpose to be there."

I had no idea what she was capable of, how she could escape a locked facility, but clearly she got what she wanted, no matter the cost. I was proof of that. I slowly inched forward, placing myself between Wendy and Ruby. No way was she going to harm the woman I loved.

"Then why are you here? What do you want?"

"I came to see your father, dear. I know he's home."

"How do you know that?"

"Do you really think your father makes a move without me knowing it?"

Ruby and I stayed silent. Brad Steel, my father, was smarter than any of us had given him credit for. He'd allowed Wendy to find out what he was doing. That way, she thought they had no secrets, and it gave him the chance to hide Daphne away without Wendy knowing.

I'll be damned.

"She's armed, Ryan," Ruby said.

"No, I'm not."

"You are."

Mom moved slowly.

"You're carrying on an ankle strap," Ruby said.

"I'm not. Where would I get a gun, coming right out of the mental hospital?"

Good question. However, according to both my father

and Ruby's father, this woman could make just about anything happen. I strode cautiously toward her. I didn't think she would harm her own son, but she was a madwoman.

I pushed up both legs of her sweat pants and found the strap. I grabbed the weapon and examined it. "Loaded too. Any explanation, Mother?"

"That's between your father and me."

"What do you want with him?" I asked.

"Closure," she said. "This all ends today, Ryan."

"According to him, you broke a promise by telling me that you're my mother," I said, seeming to enunciate my words to draw this out, give us time. "You've been the cause of everything horrible that's happened to my family. My father won't see you."

"Oh, he'll see me."

"What makes you think he will?"

"You'll make sure of it."

"No, I won't."

In a flash, she pulled another piece from inside her roomy waistband and pointed it straight at Ruby. "You will. Because if you don't, I'll send your girlfriend here to hell."

The ankle derringer had been a decoy. The woman was good. Once Ruby and I noticed the one she'd wanted us to notice, she knew we'd stop looking. Rookie mistake. I should have known better than to take anything about Wendy at face value.

She'd played me just like Brad had been playing her, letting her find out what he wanted her to find out so she didn't look any further to find Daphne.

"Don't you dare harm her, Mother," I said through clenched teeth, my hands in front of me and my heart beating like a drum, "or I'll never speak to you again." I inched backward toward Ruby.

"I don't want to harm her, darling. But I need to see your father. So take me to him and make sure I get in to see him, and your girlfriend lives."

"Don't listen to her, Ryan," Ruby said. *"Don't unleash her on your brothers and sister. They've been through enough. We can handle this right here and right now."*

Worry for Ruby rushed through me. She was good. A trained cop. But my mother was a psychopath.

"Give me the gun, Mother."

"I can't, my sweet son. I'm sorry."

"If you love me the way you say you do, please give me that gun."

"I do love you, Ryan. More than you'll ever know."

"Then take the gun off Ruby. This has nothing to do with her."

"Wrong," Wendy said. *"This involves all of you as well as your father. And I can assure you this. Someone is going to die tonight. It's up to you, Ryan, who."*

★ ★ ★

I gasp as I jerk forward and open my eyes.

"Stop, Daddy. Please."

"Breathe, baby."

I inhale, exhale. Three times. I won't have another panic attack. I know this. In my soul, I know this. But this story . . . It's incredible. My father, my mother . . . in so much danger.

"I'll tell you the rest later," Dad says.

"No. We've started this, and I've got to finish it. I've got to know the secrets to the family's past. If I don't, I won't have a future."

"Ava…"

"Please, Daddy. Just continue." I grip the arms of the recliner once more.

★ ★ ★

Up to me? Perspiration dripped from my face, but I held myself rigid. "The only person who might die tonight is you, Mother. You will not hurt Ruby. Now hand that gun to me." I extended one hand to her.

"I might very well be the one to die tonight. And after I have the closure I seek, I will not hesitate to accept my fate. But to get to that point, I need to see your father. You will take me to the main house and get me in to see him. Now go get dressed and bring her some pants."

"Hell no. I'm not leaving her."

"Have it your way." She gestured to Ruby. "We'll come along with you."

Once Ruby and I were dressed, Wendy held the gun on me while I phoned my brothers and my sister, asking them to meet me at the main house where Talon and Jade lived. I can't even remember the excuse I used, but I was desperate, and they all agreed to meet.

"I'm sorry," I said to my father and my siblings once we'd gotten into the main house. "I had no choice."

My esteemed mother was holding on to Ruby, the gun pressed into her side. Ruby was a trouper. She'd mouthed to me that she could overtake Wendy while we were walking to the main house, but I'd begged her with my eyes not to. She must have understood. I would not take a chance with Ruby's life.

I couldn't lose her. Not when happiness was finally within reach.

Ruby hadn't flinched once, and though I knew she was nervous, no one could tell by her demeanor. This was far from the first time she'd been held at gunpoint... although perhaps the first time by someone as psychotic as my biological mother.

"We understand," my father said, turning to Wendy. "How did you get out of lockup?"

"Come now, Brad," she said. "You know me better than that. You know I could have gotten out at any time."

My father nodded, clearing his throat. "Yes. I know."

"Look," I said. "I got you here. Now state your business. My family has been through enough these past several weeks. Let's just get this over with."

"I am part of your family too, Ryan," she said. "Or have you forgotten?"

How I wished I could forget. But I didn't voice the words. I couldn't risk setting her off, not when she still had Ruby at gunpoint.

"Your business is with me," my father said. "Let Ruby go."

"My business is with all of you," she said. "I came to finally get what's coming to me."

"You said you wanted closure," I reminded her.

"Yes," she said. "By the time I'm done here, we will all have closure."

My brothers and sister had been uncharacteristically silent throughout this. They stood together on one side of the large office, Jade holding tight onto Talon's hand. Thankfully, Melanie had gone to a doctor's appointment and wasn't available.

Joe's eyes betrayed his thoughts. He was getting ready to strike.

I shook my head slightly at him, hoping I was conveying my message for him to stand down. I couldn't risk Ruby being hurt.

But I knew my big brother. Once he set his mind to something—
      "Take that gun off my daughter, Wendy."
      Marjorie gasped as we all turned our gazes to the doorway. Theodore Mathias—your grandfather—stood there, gun in his hand, pointed at Wendy's head.

★ ★ ★

I gasp again. "My grandfather? The one Mom never talks about?"

Dad clears his throat. "Yes."

"He was there? But—"

"Let me finish, Ava, if you want me to. Then you may ask your mother about her father."

I nod, closing my eyes once more.

★ ★ ★

Wendy didn't turn around to face him. "I figured you'd show up, Theo. You're the one person who's better at covering his tracks than even I am."
      "I learned from the best. Now get that gun off my daughter, or I'll splatter your brains all over this room."
      "You don't have the balls," Wendy said.
      Was she kidding? This was the man who'd spent the better part of his lifetime stealing and torturing people—

★ ★ ★

I clench all over. "Stealing and torturing people?" I gasp out.

No wonder my mother never talks about her father. Just what the hell am I descended from?

"Yes," Dad says, and his voice is eerily calm. "Theodore Mathias is one of the men who abused and tortured Uncle Talon. Perhaps we—"

I steel myself. I've gone too far to back out now. "No, Daddy. Finish. I promise I won't interrupt again."

And I vow to keep that promise, no matter what I hear.

★ ★ ★

According to what Theo had told Ruby, she'd been the reason for his downfall. He should have been thrilled to do her in.

"You have something in place, don't you, Mother?" I said. "A fail-safe. Something that will take my father and Mathias down if you die."

She smiled. "I always knew you were brilliant, darling."

Of course. That was why my father and the others hadn't blown her head off years ago.

I regarded my siblings. Talon's face had gone pale. Blankly pale. He'd come face-to-face with the last of the men who'd tortured him all those years ago, and paralysis seemed to grip him. Jade snuggled into him, rubbing his shoulder, soothing him.

But no one was here to soothe Joe. His eyes were on fire, his jaw tensed.

Somehow, I had to stop him. A gun was still trained on the woman I loved, and I didn't trust the woman wielding it any more than I trusted the man threatening her.

"Mother," I said as calmly as I could. "If you love me as you say you do, please let Ruby go."

"My audience is with all of you," she said. "I will not."

"You will," Mathias said.

But before he could strike, Wendy moved with snakelike stealth.

I jumped at a gunshot.

A bullet from the gun previously pointed at Ruby had shot into Theo's stomach. He fell backward in the doorway, blood gushing from his abdomen. The metallic and raw stench permeated the air.

Did the woman have eyes in the back of her head? He could have easily shot her first.

It dawned on me then. My mother hadn't been lying when she said she might be the one to die today.

She was ready to go, which made her even more dangerous.

I had to figure out what her angle was. She might be planning to take all of us with her.

Ruby fell to her father's side and checked his pulse. He muttered some words to her that I couldn't make out, and then he grabbed her other hand.

"It's weak," she said. "I don't think he's going to make it."

Then Joe struck. He swiftly walked forward and raised his foot.

"Joe!" I said.

He lowered his foot, staring at me.

"Let him," Ruby said, dropping her father's hand. "His pulse is barely there. He's as good as dead already."

But Joe backed off as Talon seemed to reanimate. He stepped forward as well. "You bastard!" he yelled. "You fucking bastard." He knelt down and pulled up Theo's left sleeve, showing the tattoo of the phoenix. "Fucking evil bastard." He curled his hand into a fist, ready to punch.

Joe got a grip then. He pulled Talon up. "He's gone, Tal. It's over."

Talon stood, nodding. "You're right. This isn't who I am anymore. Good riddance."

I kept one eye on my mother. She still had a gun in her hand, though she wasn't pointing it toward anyone at the moment.

Ruby sat, staring into nothingness. I kneeled in front of her. "Baby, are you okay?"

She nodded, gave a sniffle, but no tears came. "He saved my life."

"Maybe. I'm not sure Wendy was going to hurt you."

"I'm calling 9-1-1," my father said.

That jarred Wendy back into action. She pointed the gun right at him. "You're doing no such thing. Besides, he's already dead. I never miss."

He put the phone down. "All right. We'll do this your way, Wendy. What do you want?"

She closed her eyes for a second, still holding the gun, and then opened them. "I was always jealous. Even when I was a tiny child, before I even met you, Brad. Did you know that one of the symbols in alchemy for copper is what we know as the female symbol?"

"Wendy," my father said, "what are you—"

"Did you ever figure it out? The symbol on our rings?"

"The symbol was nonsense," Brad said. "Now put that gun down, and we'll talk about this."

"Even then I knew I was different. My parents didn't understand me. The future lawmakers never understood me. Only you, Brad. You knew exactly what I wanted and needed. Sometimes I dream about how you used to tie me—"

"Damn it, Wendy!"

"Our son was conceived in love." She glanced to me. "You do know that, don't you? I was bound for your father's pleasure when he planted the seed that became you."

"Wendy!"

She turned back toward my father's voice, laughing. "Oh, you knew me, Brad. You destroyed me, and I let you. I coveted you. We were soul mates. But you never figured out the symbol."

"It's the symbol for evil," I said. "The devil." I pointed to Mathias's now motionless body, blood seeping all over the hardwood floor. "He figured it out. So did Larry Wade. And so did we."

"Of course you would, my brilliant son." She smiled—a sickeningly sweet smile, right out of a slasher flick. "I contorted it a little, but at its center was the symbol for female . . . and the symbol for evil. But it's also the symbol for copper. Do you know why that makes sense?"

No one spoke. I looked around. Jade was holding on to Talon. Joe's eyes moved back and forth. He was planning something. If I could take my mother down, get that gun away from—

"Copper is a soft metal, you know. Soft, like a female. Not hard like iron. Like a male."

I gathered my courage. My father might be shot in the process, but—

"And copper turns green. Green, the color of envy and jealousy." She smiled again. "I never was good at sharing. I always envied others who had what I wanted. So I took things. I made people do things to suit my purposes. But it was never enough. Never enough, Brad, because I never really had you. I could have forced you to be with me long ago. We both know that. But I didn't. I wanted you to come to me, to admit the truth about our connection. That we were always meant to be together." Her fingers tensed around the firearm. "I'm done waiting. Now I will *finally have what is mine. You and I are going to be together, Brad. The two of us and our son. One way or the other."*

Panic shredded through me. She truly was crazy. Not that I'd ever doubted that revelation. But then—

The memory . . .

"Never. I'll never believe that. You'll pay for this, Brad. I swear to God you'll pay."

What she'd said after that emerged into my mind. I could hear her say the words in the voice I now knew as I pressed my ear to my bedroom door.

"You and I are going to be together, Brad. The two of us and our son. One way or the other."

My father was no longer enough for her. She wanted us both.

I suppressed a shudder as my skin chilled around me like a cloak of ice.

She turned to me slightly, still holding the gun at my father. "It's your choice, my beautiful son. Either we're all together in this life . . . or the next. What will it be?"

"I'm not sure"—my voice cracked—"what you mean." In reality, I had an inkling of exactly what she meant. My heart thundered, and a wave of sickness traveled through me.

"Darling, you're not a simpleton. You're the son of two geniuses. You know very well what I mean. You choose. Do you and I and your father stay together here, without the rest of these people, or do the three of us go together into the next life?"

My blood pulsed in my head like a freight train. Was she truly asking me to choose whether my siblings or I lived?

No.

I'd just found happiness with Ruby.

But Talon was healing. Joe and Melanie were having a

baby. Marjorie was young, so young, only twenty-five years old.

My father was dying anyway, and Wendy's life wasn't worth anything to anyone.

But my life...

Damn it, I wanted my life! I wanted a life with Ruby, with our children, with my brothers and sister. My true siblings, even if I'd been borne to this lunatic.

"Wendy," my father interjected. "I will go with you into the next life. Our son deserves a life here. Don't put him through this."

"Why not? It's time to find out where his loyalty lies."

"You're asking him to choose between his own life and his siblings. It's not fair."

"What if the three of us go off somewhere together?" I said, the words coming out rapid and jumbled. "You don't have to kill my brothers and my sister. We can keep them away from us. You guys will leave us alone, right?"

"O-Of course," Marjorie stammered. "Won't we?"

My two brothers and Jade said nothing. Even Joe was speechless, his face pale and his eyes... something different about his eyes, something I'd never seen before. Fear. He was scared.

"No," Wendy said. "My mind is made up. I deserve closure, and this is how I aim to get it. I've waited long enough to have my family together, and I won't have anyone fucking it up for me."

I knew the answer in my heart before I voiced it. Talon, Joe, and I had recently had a conversation about the horror Talon had lived through. He'd told us that he'd have gone through it willingly if it meant saving us from the same fate. Joe and I had both agreed. We would do the same.

And I would do that now.

"I choose my siblings." My voice was strangely monotonous, but it didn't crack. "They will stay. We will go."

"No!" Ruby and Marjorie shouted together.

Ruby stood, leaving her father's lifeless body and running to my arms.

"Easy," I said, holding her tightly. "I love all of you."

Joe finally came out of his stupor. "We're not going to let this happen, Ry."

I eyed my mother, who still had the gun trained on our father. "It's okay. I'll be okay. May I please say something to each of them first?"

"Of course, dear."

"Joe." I looked to my big brother, trying to draw in his strength.

"Hey, you wait. This isn't going down like this," Joe said. "I'll fix it. Somehow."

Always the big brother. But he couldn't fix this. "We don't have a choice. You're having a baby. You need to live. You're the bravest and strongest of all of us, and you're going to be a hell of a father, Joe. Tell your child about me. Please."

I shifted my gaze to Talon, wise beyond his years, mostly from losing his innocence at such a tender age. "And Tal, you'll always be my hero. Be happy. Please. Every minute."

"How can I be happy if I lose my little brother?"

"Because you have your wife. You have Joe and Marj. You'll have children someday."

"Ryan, please!" Ruby shouted.

"Baby. Try to understand."

She gulped back sobs, still holding on to me as I turned to my sister, who represented youth and joy. "Marj, you're so young, so full of life and energy. Find your life and live it. For me."

My baby sister said nothing, just bit on her lip, sobbing.

I turned to the woman I loved. She nodded slightly at me, and an understanding passed between us.

"I love you, baby," I said. "You've shown me things I didn't think were possible. I'll always love you."

My mother pointed her gun at my heart.

I pushed Ruby away as hard as I could, and she fell to the floor, sliding against her father's body.

I closed my eyes and absorbed every fear I'd known in my short life. What would it feel like to die?

"No." My father's voice. "You will not kill our son. Not before you kill me."

"Fine."

I opened my eyes. She pointed the gun back at my father. I breathed a sigh of relief without meaning to.

"You may have your last request, Brad. You know I could never deny you anything."

She fired the gun, and my father slumped over his desk. Screams echoed, as if they were being yelled from the top of Pikes Peak.

My mother turned to me.

And a shot rang out.

$$\star\ \star\ \star$$

My jaw is clenched, and still I'm determined not to interrupt my father.

But he interrupts himself.

He stops talking.

"Dad?"

His lips are trembling. "I don't know if I can describe the sheer terror I felt when I heard that gunshot. I thought my life was over, Ava. That my psychopath mother had ended my life rather than let me live without her."

"Oh, Daddy..." Tears flow from my eyes.

"But then...there was no pain. No blood. And I could still see everyone. Perhaps I was dead, looking down, until I realized my mother had fallen, and Ruby—your mother—was on the floor, next to her dead father, holding his gun."

I gulp back my tears, determined to see this through. "Continue, Daddy. Please. Tell me everything."

★ ★ ★

Ruby ran to me and fell into my arms. "Are you all right?"

I didn't say anything, just held on to her and wept against the top of her head.

Marjorie had run to our father. I had no idea what Joe, Talon, and Jade were doing. All I could do was hold on to Ruby and never let go.

I sniffled. "You saved my life, baby."

"I'm sorry I couldn't save your father. I was so relieved when she took the gun off you that I didn't act quickly enough. I'm so sorry."

"He's ill. He would have gone to prison. You saved him suffering through cancer while he was incarcerated."

"I hoped you understood that I was going for my father's gun. I should have taken it sooner, but when she pointed that thing at you..." Ruby choked out a sob.

"It's okay."

"No, it's not. I'm sorry."

I kissed the top of her head. "You're here. I'm here. My brothers and sister are here. That's what matters right now." I pressed my lips to her forehead. "We both lost fathers today. Fathers who weren't anything close to what they should have been ... but they both ended up saving our lives."

CHAPTER TWENTY-FOUR

Brendan

After getting the Petersons to cover the bar for me again tonight, I sit back down with Ruby.

We don't speak to each other. Instead, we stare out the window into the vast backyard where the dogs are frolicking and the sun is beginning to set.

We watch the sun go down.

And we simply wait.

Until Ruby's phone dings. She reads a text and then glances up at me. "They need you now. They need both of us."

"Shouldn't we wait for them to come out?"

"No. We need to go to them."

I nod, rise, and follow Ruby down the hallway. She knocks lightly and then opens the door to what turns out to be a living room connected to the master suite.

Ryan sits on a recliner, and he rises when Ruby walks in.

On another recliner, separated from Ryan's only by a table and lamp, sits Ava.

My sweet Ava, with all the color drained from her beautiful face, her eyes glassy.

"Baby?"

She looks up at me, her blue eyes wide. She's not crying, but she clearly has been. Her nose is red, and her cheeks are stained with streaks from tears.

"Baby," Ruby says, and I'm not sure whether she's talking to her husband or to her daughter. "What have you done?"

"Only what we agreed I needed to do," Ryan says.

"Oh, God… And she knows…" Ruby looks at her daughter, goes toward her, takes one of her hands. "My sweet Ava. How I wish this could've all been kept in the past."

Ava doesn't reply. She simply sniffles.

"You do understand that I was a police officer."

Ava nods.

"I did what I had to do to save your father."

"And you've lived with that for so long," Ava finally speaks.

"Yes. And it's always difficult to take a life. Even when you don't have a choice, like I didn't."

"But apparently you *didn't* take a life," Ava says.

"No, I didn't. And I have great feelings of ambivalence about that fact."

Ava rises then and embraces her mother. "I'm so sorry, Mom."

"You have no reason to be sorry about anything, Ava. None of this has anything to do with you, and if your father and I had had our way, you and your sister would never have had to know about the dark times in our past."

I stand, not sure what to do. I have no idea what any of them are talking about, but Ava and I made a pact. No more secrets between us. Still, I won't push her on this. Clearly she needs time. Time to process whatever her father has spent the last hour and a half telling her.

I cannot push her.

All I can do is be here for her, attend to whatever she needs.

When Ava finally lets go of her mother, she doesn't come to me as I expect. She walks to her father and embraces him as well.

"This is more than I deserve, cupcake," he says to her.

Ava says nothing, sniffles into her father's shoulder for a moment until she pulls away. "You and Mom have lived through so much. So much. And then Uncle Talon, Dale and Donny... There's so much I still don't know. Why is our past so dark? So horrific?"

"I won't lie to you. Wendy Madigan had a great deal to do with all of it. Probably more than I even know. More than your aunt and uncles know. But I think my father holds a lot of the blame as well."

I'm beginning to feel like the fourth wheel in the room. I don't know what they're talking about—though I have a theory, which includes Wendy Madigan—and Ava doesn't seem to need me. Until—

She steps out of her father's embrace and comes to me. She touches my cheek lightly. "Brendan, please take me home."

"Whatever you need, baby."

"Ruby and I need you to take care of her, Brendan," Ryan says.

"Of course. Whatever she needs."

"What I've told my daughter, I've told her in confidence," Ryan says, "except for you. I gave her the option to tell you if she wishes to. All I ask is that if she does, you also keep it in confidence."

"Of course. You have my word."

Ryan nods, and then he pats me on the back. "You're a good man, Brendan. I'm sorry you've been dragged into this. I'm sorry Ava has been dragged into this. And I'm just so sorry for..."

"For what?"

"For what is inevitable," he says. "For what is to come."

★ ★ ★

Ava is quiet during our drive back to town. The sun has set, and the country roads seem darker than usual.

The sky isn't cloudy at all, so I know it's my imagination. Still, I feel the veil of darkness. I feel it surrounding Ava. Surrounding me. Surrounding us as we drive into town.

Curiosity nips at me. What did Ryan tell his daughter? And will she choose to tell me?

I vow again not to push her. I vow again to do only what she needs. Because I love her. Ava Steel has become the most important person in my life, and I will never let her down.

I pull into the alley behind the bakery, and then I see Ava to the door.

"What do you need, baby?" I ask.

"I know you have to get back to the bar, Brendan."

"I don't, actually. I got the Petersons and my father to fill in for the night. I'm all yours. Whatever you need, sweetheart. I'm here for you."

"Oh, thank God…" She melts against me, and I gladly take her weight upon me.

Anything for my sweet Ava.

I take her key from her, unlock the door, and we walk into the bakery. The aromas of yeast and the warm cinnamon of the baklava she made two days ago waft toward us.

Tomorrow is Monday, of course, and she'll need to get up early to begin the day. It's not late, though. In fact, neither of us have eaten dinner.

"Are you hungry?" I ask.

"I may never eat again."

I kiss her lips. "You're going to need to eat something, sweetheart. Do you have anything in the house? If you don't, I'll go over to my place and pick up some supplies."

"If you're hungry, make yourself a sandwich. I have some meat in the refrigerator in the bakery. It has to be used up, as I'm getting a new shipment in tomorrow. It's still good."

"All right, baby. But I'm going to make you a sandwich as well." I take her up to her apartment, make sure she's okay, and then I go downstairs to the bakery, flick the lights on in the kitchen, and open the industrial refrigerator.

The deli meats—Steel Acres roast beef and Steel Acres London broil. Hedge Farms turkey and cracked pepper turkey. Dodge City Black Forest ham. She is running low. I don't trust myself to fire up her industrial slicer, so I find a butcher knife and a cutting board, and I hack off turkey for both of us. After hearing about her little calf named Buster, I'm not sure I ever want to eat beef again. I can't believe she still eats it. I add a slice of cheddar cheese and slap it all between slices of her day-old sourdough.

I add mayonnaise and mustard, and nothing else. Ava has already gotten rid of the produce in the industrial fridge. Fresh produce will be delivered tomorrow before lunch.

I clean up the counter until it's ready for tomorrow, and then I take the sandwiches up to Ava.

But sweet Ava...

She's still in the kitchen, her head on the table.

She's asleep.

CHAPTER TWENTY-FIVE

Ava

I'm running...
> *Racing, my breath catching, my legs aching...*
> *I have to run...*
> *Run from the fire and the falling rubble...*
> *Run from the tower collapsing behind me.*
> *A pit lies before me... the bottomless pit...*
> *If I stop, the debris and flames will get me.*
> *If I move forward...*
> *I fall.*
> *And I'm falling... falling... falling...*

★ ★ ★

I jerk upward, and for a moment, I don't know where I am.

Until I see Brendan. Strong and handsome Brendan. His arms secure me.

"Shh. It's okay, baby."

Except it's not okay. It will never be okay again.

"I made you a turkey sandwich," he says. "You need to eat."

My stomach is a void, but I'm not hungry. The nausea climbing up my throat won't let me eat. I hold up a hand, refusing the food.

"You have to try, Ava. Please. For me."

For me.

For Brendan.

I think I'd do anything for Brendan. He's the only part of my life that is who he says he is.

I think, anyway.

I look up at him, into his searing blue eyes.

I see the love he feels for me. And reflected in the cerulean depths, I see the love I feel for him.

"For you," I say.

He nods and takes the seat next to me at the table. He hands me the turkey sandwich on a plate along with a napkin and a glass of water.

I take a bite of the sandwich.

It's dry, like sawdust. It shouldn't be, as Brendan has added more than a dollop of mayo, but still . . .

Dry.

I choke it down.

Then another bite.

It gets easier after a few bites, and I manage to eat a little more than half the sandwich and drink the entire glass of ice water.

He polishes off his whole sandwich, but he seems satisfied with the half that I ate. He doesn't push. Another thing I love about Brendan Murphy.

He never pushes.

I love him for that. I love him for so many reasons.

He rises, helps me up. "Let me put you to bed."

"Will you stay?" I ask.

"I'll do whatever you want me to do." He kisses my cheek. "Whatever you need, Ava, because you're mine."

Mine.

All my thoughts—everything my father told me—crash together into that one word.

Brendan is mine. I'm his.

And in this moment, nothing else matters. I need him. I need Brendan's body. We walk to my bedroom, and I grab him, dig my fingers into his shoulders, lever against him. His cock is hard through his jeans, and my God... I want it. I want *him.*

He leans down, takes my lips, and my heart races as he pushes his cock against me. He grinds it against my belly and pushes his tongue farther into my mouth.

I moan softly.

Mine.

He breaks the kiss and lifts me, carries me to the bed.

"Brendan..."

"No more talking," he says. "Nothing but me inside you."

Already I'm wet. Brendan undresses me in what seems like a flash, and he slides his hand beneath my panties.

"God, so slick, baby. So wet and ready."

He nearly rips my panties from me, and an instant later, he's undressed, on top of me, our gazes fiery with the heat that's between us.

This is where I belong. Where Brendan belongs. He thrusts inside me, his huge cock burning through me.

"Brendan," I moan. "Mine. All mine."

"Mine," he groans as he pushes into me again and again. "Always mine."

Brendan doesn't last long. Within seconds, he's releasing into me, and I feel every contraction of his cock.

"Mine," he growls again. "Mine."

I didn't come, and I don't care. I got what I was after.

Fullness. Completion. I close my eyes, reveling in the joy of our joining.

"Open your eyes, Ava."

I obey Brendan's command. His blue eyes are on fire. "What makes you think we're done?"

I smile, my eyes heavy lidded.

"I'm going to give you an orgasm that's going to blow your mind, baby. Then I'm going to give you another. Maybe a third and fourth."

My breasts are sensitive, my nipples erect and yearning for his touch. I finger one, squeezing it, and Brendan lets out another groan.

I arch my back, and he gets the message. He sucks a nipple between his full lips. I inhale the woodsy fragrance of Brendan's hair and undulate my hips. If only he could spend hours on my nipples . . . but I need him between my legs.

He moves to my other nipple and fingers the first, twisting it and tugging on it. Then he squeezes both my breasts, kisses down my abdomen, where he spreads my legs.

He inhales, groans, inhales again. "So beautiful, Ava. So pink and fleshy and beautiful." He kisses my pussy, tugs on my labia. He swirls his tongue over my slit and tugs again at my lips.

I arch again, bending my legs toward me so Brendan can dive deeper into me.

Lust fills me.

Love fills me.

But my God, I need to come. I grab his head, tangle my fingers in his gorgeous long hair, and push him against my clit.

His eyes smile up at me, and when he slides two fingers inside me, I shatter.

"Yeah, baby." He thrusts into me with his fingers. "That's it. Come for me."

I jump. I fly. I soar . . . and just when I think I can't go any further, he clamps his firm lips around my clit, adds another finger to my pussy, and I rocket into another climax.

I fist the blanket as he torments me, drives me into orgasm after delicious orgasm until I'm limp.

Finally limp.

Finally spent.

Then his cock is in me, and he's fucking me, and his lips come down on mine.

We kiss, our tongues tangling, and my clit and pussy are so sensitive, I feel the head of his cock sliding against every ridge inside me.

He breaks the kiss, his hair flowing around me like an auburn curtain.

"Mine, Ava," he grits out. "Always mine."

CHAPTER TWENTY-SIX

Brendan

Monday morning, and Ava's gone when I wake up. I'm surprised I didn't hear her leave.

I take a quick shower in her bathroom and head down to the bakery, where I find her near the ovens, while Maya and Luke are handling the counter.

Her black apron is covered in flour, her beautiful pink hair pulled up in her hairnet. She's adding a few dashes of salt to the dough that's in the bowl of her Hobart mixer.

"Good morning," I say softly.

She turns. "There you are. It's nearly eleven."

"I know. I slept really well. Very relaxed."

She doesn't reply.

"Did you sleep okay, Ava?"

She touches my cheek with her floury hand. "Can we talk later, Brendan? I need to focus."

"Of course. But I'm working tonight. I don't see how I can get out of it. I've already imposed on the Petersons and my dad more than I should."

"I know. I understand." She stops the mixer and pulls the blob of dough onto the counter. "We're both married to our jobs, aren't we?"

"When you own your own business, that's kind of how it is."

The truth of the matter is that Ava and I both love what we do. I love tending bar, and she loves baking. Neither of us wants to stop, but the hours certainly don't mesh well with each other.

"Can you spare an hour for dinner?" she asks.

"I'll have to let you know. I'll see if I can get someone to cover the bar for an hour while I'm gone."

"I close at six. The bar doesn't get hopping until around eight or nine, right?"

"Monday night? It's usually earlier, baby. Sorry."

She sighs. "Right. Monday Night Football."

"Exactly."

"I suppose I could come help you tend bar again," she says, "but that won't really give us time to talk."

"No."

"Damn." She fiddles with her lip ring, making me crazy.

"You take as long as you need, Ava. I'm not going anywhere."

"Last night you gave me what I needed, Brendan. And then, when you fell asleep, I didn't want to disturb you."

"You come first with me." I give her a wink. "You came second and third last night as well."

Ava blushes.

"Feel free to disturb me whenever you need to," I continue.

She smiles. "You looked like a Greek god sleeping. Okay, more like an Irish god, if there's such a thing."

I smile. She's so adorable, my Ava.

"I'll see what I can do about tonight." I lean forward and brush my lips across hers. "I'll check in with you later and let you know."

"Okay. Thanks, Brendan."

"Anything for you. Anytime."

I leave the bakery, walk the back way, and head to the bar.

Anytime, I said.

Those words weren't truthful. *Anytime* would mean giving her an hour tonight like she asked. I need to find a way to make that happen.

I get to the bar, take the stairs to my apartment, where I change into a clean pair of jeans and a green-and-white striped button-down. I towel the dampness out of my hair, and then comb through it and tie it behind my neck in a low ponytail.

The copies of the Steel documents are still sitting out on my table from when Ava found them in my copy of *Tom Sawyer*.

Grandmother.

Wendy Madigan. Wendy Madigan, who had a child with Bradford Steel.

Jeremy Madigan, who my father bought this bar from so many years ago.

Ryan and Ruby Steel.

I don't know what Ryan told his daughter yesterday, though I have a hunch. I believe Ryan Steel may be the child Bradford Steel had with Wendy. Perhaps she forced him to sign over all his property to Ryan, her son. Makes sense. But Ava hasn't spoken to me about it, and I have to accept the fact that she may *never* speak to me about it. We said no more secrets, but this is big. This is the tower.

And if she chooses to keep it to herself, I have to be okay with that.

But still, I wonder...

What exactly is *my* family's involvement in this? Why did my father and I get the same messages?

And why did Pat Lamone, as well?

I go downstairs to the bar and check the schedule. Laney and Johnny are both on tonight, which would be enough for a normal Monday night. Not a Monday night during football season, though.

But I need to be there for Ava. I made that promise to her. I call my dad quickly.

"Hi, Brendan," he says into my ear.

"Hey, Dad. You feel like getting out of the house tonight?"

"It's football night, son."

"Yeah, but the Broncos aren't playing."

"True enough."

"I need to see Ava for about an hour when she shuts down the bakery at six. Could you cover me at the bar?"

"Your mother will be pissed. You know she likes to have dinner at six o'clock on the dot."

"All right, Dad. Thanks, anyway."

"This is important to you, isn't it, Brendan?"

"It is, but I'll deal."

Dad chuckles. "If I tell your mother that her precious son needs a favor, she won't give me too much crap."

"So you'll do it, then?"

"Yeah, Brendan. I'll be there."

"Thanks, Dad. You're a lifesaver."

"Depending on how busy it is, I may stay a little longer after you get back from seeing Ava."

"Why is that?"

"Because," he says, "we need to talk. You and I."

My heart drops to my stomach. "We do? What's wrong?"

"Nothing's wrong," he says. "At least I don't think anything is wrong. But I found something. Something that may be relevant to all these things that we're investigating."

"Oh?"

"Yes. I found an address for Lauren Wingdam."

I wrinkle my forehead, thinking. Who is Lauren Wingdam again? "Right. Pat Lamone's mother. Biological mother, that is."

"Yes. The one he hasn't been able to find."

"How were *you* able to find her?" I ask.

"I called in a favor," my father says.

I recognize his tone. Though I'm itching to know who helped him, my father has said all he's going to say on that subject. I know him too well.

"All right. I should be back at the bar around seven. If it's not too busy and Laney and Johnny are handling things, you and I can take some time to chat."

"Good enough. I'll be there about five forty-five."

"Thanks again, Dad."

I end the call and take a look at the bar.

Everything is clean and in its place.

If only life were like that.

CHAPTER TWENTY-SEVEN

Ava

Luke approaches me at one thirty. "Aren't you taking lunch, Ava?"

Normally I go earlier, but today? I need to keep busy. I don't want to think.

I need to keep busy until tonight, when I spill everything to Brendan and ask for his help.

"No, not today."

"You want me to fix you a sandwich that you can eat while you're working?" he asks.

"Not hungry."

"Okay. Is it okay if I take my normal one-thirty lunch?"

"Absolutely. Enjoy yourself."

Maya and Luke only take half-hour lunches, although I give them an hour. They usually make themselves a sandwich and eat in the back.

"Take your whole hour today," I say. "I'll be here."

"I don't have anywhere else to go." Luke smiles. "But I will take my lunch. A corned beef sandwich is calling my name. Don't think I'm strange or anything, but I think I'm going to try it on that cranberry walnut bread you make."

"Should be delicious," I say.

Cranberry walnut is one of my favorite holiday breads,

but it doesn't sound good to me today.

I haven't eaten anything since half the sandwich Brendan brought me last night. My stomach is again a void, and I know I need to fill it. But it's so difficult when my throat feels like nothing will go down.

I've been sipping water all day, which is keeping me going, but eventually I'm going to require sustenance.

I hope Brendan will be able to come by at six. I need him so much, but I can't expect him to drop everything and come to me.

This relationship is a two-way street, and we both have businesses that we love. Unfortunately, the hours of said businesses conflict big time.

So I work.

Until I hear the ding of my text.

Good news. I can come by at six for an hour. I got my dad to fill in.

Thank God.

I text Brendan back quickly.

Thank you so much. I know this is difficult for you, and I appreciate you making time for me.

I'll always make time for you, baby.

My heart warms, and then I go back to work.

★ ★ ★

At six o'clock, when the bakery closes, I leave Maya and Luke on cleanup duty and head straight out to the alley. Brendan is arriving. I grab him, pull him to me, and kiss him deeply.

His tongue meets mine, and the kiss turns me into jelly all the way to my toes.

But I can't be jelly. Not right now.

So I break the kiss. "Thanks for coming. Let's go to my place."

"Whatever you need, baby."

I throw my dirty apron in the hamper and then lead Brendan up to my apartment. I wash my hands quickly in the sink, and then I take Brendan into my living area and sit on the couch, beckoning him to take the spot next to me.

"I'm sorry," I say. "Do you need anything to drink?"

"I'm fine. I'm more concerned about what you need right now, Ava."

He's such a strong, sweet, loving man. And he's totally focused on me.

"I promise you, Brendan, when all of this shit with my family blows over"—*if it ever blows over*, I add to myself—"I'm going to focus on you like you've never been focused on before."

"You do a fine job of focusing on me, Ava." He grabs my hand. "You're all I want. All I need."

"But I'm going to show you that I'm not just a bunch of Steel problems wrapped up in a pink-haired woman. I'm actually pretty good at relationships. Or at least I think I could be. I haven't really had one."

He smiles. "I know you're going to be great at this. It's okay that we need to focus on you right now. Perhaps one day you'll need to focus on me. And when that day comes, I know you will."

I can't help but smile, despite the fact that I've felt perpetually sick since my father laid our twisted family history on me—with the exception of making love with Brendan.

"I'm not sure I'm ready to tell you what my father told me. Are you okay with that?"

He takes my hand. "I won't deny that I'm curious, but Ava, this isn't about me. This is about you and what you need. If you're not ready to talk about it, that's okay."

"The thing is . . . I want to talk about it. I want to get it off my chest. But I'm just . . ." I sigh. "I think I want to draw a card."

"You want me to get your deck for you?"

I rise. "I'll get it." I grab the scarf-covered tarot deck out of the mahogany box and bring it back to the couch. "I normally read at the table, but the coffee table will do for now."

I unwrap the deck, shuffle it three times, and hold it to my heart.

I don't think in words, simply infuse the deck with love and energy. Then I cut the deck, draw a card, and place it faceup on top of the old steamer trunk I use as a coffee table.

And I can't help myself. I burst into laughter.

Brendan lifts his eyebrows at me. "Ava?"

The card on the table is the five of cups. A lonely figure in a black cape stands, saddened by the five cups on the ground. Every time I've drawn this card, the first feeling that comes to mind is negativity.

Nega-fucking-tivity.

As if I needed a reminder.

"You're starting to freak me out here," Brendan says.

"Sorry. It's just . . ." I shake my head. "This is the five of cups."

"You're going to have to go into a little more detail for me. Tarot novice here."

"Right. This card is just pulsing negativity, Brendan. Anger. Loss. Instability. You name it. I was hoping for some enlightenment, but I got more darkness. Serves me right, I guess."

"I don't want to push ... but does this card make sense to you given what your father told you?"

I scoff without meaning to. "This card is the personification of what my father told me."

Brendan trails his finger over my forearm. "Let's attack this from a different angle."

"What other angle is there?"

"I don't know. Tarot novice, remember? What I mean is, you've always said that you try to put a positive spin on each reading, but that you weren't able to when you drew the tower card."

"Yeah. And I'm thinking my positivity has gone on hiatus because I sure can't see anything good in this damned card."

He grabs my hand and squeezes. "Try, Ava. It's just a card. It's not your fortune. It's just a card."

I open my mouth to contradict him, but then I stop myself. He's right, after all.

It's just a freaking card. It's an image printed on cardstock. Most people in the world would give it no meaning whatsoever.

Maybe it's time to take a break from the tarot. God knows I've got enough going on. In the past, the tarot has been a source of comfort and guidance for me. If it's no longer a positive influence in my life, why give it any influence at all?

I shove the card back into the deck, wrap it up in Grandma Didi's scarf, and take it back to the box. Then I return to the couch.

"Aren't you going to make any notes?" Brendan asks. "You always write in your journal after a reading."

"No, Brendan, I'm not."

"How come?"

"Because that's the last card I'm drawing. At least for now."

Brendan drops his mouth open.

"Does that surprise you?"

"Uh...yeah. The tarot means a lot to you, Ava. Are you sure now is the time to give that up? With...everything going on and all?"

"You don't even know what's going on, Brendan." I pull away from him.

His lips turn downward. "I didn't mean—"

"I know." I sigh. "It's just all too much right now. I want to tell you, but I don't want to rehash it all, you know? It's so... awful."

He reaches for me but then pulls his hand away.

Jeez. Now he thinks I'm rejecting him. Maybe a part of me is. I don't want to reject him. I don't want to reject the tarot. I don't want to reject my family.

I don't want to reject anything...but I'm just in a negative, rejecting sort of mood.

"Thanks for taking the time to come over, Brendan," I say, "but I think I want you to leave now."

He furrows his brow. "Ava? Come on. What's going on?"

"Nothing. I just don't want to talk to anyone. I don't want to kiss or be cuddled or any of that either. I think... I think I need to get my hands in a ball of really stiff dough."

"You did that all day."

"I didn't. The big Hobart does most of my kneading." I rise

and head to the kitchen. "Thanks again, Brendan. Good night."

"You're really doing this?" He stands and follows me to the kitchen. "You're dismissing me?"

"I am." I grab my canister of flour. "See you later."

He shakes his head. "Whatever."

And then he's gone.

Loss. Profound loss envelops me. I love Brendan so much, but my mood is fucked up.

Will I ever see him again?

Does it even matter? Negativity is surrounding me, so it's only a matter of time before he breaks my heart. Not a problem. I'll put my emotions on hold because in the end, none of this matters anyway.

The tower is falling.

CHAPTER TWENTY-EIGHT

Brendan

"Back so soon?" Dad asks when I head behind the bar.

"Yeah. Ava's acting weird."

"Cut her some slack, son. Things are getting real for her."

I raise my eyebrows. "Do you know something I don't?"

"Only that the Steels are headed into something. Something that may not be pretty."

I grab a bar towel. "Why the hell would you say that?"

"The ominous messages."

I expected Dad to say something about the child born to Brad Steel and Wendy Madigan. When he doesn't, a chill lands on the back of my neck. "Last time I checked, they're coming to us as well. Does that mean things are getting real for us too?"

Dad fills up a pilsner glass from the tap and hands it to a customer. "I'm only saying that things were bound to come to a head sooner or later. Something about the Steels has never sat right with me."

"Because of your uncle."

"Yeah. Because of my uncle."

"But you know that the Steel brothers weren't even alive yet when your uncle died."

"My uncle didn't die, Brendan. He was murdered."

I don't argue that even Dad himself couldn't find proof.

He's convinced his uncle was murdered, and nothing I can say will change that fact.

"Sixty years ago," I say.

"Yes. Over sixty years ago. And I may finally find out what the hell happened."

"How can you when no one is alive to tell you? When you exhausted all avenues decades ago?"

My father doesn't answer. I wouldn't be able to hear him anyway because the entire bar erupts in shouts from people watching the game.

"You call that a pass!" someone yells at the television. "My sister can throw better than that."

"Fucking pussy." From another.

I scan the bar. It's hopping, with most patrons glued to the several television sets, watching the game. A few stragglers are playing pool . . . including Brock Steel and Dave Simpson.

"Could you excuse me for a minute, Dad? I want to talk to Brock and Dave."

"About what?"

About the rash on my ass. Damn. My mom was right. Dad is getting all worked up again about his uncle. I hate to tell him that he's chasing ghosts.

"Ava wanted me to give them a message for her."

"All right. I've got the bar covered. Johnny's in the back. I'll get him out here."

"Great. Thanks." I head toward the back of the bar to the pool tables.

"I need to start laying some money down," Dave Simpson says to Brock. "I haven't lost a game in a week."

"Your winning streak won't hold out much longer," Brock says. "You still suck at pool, cuz." He looks up at me. "Hey, Brendan. What's up?"

"Maybe the two of you can tell me."

Brock sets his cue down and takes a drink of his beer from an adjacent table. "What's that supposed to mean?"

"It's Ava. Her father told her a bunch of stuff, and now she's giving up the tarot. And she may be giving up our relationship as well."

Brock eyes me. "What exactly did Uncle Ryan tell her?"

"I don't have a clue. I figured the two of you might. You're the closest to her in the family."

"We're not closer to her than her parents," Dave says.

But Brock's expression says differently. His eyes change. They widen just a bit but then go back to normal. I meet his brown-eyed gaze, but I don't say anything.

He seems to get my meaning. "I've got to hit the can."

"Okay," Dave says. "Don't be surprised if this game is over by the time you get back."

"You guys okay on drinks?" I ask.

"Yeah, I'm good." Dave measures out his pool shot.

"All right. I've got to get back to work."

I head to the men's room by way of the bar. Brock is in there, but we're not alone. "Follow me," I say quietly.

I lead him to the secret staircase that leads to my closet.

"Whoa," he says when we end up in my apartment. "That's some Narnia shit right there."

"I got a huge payout from my insurance company, so I really fixed up this place. In record time too."

Again, Brock's eyes do that weird thing. "It looks great."

"Yeah. I love it." I narrow my gaze. "But we're not here for social hour, Steel. What gives with Ava?"

"I couldn't say anything in front of Dave because he's not wholly in the know about everything yet."

"What is up with you people?" I shake my head. "You have more secrets than the royal family, I swear."

Brock sighs. "I shouldn't be talking to you. Especially if Ava won't."

"Here's the thing. Ava's not acting like herself. I don't know what Ryan told her, but he took me aside afterward and mentioned that he told her to keep it in confidence except for me. That she could tell me if she wanted to, but that was it."

"And...?"

"And... I'm concerned. I don't want to push Ava, but she's acting... I don't know. She hasn't been eating well, and she decided to give up the tarot and kicked me out of her place tonight."

"That's just good sense. The part about kicking you out, I mean." Brock chuckles.

"Brock, damn it, this isn't a joke. Something's going down with Ava, and I care too much about her to let her go through it alone."

Brock sighs. "I only know bits and pieces, and though I sympathize with you, I'm not comfortable telling you the little that I know. Not without Ava's permission."

I plunk down on my couch. "I understand. Thanks anyway."

Brock raises his eyebrows. "You giving up that easily?"

"What else can I do? I'm involved, Brock, whether Ava wants me to be or not." I rub at the stubble on my jawline. "I—or my family—got those same messages. I feel like we're about to fall into a rabbit hole. Like a bottle that says *drink me* is going to show up."

"I mean, that secret staircase leading into your closet *was* pretty Wonderland."

"Could you be serious for one damned minute?"

He sits down on the other end of the couch. "Look, Brendan. I *am* being serious. I love Ava. She's like a sister to Dave and me. But I've had about all the family drama I can handle for the moment. I've seen things I never imagined. Learned things that made me question everything. I need a break. Rory and the band are going on that European tour with Emerald Phoenix, and I'm going along. I need a break from the Steels. If that's what Ava's feeling, I can relate."

"You'd leave even if Ava's in trouble?"

"She's not in trouble, Brendan. She's just questioning a lot of things. Trust me. I've been there."

I cock my head. "Has Ava shared any of her recent tarot readings with you?"

"No. Why?"

"Because that seems to be the focus of a lot of them. She seems to think she'll be questioning who she is."

"I don't put a lot of stock in that stuff."

"Neither do I. At least I never used to. But Ava does, and it's got her freaked. And now, whatever her dad laid on her has freaked her out even more."

"Look, I—"

We both jerk as someone pounds on my door.

I rise. "It's probably my dad. It's busy down there, and I'm shirking."

Brock stands and wipes his hands—are they clammy?—on his jeans. "I should get back anyway. Dave has probably placed all the balls in the pockets, and he's going to try to convince me that he nailed the shots."

I walk to the door, open it.

Pat Lamone stands there.

"Oh, for God's sake." Brock rakes his hands through his dark hair. "What the fuck, Lamone?"

"I came to see Murphy."

"Looks like you're going to see both of us, then, because I'm not leaving." Brock shoves his hands into the pockets of his jeans.

"Do you two know each other?" I ask.

"Yeah, we do. This jackass drugged my cousin and tried to have sex with my fiancée. We're not the best of buddies."

"Wait, wait, wait…" I regard Lamone, my ire rising. "You're the one who drugged Diana Steel at the bonfire… Fuck, when the hell was that?"

"Ten years ago," Brock offers. "I was still in middle school. Rory was homecoming queen, and this asshole thought it was a good idea to lace Diana's punch with angel dust."

"I thought we'd gotten past that," Pat says.

"You did? Because I paid off some jerk so you could find out what your grandmother's alias is? I believe your end of the deal was to leave my family's fortune alone as long as we cared for your ailing grammy."

"Right. I stand by that. The woman is all I have."

I rub my forehead against the headache that's forming. "Too much information. What the fuck are you two talking about?" I turn to Pat. "And why the fuck are you here?"

"Your dad was tending bar when I came in. He told me to come up here and wait for him."

Right. My dad wanted to talk to me… about an address for Lauren Wingdam, Pat's birth mother.

Except… Why would Dad send Pat up here? He's covering the bar, and—

"So you came to the bar to see my father?" I ask.

"Yeah. He texted me earlier today. Said he had some information for me and to meet me at the bar."

"My dad didn't even know he'd be here tonight until I asked him to cover me."

Pat pulls his phone out of his pocket. "That makes sense. The text says it came at ten after six."

I look at Brock.

"What?" he says. "I'm not going anywhere."

"What about Dave and the game?"

"Someone else will be happy to play him and win. I have a vested interest in anything Lamone here has to say."

"I don't have anything to say," Lamone says. "I came to hear what Sean Murphy has to say."

"Whatever." I turn to Brock. "So you're taking care of this Dyane Wingdam?"

"Yeah. She's nearly ninety. She can't last that much longer anyway."

"Whoa," Lamone says.

"Hey, I've got nothing against your grandmother," Brock says. "But taking care of her for her few remaining years is a lot better deal than giving you a piece of the Steel pie."

Right. Dyane Wingdam. Pat's grandmother, who goes by the alias of Sabrina Smith. Funny. Maybe Dyane Wingdam is an alias too. Sometimes people go by several.

Dyane Wingdam. An interesting name. A name that—

I head to my kitchen, open my junk drawer, and pull out a pad of paper and pen. Dyane Wingdam.

DIANEWINGDAM

I need Ava's anagram maker. But I have a feeling...

Nope, doesn't work.

Except...

Lamone told me Friday morning. She spells Dyane with a Y, not an I.

DYANEWINGDAM

I move the letters around, looking for words. I could pull up the anagram maker on my phone but—

Fuck it all.

Wendy Madigan

CHAPTER TWENTY-NINE

Ava

I jerk upward when my phone rings.

It's Brendan.

"Hi," I say softly.

"Ava, I'm coming over."

"Aren't you working?"

"My dad's covering me. But I've got to talk to you. I'm bringing Brock."

I stand up quickly. "Brock? Why? What's going on?"

"I don't know, but I just figured something out. I'm on my way. Meet me down in the alley and unlock the door."

"Bren—"

"Damn it, Ava! This is important!"

Something in his voice makes me agree. "Okay. I'll go down now."

Brendan and Brock are already standing outside when I open the door.

"Come on up."

They follow me up the stairs to my place.

"If you're hungry, I don't have anything. You can go down to the bakery and make yourselves a sandwich."

"Have you eaten yet?" Brendan asks.

I sigh as I slowly shake my head.

"For God's sake, Ava. I have no idea what's going on, and you don't have to tell me. But I will not sit by and watch you starve yourself." He opens my refrigerator. "You weren't kidding."

"Told you."

"She's got eggs." Brock grabs the carton. "I'm making you scrambled eggs, cuz. And you'll eat it. You and Brendan sit down and talk."

"I don't have anything to say." Though I do obey him and take a seat at the small table.

"That's okay," Brendan says. "I do."

He shoves a piece of paper in front of me.

"Who's Dyane Wingdam?" I ask.

"Pat Lamone's grandmother. Only it's an alias." He turns the paper over. The letters are rearranged.

My stomach drops.

"Wendy Madigan."

"Yup. Wendy Madigan. Just like the acrostic."

"*Grandmother,*" I say softly.

"That's the other clue," Brendan says. "From the first message. So what do they mean together?"

"They mean"—I draw in a deep breath—"that Wendy Madigan is my grandmother."

Brock drops an egg on the kitchen floor. "Shit. Sorry. I . . . My father told me some stuff, Ave. He . . ."

I rise. "You knew?"

Brock scratches his shoulder and looks down. "No. I mean, sort of."

I punch him hard in his left upper arm. "And you didn't tell me?"

"Easy, cuz. That hurt." He rubs his arm—the right one.

"I hit the other arm, douchebag. You'd better tell me what you know and now, or I'll aim lower next time."

He rubs his other arm. "Fuck it all. This means that dickhead Pat Lamone is your cousin, right?"

I look to Brendan. He doesn't look nearly as surprised as Brock.

"Lauren Wingdam is the daughter of Dyane Wingdam. She's Pat Lamone's birth mother."

I plunk back down in my wooden chair, making my tailbone ache. "This is all too much. We don't know for sure that Dyane Wingdam is an anagram for Wendy Madigan."

Brendan caresses my forearm. "Babe..."

I shake my head. "I know. I know. It all fits. My God..."

Brock kneels with a rag to clean up the broken egg. "Eggs will be another minute."

"I don't want to push..." Brendan urges.

"What the hell? I've already spilled that the woman is my grandmother. But first, Brock, you need to tell me what *you* know."

He turns off the burner. "Okay. Eggs will have to wait, then."

"Do I look like I care about the fucking eggs?" I nearly scream at him.

He takes a seat on my other side. "I honestly don't know a lot. Only that Uncle Ry had a different mother than my dad, Uncle Tal, and Aunt Marj."

"And who told you this?"

"My dad."

"Jesus Christ." I massage my forehead. The headache is massive now. "So your dad, my uncle, thought you had the right to know this fact before I did?"

"No." Brock shakes his head. "It wasn't like that at all. He just felt your parents should be the ones to tell you. Not him or me or anyone else."

"My God . . ." This time I massage my temples.

"What can we do for you, baby?" Brendan asks.

"You can both buckle up," I say. "Because you're in for a wild ride."

CHAPTER THIRTY

Brendan

Brock and I sit, mesmerized, as Ava spills out what she learned from her father. She confirms my theory, but there's so much more.

Her words fade in and out.

Wendy Madigan

Bradford Steel

Lovers

Affair

Ryan

Daphne Steel

Dissociative Identity Disorder

Dale and Donny

Talon

Human trafficking

Theodore Mathias

Ruby's father

Shots

Wendy dead

Brad dead

Ruby killed Wendy

Brad not dead after all

And Wendy?

Now she's alive too, hiding in plain sight under the alias Sabrina Smith.

By the time Ava stops speaking, her pallor has faded, and her eyes are glazed over. She's not crying. She hasn't even sniffled since she began this story.

Perhaps she got all that out of her system earlier—or more likely, she's become numb out of pure defense.

Silence reigns for a few moments, until—

"I'm not Daphne Steel's granddaughter," she says. "So I don't have to worry about inheriting her mental illness." Then she laughs. A sarcastic laugh. "Instead, I'm descended from two psychopaths. My father's mother, Wendy Madigan, and my mother's father, Theo Mathias. What a fucking genetic jackpot."

I touch her hand gently. "Have you eaten anything, Ava?"

She doesn't answer, but Brock rises.

"I'm pretty sure the eggs are ruined," he says.

"I don't want anything anyway," Ava says.

"Sweetheart, you have to eat something." I look at my watch. "And I have to get back to work. I left my old man to deal with the bar and Pat Lamone."

"Pat Lamone?" Ava asks.

"Yeah. He showed up at my place when Brock and I were talking. We shoved him off to Dad at the bar to come over here. I had to see you once I figured out Dyane Wingdam and Wendy Madigan are one and the same."

"I don't know anything about Pat Lamone."

"I do." Brock scoffs. "He's a dick. He's the one who poisoned Diana back when she was a freshman in high school."

Ava's jaw drops. "What?"

"Not only that," Brock continues, "he made Rory and

Callie's lives hell. He and Brittany Sheraton."

"The vet's daughter?"

"One and the same. God, do I have some stories to tell."

"Then spill them," Ava says. "I'm sick to hell of being left in the dark here."

"I should check with my fa—"

"Fuck that!" Ava snaps. "I'm done with caring what our parents have to say about any of this. They've kept important stuff from us our whole lives, and now we're getting bombs dropped on us as adults. It's fucked up."

"I won't disagree with you there," Brock says. "Suffice it to say that the trafficking ring that's responsible for Dale and Donny—and probably Uncle Talon's abduction too—was still operating up until a few weeks ago."

"Jesus," I say.

"On Steel property," Brock adds.

Ava's mouth is open, and she tongues her lip ring. Is she going to say something? She's got to be feeling something. Anything.

"Ava..." I begin.

"I could go into the gory detail," Brock continues, "but I'll save that for another time. Dad and Uncle Bryce took care of it. Destroyed all the evidence and ran the fuckers off. Turns out Brittany Sheraton clued us in on the whole thing. And Brendan, you probably know the story of Patty Watson, my grandmother's best friend."

I swallow. "She disappeared. After my great-uncle died at your grandparents' wedding."

"He didn't technically die at the wedding," Brock says. "He passed out at the reception and then died at the hospital."

"Fucking close enough," I grit out.

"Turns out," Brock says, "that Dale, Donny, and I found Patty Watson's remains on the edge of Steel property, right at the Wyoming border."

If possible, Ava goes even paler.

"Who the hell killed Patty Watson?" I demand. "Why was she on your property?"

"The story is that Patty disappeared while shopping in Snow Creek when she and her then boyfriend were visiting." He turns to Ava. "Remember the original Steel winemaker, who taught your dad? Ennis Ainsley?"

"Yeah. The Brit. I know the name, but I don't remember him."

"Right. He was Patty Watson's boyfriend back in the day. He never knew she was killed. He was told some story that she up and left the country to join the peace corps, but he didn't buy it. Rory and I went to London to meet with him, and out of sheer luck he had some of Patty's old belongings. We found a viable DNA sample, and it matched the bones we found on our property."

"Oh my God . . ." Ava shakes her head, her lips trembling.

"I'm betting whoever is responsible for Patty's death is also responsible for my great-uncle's."

"Most likely," Brock agrees, "but this all happened half a century ago. Who the hell could have been responsible?"

Ava finally raises her head and speaks. "Wendy Madigan. My grandmother."

"Why would she be involved?" Brock asks.

"She was obsessed with my grandfather. My dad told me. What better way to send him and the woman he married a message than to have both of their best friends murdered?"

"Madigan." I shake my head. "Jeremy Madigan, who Dad

bought the bar from. All this time... All this time, the answer was hidden under our own damned floorboards. And now this bitch is still alive?"

Ava trembles at my words.

I recalibrate. "Oh, God, sweetheart. I didn't mean—"

"Yes, you did," she says. "You totally meant it. She was— *is*—a bitch. If I could erase her from my DNA, I'd do it."

I squeeze Ava's hand. "I wouldn't."

She scoffs. "How can you say that? The woman's a menace. A psychopath. A murderer!"

"Because then you wouldn't be you." I stare into her beautiful blue eyes, into her soul. Damn, I stare nearly into her DNA. "Look at your father. Look at Gina. You're all fine. Whatever is wrong with Wendy isn't affecting any of you."

She shakes her head, says nothing.

I squeeze her hand again, but she doesn't respond.

"Ava," I say. "We're getting you something to eat."

"Not hungry."

"I don't care. You're going to eat something. I'm not taking no for an answer."

CHAPTER THIRTY-ONE

Ava

I don't have the strength to argue with Brendan. Especially not when Brock joins in.

"I've been there, Ave," he says. "I get what you're feeling. You're angry about the secrets. You're resentful. You're freaked. Our family history is dark and gruesome. Appalling. But this all happened forever ago. You need to focus on today."

"And today," I say, "my grandmother is alive."

"She is," Brendan says. "And we'll deal with that. But *your* life hasn't changed."

"How can you say that?"

"You know something you didn't know before. Your father is a half-sibling to your uncles and aunt. But he always was. You always were who you are. Nothing has changed."

I rise then. "I'm going out."

"Where?"

"Where do you think? I'm driving to Grand Junction. To visit my grandmother."

"Not until you eat something," Brendan says.

"Fine. I'll grab something on the way."

"I'm going with you."

"You have to get back to the bar."

He grips my shoulders. "Damn it, Ava! You're more important to me than any bar."

"Brendan . . . this isn't something you can do for me." I swat Brendan's hands away and grab my jacket. "I have to go. Alone."

"Hell no, you're not going alone."

"The woman's unconscious. And she's an octogenarian. I'll be fine. Besides, what other time do I have? I have to open the bakery in the morning."

"Will they even let you see her at this time of night?" Brendan asks.

"I can go with her," Brock says. "My mom is a big deal at that hospital, and the Steels are major donors to the foundation. All Ava and I need to do is drop our name. But if you don't want her going alone—and I understand—I'll go. I just need to text Rory."

Brendan sighs. "All right. But you call me as soon as you get home, all right? And you"—he turns to Brock—"take fucking good care of her and see that she gets something in her stomach." Then he kisses my lips. "I love you," he whispers.

I move my lips to his ear. "I love you too. Thank you for understanding."

★ ★ ★

"How about a taco?" Brock asks me once we're in the car. "That new Taco Bell at the edge of town is open until midnight."

"The dining room? Or the drive-thru?"

"It's only eight o'clock, so the dining room is still open. We can use the drive-thru, but tacos are a mess to eat in the car."

"Fine." I sigh. "I'll choke down a taco."

"Two," Brock says. "One taco isn't enough for a small child."

"My God . . . You're going to report back to Brendan, aren't you?"

"Guilty." He grins. "Look, cuz. That man looks at you the way I look at Rory, and I'd fucking kill anyone who didn't take care of her."

Despite everything going on, I can't help a slight smile.

"So he loves you." Brock pulls into the Taco Bell parking lot.

"Yeah."

"And is the feeling mutual?"

My cheeks warm.

"I'll take that as a yes."

"Take *what* as a yes?"

"The blush. You've been pale as a ghost all evening, Ava. The mention of Brendan loving you finally put some color back into those cheeks."

He puts the car in park, and we go into the restaurant. It's surprisingly busy for a weeknight on the edge of a small town, but we don't have to wait too long to put in our order.

"Six tacos," Brock says. "What'll you have, Ava?"

"Six tacos?" I say.

"They're not that big. And I had a light dinner." He turns back to the cashier. "My cousin will have three."

"Two," I say.

"Three," he repeats. "And two fountain drinks. Oh, and one order of those churro things."

"Cinnamon twists?" the cashier asks.

"Yeah, whatever. An order of those. You want any, Ava?"

"Uh . . . no. Thanks."

Brock taps his credit card on the reader and glances over his shoulder. "There's a table in the back. Why don't you snag it while I wait for the order?"

"Okay."

"What do you want to drink?"

"Just water."

"I paid for a fountain drink, Ave."

"For God's sake. So what?" Then I berate myself. I may not use my family's money, but I don't want it wasted. Even the few cents for a soda. "Diet Coke."

"They don't have Coke products."

"Pepsi, then. I don't care."

"You got it."

I head to the table Brock gestured to and take a seat. A few crumbs are scattered on top. Great. Something about fast-food places always makes me want to bathe in hand sanitizer. My bakery is always spotless. I get perfect scores on all my reports from the Department of Health. No one will ever find a crumb on one of my tables. Maya wipes them down a millisecond after a customer gets up.

Makes me wonder if the newfound crumbs of my family history will ever be wiped from my mind. If only I had a Maya inside my head brushing away all the unpleasantness.

Brock returns with our order. I grab a taco and a packet of sauce.

"Which drink is mine?"

"Doesn't matter. They're both Diet Pepsi." He grabs one and shoves in a straw.

I open the sauce packet and squeeze it onto my taco. Then, against my better judgment, I take a bite.

Brock lifts his eyebrows at me as I chew and swallow.

It's good. What is it about tacos? You can be feeling like complete crap and a taco will still taste good.

I nod at him.

He smiles. "Eat every bite."

He downs all six of his plus the cinnamon twists before I get through my second. But it is good. Something about the crunchy shell scratching my throat a bit as it goes down puts me in a better mood.

I unwrap my third taco. "It feels weird, us being here."

"How so?" Brock takes the last sip of his drink, the straw making gurgling sounds.

"I mean, the two of us without Dave. You know. Huey, Dewey, and Louie."

"You went to a different college than Dave and I did," he says. "The whole duck thing kind of dissipated after that. And it should have dissipated a lot sooner." He rolls his eyes.

I swallow my bite of taco. "I know. But when things were serious, the three of us always stuck together, just like the awesome foursome does."

"Who the hell came up with that name, anyway?"

I take a sip of drink. "They probably came up with it themselves." Gina, Angie, Sage, and Bree are the youngest of the Steels, and the most fabulous, to hear them tell it.

"Actually..." Brock fiddles with his phone. "Rory came up with the Three Rake-a-teers, and I'm betting..."

His phone dings.

"Yup. Just as I suspected. The Pike sisters strike again."

"What are you talking about?"

"Rory says Maddie came up with the awesome foursome. I wonder if the four of them know that Maddie always feels like a fifth wheel with them."

"She's not a member of the family."

"No, but she's their same age, and they all still go to college together."

"I don't get that," I say. "That feeling of not belonging."

"That's because you never cared whether you belonged or not."

I can't help a chuckle. "That's the truth, for sure. But it's more than that, Brock."

"What do you mean?"

I look away and scrunch the wrapper from my taco into a ball. "I can't believe I'm about to tell you this."

He smiles. "You're going to have to tell me now, after that lead in."

"I stopped caring so I wouldn't have to compete with Gina."

"Why would you have to compete with Gina?"

"Come on. You know why. She's beautiful, brilliant, talented. She's everything I'm not."

"She's got a few inches on you in height, but that's about it, Ave. You're just as beautiful, brilliant, and talented as she is."

"I can't paint."

"So what? Gina can't make the fluffiest croissants on the planet."

I finish up my final taco. "That's right. She can't. See? I'm not competing with her."

He rolls his eyes. "I'll never understand women. I'm getting a refill." He rises and heads toward the soda fountain.

I shrug. He doesn't get it. That's okay, though. I know what I mean.

He returns to the table with his refilled cup. "You ready?"

"Yeah." I grab the tray and head to the wastebasket.

You ready?

Not in the slightest. But I want to see this woman. This grandmother. I want to know the secrets she still hides.

Because I'm fucking done with secrets.

CHAPTER THIRTY-TWO

Brendan

By ten, the game is over and the bar has settled down to its normal Monday-night atmosphere.

"Let's go," Dad says. "You and I still need to talk."

I pop the cap off a Fat Tire and hand it to a customer. "All right. Where's Johnny?"

"In the can." He gestures at Johnny, who's walking toward the bar, wiping his hands on his jeans. "There he is."

"Fine." I move toward the staircase to my apartment.

Dad is right behind me. I unlock the door and enter.

"You want anything? A sandwich?"

Dad takes a seat at my small table. "No. Sit down, Brendan."

I grab a bottle of water from my fridge and sit next to my father. "So ... Lauren Wingdam?"

"Yeah. I've got an address."

"Did you give it to Pat Lamone?"

"I did. She's his mother. His birth mother, that is."

"She's his only mother now," I say. "His adoptive parents were killed in a car accident."

"That's a damned shame."

"It is. But Pat Lamone is no saint, Dad."

"Neither am I. Neither are you."

He's not wrong. "But Lamone's bad news. I was talking to Brock—"

"Brock Steel?"

"Yeah."

"Let's keep the Steels on a need-to-know basis, Brendan."

"They've been getting the same cryptic messages. The Steels aren't our enemies, Dad."

"Did I say they are?"

"No, but . . . Pat Lamone isn't a good guy. I'm sorry he lost his parents and all, but he tried to destroy the Pike sisters back in high school. And . . . he drugged Diana Steel."

Dad raises his eyebrows. "You got proof of that?"

"Brock does."

"Are they filing charges?"

"They can't. Statute of limitations."

"You mean they only just found out?"

I nod.

"The Steels have their hands in everything. Damn."

"This isn't the Steels' fault. And Pat—"

I stop. As much as I hate keeping things from my father, I can't tell him that Lauren Wingdam is Wendy Madigan's daughter, and that Wendy Madigan is Ryan Steel's birth mother. I promised Ava I'd keep it all in confidence.

"Pat what?"

"Nothing. Just don't let him fool you."

"You have to get up pretty early to fool me, Brendan."

I clear my throat. "I'm in love with Ava, Dad. She's important to me, and her family is important to her. So I don't want to get into anything that will bring down the Steels."

"Even if they're behind your great-uncle's death?"

I stop myself from pounding my fist on the table. "Dad, for

God's sake. That was over fifty years ago. I didn't even know the man, and you were just a kid yourself. Was Bradford Steel involved? Maybe. Does it really matter at this point? None of the Steels alive today were even born yet. They couldn't have been involved."

"That doesn't mean they don't know something."

"They don't."

"How can you be sure of that?"

"Because they're good people, Dad. If they knew something, they'd tell you. We're talking about Brad Steel here. A man who faked his own death, not once but twice. He was shrewd, brilliant. And he's dead, Dad. For good this time. He's been dead for twenty-five years."

"I see your point. The trail is cold, for sure." Dad shakes his head. "But it doesn't sit well with me."

"Do yourself a favor," I say. "Do Mom a favor. Let this go."

"But the messages . . ."

"Right. The messages. Whatever's going on with the Steels involves us somehow. And you're right, your uncle seems to be the only commonality, but still, for Mom, let this *go*."

"I love your mother."

"I never said you didn't. But this relentless pursuit isn't going to help your marriage."

"My marriage is my business, Brendan. Mine and your mother's. None of yours."

"That'd be nice if it were true, Dad, but it isn't. You're my parents, and I love you both. Your happiness is important to me."

Dad doesn't reply, and just when I'm sure he's done talking altogether—

He slides a piece of paper across the table to me.

On it is written an address for Lauren Wingdam.

"Damn. She lives in Barrel Oaks, the next town over."

"Surprised me too."

"You doing anything tomorrow morning?"

"Going to Barrel Oaks," he says.

"Good. Me too."

CHAPTER THIRTY-THREE

Ava

"She looks so old and helpless," I say to Brock.

I'm staring at Sabrina Smith, aka Dyane Wingdam, aka Wendy Madigan.

"Did I tell you about Dyane Wingdam's rap sheet?" Brock asks. "That's no helpless old lady there. She's sedated. And strapped down."

I move her sheet down to regard her wrists. They are indeed strapped down. Her skin tone is good for her age, and her hands still look young. Her fingernails are painted. Odd. Who would have painted them? Surely not Pat Lamone.

Her face is wrinkled yet serene, and her lips are a soft pink. I can see that she was a beauty when she was young. And her nose. I absently touch my own. It's just like my father's . . . and mine.

"Why do they have her strapped down?" I ask.

"Probably because she's psycho." He twists his lips. "Sorry, Ave. I didn't mean—"

"Yeah, you did. It's okay. She's messed up. Or she's not, and that makes her even scarier. What if she doesn't have any mental illness? What if she's just *that* evil?"

He cocks his head. "You're right when you say she looks the part. Old and helpless. But her record is a mile long. Felony forgery, bank fraud, insider trading. Never did any time, though. Somehow she managed to get away with everything."

"She just changed her name and went into hiding."

"I had our PI team look into her. Into Dyane Wingdam, that is. Her crimes were all committed within the last twenty-five years."

"After Wendy Madigan *died*," I say.

"Right. The alias goes back about forty-five years, but she didn't commit any crimes as Dyane until later."

"So she faked her death and became Dyane for good."

"That's how it looks."

"And Dyane has a record, so later she created the new alias of Sabrina Smith to evade capture."

"Makes as much sense as any of this does," Brock agrees.

I let out a heavy sigh. "This woman is my grandmother. The nose. I have her nose. What color are her eyes?"

"Apparently they're blue, according to my dad. Daphne's were brown."

"Have you heard how my father was always considered the handsomest and most jovial of all the Steel brothers?" I ask.

"Who hasn't?"

"I've seen photos of Daphne. She was classically beautiful. And our grandfather was ruggedly handsome. Looked just like your father. So how could my father be the handsomest when your dad and Uncle Tal came from Daphne?"

"Genes are funny things," he says. "Who knows? We don't know what Dyane—or Wendy—looked like. She could have been gorgeous too."

Yes, she was gorgeous. Even in old age, it's clear. But none of this matters. Whether my father is the best-looking Steel brother doesn't matter. And this woman... This woman can't do anything to my family. She's old and frail and strapped to a hospital bed.

This? This is my collapsing tower?

She's nothing.

She's nothing to me.

Except I feel her. I felt her when I drew those cards. I always knew I wasn't feeling Daphne Steel. I just didn't realize there was a reason for it.

Even now, as my grandmother lies here, sedated, I feel that she's a part of me.

And I hate the feeling.

So I choose to think of her as nothing.

"Let's go." I turn and walk toward the door.

Then I jerk.

"Who the hell are you?" I say to the young man entering.

Brock turns. "Lamone. What the hell?"

"I came to visit my grandmother."

"At ten p.m.?"

"Yeah, at ten p.m. What the hell are *you* doing here?"

"This is my cousin Ava," Brock says.

"Hi. So what the hell are the two of you doing here?"

I clear my throat. "It seems—"

I stop. I promised my father I wouldn't tell anyone, other than Brendan, what he told me. I was about to spill that this woman is my grandmother too.

"It seems what?" Lamone asks.

"Nothing. We're done here." I leave the room.

Brock doesn't follow me, and I listen through the door.

"You take care of everything?" Lamone says to Brock.

"I'm a man of my word."

"I just want her comfortable. I'm going to see my mother—my birth mother—tomorrow. I hope I can get her to come visit."

"Maybe you should be asking yourself why she *doesn't* visit."

"You're a Steel," Lamone says. "I thought you people were all about family."

"If that were the case," Brock says, "we'd be embracing you with open arms. Of course, you haven't proved anything yet. Only that you're the grandson of this woman. I haven't seen any proof that you're a Steel."

I widen my eyes. There's no proof?

"I'll get proof," Lamone says. "As soon as I talk to my mother."

"Doesn't matter, anyway," Brock says. "You agreed not to make any claims against the family fortune as long as we take care of the old lady."

"Too bad we never signed anything."

Brock chuckles. "I should have known. Anyone who would poison an innocent young girl. You, Lamone, are *not* a man of your word."

"I just want to see what my birth mother has to say. I want answers."

"So do we all. But the answers we need are inside this sedated woman's head."

"My mother may know what's going on."

"She may. She may not. But I think it's safe to say that if she gave a shit about *her* mother, she'd be here. She wouldn't have left her in your care."

"She didn't. Or...I don't know if she did. I got an anonymous tip that this woman was my grandmother, and as you know, I had our DNA run and it's true. I'm her grandson."

"Another anonymous tip. How convenient."

"Look, Steel, I didn't ask to be dragged into your family chaos, but I'm here."

"You certainly are. I don't give a rat's ass if you're a direct descendant of Brad Steel himself. You'll get nothing. Not after you violated Rory and Callie and poisoned Diana. You can burn in hell."

Brock is angry. I can hear the tension in his voice. I don't blame him. I'm angry too.

"I was a kid, damn it! And all those photos of Rory and Callie have been destroyed. We've been through this."

"Funny. I don't feel like it's over at all. Call me a skeptic, but I don't trust you, Lamone. I'm pretty sure you're here to stay, and let me make myself perfectly clear—you will never get a penny of Steel money. I'll die first."

Brock whooshes out of the room. "Let's go, Ava."

"What was all that about?" I ask as we walk to the elevator. "He took photos of Rory and Callie?"

"It's a long story, cuz. Suffice it to say that ten years ago, he and Brittany Sheraton drugged the Pike sisters, disrobed them, and took incriminating photos. Then blackmailed them."

"Why?"

"Because they had proof that he drugged Diana."

"Oh my God…"

"He's not a nice guy, Ava. Don't be getting all soft just because you're cousins or whatever."

"Oh, God. I *am* his cousin. His mother and my father are both children of…" I swallow back nausea.

"Like I said…"

We get into the elevator, and as it plummets, so does my stomach.

Just like the tower.

CHAPTER THIRTY-FOUR

B r e n d a n

I'm home.

I regard the text from Ava. It's nearing midnight, and the bar is emptying out.

I text her back.

Do you want me to come over?

She doesn't respond for a few moments, which troubles me, and then the three dots begin to move.

If you want to.

Women. Why don't they just say what they mean?

I'm coming.

Then I head over. She's waiting for me at the back door of the bakery. Her hair is soft and wavy around her shoulders, and the color has come back into her beautiful face.

"Did you eat?" I ask.

She nods. "Tacos. Brock made me."

"Brock's a good man." I enter and follow her up the steps to her place. Once we're inside, "Do you want to talk? About your grandmother? Or anything else?"

"Not especially."

"All right. Let me get you some water."

"I'm not thirsty, Brendan."

I sigh. "Then why am I here, Ava?"

She shrugs. "That was your choice."

I grip her shoulders. "Damn it, don't do this. Don't play games with me."

"I'm not."

"The hell you're not. Maybe it's the age thing. Maybe you're too immature—"

Her cheeks redden with anger. "Excuse me?"

"I'm sorry. You're not immature, Ava, which is why I don't understand why you won't just tell me what the hell you want."

"I . . . I don't know what I want, Brendan." She balls her hands into fists. "I'm twisted up in knots inside. Everything I've counted on, believed in, is a lie. How am I supposed to deal with this? It's the tower."

"I thought you were taking a break from the cards."

"I am. But that doesn't negate the tower and how it affected, and continues to affect, me."

"Okay. So you don't know what you want. What do you need, then? What can I do for you?"

She shrugs. "It's crazy, but I want you to take me to bed."

I smile, finger a lock of her pink hair. "Why is that crazy?"

"Because how can I be thinking of sex at a time like this?"

"Easy."

"Easy for you. You're a guy. You're always thinking about sex."

"Well…"

She shakes her head. "Don't even try to deny it."

"I wasn't going to."

"I'm sorry," she says.

"For what?"

"For…" She sighs. "For…you know. I should have just told you I wanted you to come over and take me to bed."

"Instead of leaving it up to me. But you knew I'd come."

"I did. I'm sorry. I wasn't trying to be manipulative."

"Yeah, you were."

She frowns. "Hey, wait a min—"

"Look, Ava. I love you. You're the most important thing in the world to me. But I'm not going to use kid gloves with you. I respect you too much for that."

She plays with her lip ring. My groin tightens.

"So let's make a deal. You tell me what you want when you want it. I'll do the same. I understand you're going through some major stuff right now with your family, and I can't even begin to understand just how much seeing your grandmother tonight affected you. I'll talk to you about it if you want. I'll listen. Or I'll throw you onto your bed and fuck the daylights out of you. Whatever you want, Ava. All you have to do is tell me."

She looks down. "The second one."

I tip her chin up so she meets my gaze. "Tell me. Tell me exactly what you want."

"I want you to throw me onto my bed, Brendan. I want you to fuck the daylights out of me."

"Good enough."

I lift her, sling her over my shoulder, and march into her bedroom.

CHAPTER THIRTY-FIVE

Ava

"Undress," Brendan commands, after he throws me onto my bed.

I don't hesitate to obey. Within a minute, my clothes and shoes are flung onto the floor, and then I watch, mesmerized, as he gets rid of his clothes. Then he hovers over me, naked, his hard cock pressing into me. He kisses me, deeply, and then he breaks it and slides his tongue over my breasts, down my abdomen, until he stops between my legs.

"God, you're slick and wet and gorgeous." He cups my pussy. "I'm going to eat you until you can't take it anymore."

Though I desperately want him inside me, this sounds good too.

I close my eyes—

"Oh, no," he says. "You keep those eyes open. You watch me eat this sweet pussy, Ava."

Then I gasp as he slides his tongue over my wet folds. I want to relax, to close my eyes, but I don't want to disobey Brendan. Strange, but true, so I watch.

I watch as he slithers his tongue over my slit, down to my perineum, and then back up to my clit. My flesh is on fire, and with the touch of his tongue and of his lips, I grow hotter.

"Mmm, delicious." He groans as he continues licking me.

"Brendan..." But it comes out more like a soft moan.

He works my pussy, licking, sliding, nipping. My nipples are hard and aching, and without thinking, I cup my breasts, still focused on Brendan.

"Yeah, baby," he says. "Play with those nipples. Make yourself feel good."

Careful not to close my eyes, I obey him again. I touch both nipples, squeeze them gently. The sparks travel straight between my legs—where Brendan is feasting.

Each tug on my nipples makes the currents running through my pussy more intense.

And watching Brendan... His handsome face between my legs... His hair unbound and tickling my thighs...

"Oh!"

The climax sneaks up on me and rocks through me like an earthquake. When Brendan shoves two fingers inside me, the rumbling strengthens, and I cry out his name.

"Easy, baby," he says, his chin glistening. "We're just getting started."

"So good..." I sigh, still plucking at my nipples. They're hard and needy and still aching, and I twist them, loving the sensation.

Brendan removes his fingers and sinks his tongue deep into my pussy. The sensation is less intense, but the velvety softness of his tongue is heaven.

In a flash, though, his lips are around my clit, his fingers tunneling into me once more. I'm on the brink of another orgasm, and I tug at my nipples—

"Yes!" I come with more force this time, arching my hips and grinding against Brendan's face. His stubble scrapes my sensitive inner thighs, and God, it feels heavenly.

I come again and then again, and when Brendan finally pulls his fingers out of me, I'm a heap of mushy flesh.

Mushy flesh that wants to be fucked. That aches to be fucked.

He crawls toward me, his eyes on fire, but instead of plunging into my pussy, he comes closer, dangles his dick between my lips.

"I need to feel your mouth on me, Ava. Please."

I open for him, and he slides his cock inside my mouth.

"Fuck," he grits out. "That lip ring. Nothing like it."

He fucks my mouth slowly at first, but then he glides in and out faster. Part of me yearns for my pussy to be filled, but another part is loving his groans of pleasure as I suck his big cock.

And it's a damned big cock.

I don't want to stop, but he pulls out swiftly. "Fuck. Need to be inside you."

And then he is . . . thrusting, thrusting, thrusting . . .

That ache . . . That empty ache . . . It's filled. Completely filled by Brendan's magnificent cock.

He slides in and out of me, each time jarring my clit, and each time sending me closer, closer, closer . . .

Until I shatter once more, clamping around him as he thrusts.

"Yeah, baby." He squeezes his eyes shut. "So. Fucking. Good." He pounds into me one last time, releasing.

I'm still on the edge of my own climax, and I feel each contraction as he spurts inside me.

And for a moment . . .

I forget about my grandmother.

I forget about the tower.

I forget about my family's secrets and lies.

Only Brendan and I exist.

And I wish it could stay this way forever.

★ ★ ★

Nothing lasts forever, though. The alarm clock wakes me early, and I rise and pad into the shower. The warm rainfall on my head is both relaxing and exhilarating, and I give myself a good exfoliation with my shower pouf.

Until—

A warm body touches mine.

I turn into Brendan's arms. "Hey... What are you doing up so early?"

"Showering with the love of my life."

"You should sleep."

"Mmm." He kisses my lips. "Can't. I'm meeting my father for breakfast, and then we're going to go see Lauren Wingdam."

"My aunt." The words come out of my mouth before I can think about them.

"Yeah. In a technical sense."

"In a genetic sense," I say. "I wish I could come along."

"Can Luke or Maya take care of the bakery this morning?"

"No." I squeeze some shampoo into my palm. "Maybe. If I get the morning bake started. But I don't like to be out of the bakery during business hours."

"I know what you mean."

I kiss him. "I know. And you've been really good about leaving your place of business when I need you."

"You're number one with me, Ava. But don't feel like you have to be there this morning for my sake."

"You don't need me?"

"I always need you. But this is more for my dad."

"All right. But tell me everything."

"Of course." He lifts me, sets me onto his hard cock. "But first..."

I sigh. True completion. In the shower, only Brendan and I exist, as if we're in a secluded pond under a waterfall.

I close my eyes and let myself slide into the fantasy... for as long as I can.

CHAPTER THIRTY-SIX

Brendan

Dad and I drive up to a large brick ranch house on the edge of Snow Creek's sister town, Barrel Oaks, Colorado. Don't blink or you'll miss it. Barrel Oaks makes Snow Creek look like a thriving metropolis.

But this house...

It's sprawling, and the lawn is green—not always the norm in the dry desert climate of Colorado—and well-kept.

The driveway is fine gravel and leads to a detached three-car garage. Instead, we park on the street and take the stone walkway to the front door.

An ornate antique door knocker graces the door that's painted dark red. I choose the doorbell, pressing it lightly.

No response.

I ring it again, while Dad lifts the door knocker and brings it down loudly once. Then again.

Finally the door opens. A young man in jeans, a white button-down, and a bolo tie—seriously—stands there. His reddish-brown hair is cut short in a professional style.

"Yeah? Can I help you?"

"We're from Snow Creek," Dad says. "We're looking for Lauren Wingdam."

"What for?" he asks.

"That's between us and her," I say.

"And me," the man says. "She's my mother."

I stop myself from dropping my jaw to the ground. Pat Lamone has a brother. Now that he says it, I see the resemblance, although this guy is much better looking than Lamone. Perhaps they don't share the same father.

"Good enough," Dad says. "We have some questions about your grandmother. Dyane Wingdam."

"Then we can't help you," the man says. "My mother had a falling out with her mother years ago."

"We'd still like to talk to her." I hold out my hand. "I'm Brendan Murphy."

He doesn't take my hand. "Murphy?"

"Yeah. This is my dad. Sean Murphy."

"*Sean* Murphy?"

"I'm not getting out my ID," Dad says, "but yeah, I'm Sean Murphy. Now that you know who we are, maybe you can clue us in on your name."

He looks to me and then to Dad. Then he finally takes my outstretched hand and gives it a firm shake. "My name is Jack. Jack *Murphy*."

This time I let my jaw drop.

Have we just found the link between us and the Steels?

The reason why we've been getting the same messages?

"I think," Dad says, "you should let us in. Seems we may have more to talk about than we thought."

Jack holds the door open. "Yeah, maybe. Because Sean Murphy is . . ."

Dad walks in. "Me. Sean Murphy is me."

The foyer is tiled with marble and leads into a lush living area, complete with a baby grand piano in black lacquer and white-and-gold wallpaper.

"Have a seat." Jack points to the blue-and-burgundy brocade chairs and sofa. "I'll get my mom."

"Thank you." I take a seat.

"I'll send Margaret in. She'll get you a drink if you want one."

"That's kind of you." Dad sits in a chair across from mine.

They have help? I mouth to Dad.

He simply shrugs.

Clearly Lauren and Jack aren't hurting for money, which is a good thing. If they're somehow related to the Steels, maybe they won't go after more money.

A young woman in a blue maid's uniform enters with a smile on her face. "Good morning, gentlemen. Could I get you a cup of coffee? Some breakfast?"

"We've had breakfast," Dad says, "but I could go for a coffee."

"Of course." Margaret—presumably—smiles. "Cream and sugar?"

"Black."

"And you, sir?" She nods to me.

"Same. Coffee, black."

"I'll be right back." She turns, still smiling, and leaves the living room.

Margaret returns a few moments later with a tray and sets it on the glass-topped coffee table. Fine china cups and saucers and a silver coffee service. The Steels themselves don't put on this much of a show when they serve coffee. Margaret pours us each a cup and then leaves again.

I take a sip. Strong and a little bitter. Perfect.

"She knows how to brew a damned fine cup," I say to Dad.

He doesn't reply right away. Until, "Red hair."

"Jack?" I ask.

He nods.

"I'd call it reddish brown."

"It's still red."

"We're not related to every Murphy in the world," I tell him.

"That kid knows something about my uncle," Dad says. "I can feel it."

"Dad..."

"The name Sean Murphy means something to him, and I don't know this guy from Adam, so it's not me he's talking about."

"Sean Murphy is a common name for people of Irish descent, Dad. So is Brendan Murphy, for that matter."

Dad opens his mouth but then closes it when Jack returns, this time with an attractive older woman. Her hair is medium brown and cut short, and her eyes a searing blue. Dad and I both rise.

"This is my mother," Jack says, "Lauren Wingdam. Mom, Sean Murphy and his son, Brendan."

"It's a pleasure." Lauren shakes Dad's hand and then mine. "I understand you have some questions about my mother."

"We do," Dad says, "and also about how you're related to the Murphy family. Specifically a Sean Murphy."

"First things first, though," I say. "Your mother. Dyane Wingdam."

Lauren takes a seat on the sofa, and Jack sits next to her. "My mother..." She sighs. "There's no better way to say this. My mother is a psychopath."

Dad widens his eyes. "Why would you say that?"

"Because it's the truth." Lauren pulls a small bell off the

tray and rings it. "Just getting Margaret to bring me some tea. Now, what is your interest in my mother?"

"Apparently I bought the bar that I own in Snow Creek from her uncle," Dad says.

"Okay." Lauren blinks her blue eyes. "So?"

"That's not the main thing," I say. "I don't mean to bring up anything that's difficult for you to discuss, but did you give up a son for adoption about"—I calculate in my head—"twenty-seven or so years ago?"

Lauren looks down.

"I'm sorry, I—"

She meets my gaze. "No. It's all right. Yes, I did. The child was..."

Jack pats his mother's hand. "You don't have to do this, Mom."

"It's okay, honey." She swallows. "Jack was—"

Margaret enters. "Yes, ma'am?"

"Some tea, please, Margaret. And coffee for Jack."

"Right way."

Lauren sighs. "Now, where was I?"

"The child you gave up," I prompt.

"Right. Jack was only three at the time. He was on a sleepover at my mother's house, and I was home alone."

"Here?" I ask.

"Oh, no. We didn't have this house back then. Jack and I lived in a mobile home in north Denver. Anyway"—her voice cracks—"a group of three men broke in while Jack was gone and they..." She closes her eyes. "Well, you can guess what they did. The child was the result. I didn't want to terminate the pregnancy, but I couldn't keep him. Every time I looked at him, I would have remembered. Carrying him for nine months was difficult enough. So I gave him up."

Dad and I don't speak. What can we say to that?

"I suppose you must think me callous," she continues, "but I've rarely given him a thought all these years. I couldn't, for my own sanity."

"No one's judging you, Mom," Jack says.

"No, of course not," Dad agrees. "But you should know that he is in Snow Creek. His name is Pat Lamone...and he has this address."

Lauren covers her mouth with her hand as she gasps. "How did he find me?"

"I'm sorry," Dad says. "I got your address from my private investigators—"

"Why the hell would you be looking for my mother?" Jack interjects.

"It's a long story," I say. "Go ahead, Dad."

"Your son got an anonymous message," Dad says, "and my son and I got the same message. It was an acrostic puzzle, and the answer was Wendy Madigan."

"Who's Wendy Madigan?" Jack asks.

But Lauren looks at her lap.

"I believe your mother may know," I say.

Lauren trembles and then turns to Jack. "Wendy Madigan is my mother. Dyane Wingdam is an alias she used off and on, and twenty-five years ago, she began using it exclusively. Wendy Madigan no longer exists."

"So your real name..."

"Is Lauren Madigan," she says. "But twenty-five years ago, my mother somehow got everything changed. I have no idea how she did it, but your birth certificate, mine, everything, now shows my name as Lauren Wingdam."

Margaret returns with the coffee and tea.

"I'm going to need something a little stronger," Jack says.

"It's ten a.m.," Lauren admonishes.

"Yeah, and I think I'm going to be drinking all day."

"Dyane Wingdam." Jack wrinkles his forehead. "Wendy Madigan."

"It's an anagram," I say.

"I'll be damned." Jack looks up. "Margaret? I'm going to need a scotch. A double. Fuck. A triple."

"Jack . . ." Lauren says.

"Mom, I'm not even kidding."

"Right away, Mr. Murphy," Margaret says.

"Okay." Dad takes a drink of his coffee and then wipes his lips with a napkin. "So we have two more questions. First, Lauren, who is your father? And second, Jack, how exactly are you a Murphy?"

CHAPTER THIRTY-SEVEN

Ava

I throw myself into baking, trying desperately not to think about all the new revelations about my life.

My normal response when I'm feeling this way would be to draw a tarot card, but I'm determined to keep to my promise of taking a break from that world. After all, the last several cards have given me nothing but negativity.

There's enough negativity in my life now without the cards.

Still...

No. No. No.

I punch the ball of sourdough I'm kneading. Then I punch it again.

No cards.

No cards.

No cards.

"Ave?"

I look up at Luke's voice.

He wipes his hands on his apron. "What the hell did that dough ever do to you?"

He's right, of course. The dough ball has had enough. I place it in an oiled stainless-steel bowl, turn it to coat, and cover it with a piece of cheese cloth.

Time to do something else.

I head to the front counter to relieve Maya.

The breakfast rush has died down, and I clear out the croissants and place freshly baked loaves of sourdough and whole-grain bread in the glass case. Time to slice for the lunch rush that will start in less than an hour.

I gear up the slicer when the bells ding as someone walks in the door.

Brock.

"You doing okay?" he asks. "I wanted to check in this morning."

"I'm fine," I say with as much nonchalance as I can muster.

Brock narrows his gaze. "I don't buy it. At least your cheeks have color. I hope you've eaten."

"Not since our tacos."

"Ava, come on. This isn't the end of the world."

I dart my gaze around. "Quiet down, for God's sake."

"No one's here. Just a few customers at the back table and Luke and Maya, and since I don't see them, I assume they're in the back."

"They still have ears."

"With supersonic hearing?"

"Brock, I swear..." I remove my gloves, toss them in the trash can, and head into the kitchen. "Maya, I need you out front."

Once Maya is handling things, I grab Brock and pull him out the back door into the alley.

I shiver against the chill in the air. "You can't just come into my place of business and start talking about this stuff. I promised my dad I wouldn't tell anyone."

"I'm not asking you to tell anyone. Fuck, Ava, I was just concerned."

"I'm fine."

"You're not. If I hadn't forced you to eat tacos last night, you still wouldn't be eating."

He may be right. My stomach is still full of knots. But the tacos did taste good. I can't starve myself forever. I don't want to do that. I love my life.

Yeah, I do love my life.

My business is thriving, and I'm in love with a wonderful man.

Time to get over myself.

"Ava?"

"Sorry, just thinking." I wipe my hands on my apron. "I'm good, Brock. Truly. So I'm not descended from Daphne Steel. I'm descended from two psychopaths instead."

"How much do you know about your grandfather on your mom's side?" he asks.

"Not much. I need to talk to my mom. In fact, I'm going to talk to my mom. Now."

"You're going to leave the bakery?"

"I am. I love this place, but it can function without me."

"The lunch rush is coming."

He's right. "I'll leave after the lunch rush. Luke and Maya can handle things after that. The day's bake is done, and if we run out of bread, they can close early."

"Ava, this isn't like you."

"No, but I'm not *me* anymore."

"Ave..."

"Seriously. I'm okay." I grab Brock's forearm. "That didn't come out right. But I will eat. I promise. I'm not going to let myself wither away to nothing. I love my life. I love my family, despite their obvious flaws. I love Brendan."

"We've all—well, Dale, Don, and me, at least—been through the same thing. I mean, none of us found out we had different ancestors than we thought, but we got a heavy dose of Steel secrets. None of it is pretty, Ave. We got through it, and so will you."

"I know that. But I'm going to get answers from my mother, and I'm going to get them today." I grab a clean pair of disposable gloves from the dispenser. "Now if you'll excuse me, I have to get back to work."

CHAPTER THIRTY-EIGHT

Brendan

"That's a long story," Jack says.

I take the last sip of my coffee. "We don't have anywhere to be."

Jack turns to Lauren. "Mom...maybe you'd better do the honors. Not that it's any of their business, but I don't have anything to hide."

"You know, Jack," Lauren says, "maybe it's time to get all this stuff out in the open. I'm tired of covering for my mother. She's made my life hell, but I got you out of it, and you've been the most amazing gift. I just—" She chokes back a sob.

"It's okay, Mom." He pats her knee.

"You have no idea the guilt I still feel about giving up my other son," Lauren says. "I try not to think about it, but now that you've brought it up..."

"We didn't mean to bring up painful memories," I say. "We're just looking for answers."

"Believe me, I understand." She draws in a deep breath. "Jack was conceived through a sperm donor. A sperm donor named Sean Murphy."

Dad's eyes widen into circles.

And I glare at him. "Dad..."

"For God's sake, Brendan. It wasn't me. I never donated

243

any sperm. You're my only child. Your mother and I tried after you, but it just never happened."

I nod. "Sorry. Of course you're not Jack's father."

"I hesitate to even tell you this," Lauren says, "but we're all in now, I guess. You know more about me than most do, and we just met, but somehow I feel like..." She shakes her head. "Let me just get this out. My mother made all the arrangements. I'd always wanted to be a mother, ever since I was a little girl, and I was ready to get married to the man I thought was the love of my life when he disappeared. I'm sure my mother was behind it. She never liked him, but I was young and naïve and didn't know what she was capable of back then. Anyway, she offered to pay for artificial insemination and said she knew of the perfect donor."

"So your mother got the sperm sample for you?" I ask.

"She did." Lauren clears her throat. "I was just so desperate and heartbroken after Michael left me, and I wanted a child so badly... I didn't ask a lot of questions."

"And the sperm donor's name was Sean Murphy."

"Yes. That's all I know. Mom arranged for it and said he wouldn't be involved in the child's life but asked that Jack take his surname."

"Did you know that Sean Murphy was my uncle?" Dad asks.

"I didn't know who he was."

"And my uncle died of a drug overdose over fifty years ago."

"Dad," I begin, "Sean Murphy is not an uncommon name. It may not be—"

"For God's sake, Brendan, look at him. His hair, his facial features. Look at that jawline and that nose. He's related to us for sure."

"A simple DNA test can prove that," I say.

"Hold on," Jack says. "I never knew Sean Murphy, and if he died fifty years ago, how the hell could he be my father? I'm only thirty-one."

"Jack makes a good point, Dad," I say.

"You're right." Dad sighs, takes a sip of his coffee. "I'm just so determined to figure out what happened to him."

"Maybe it's time to take what happened to him at face value, Dad. He passed out at Brad Steel's wedding, and he died in the hospital of a drug overdose."

"But he didn't do drugs."

"That you knew of. That anyone who knew him knew of. But drug addicts aren't always forthcoming about their usage."

Dad punches the arm of his chair. "My uncle was not a damned drug addict!"

I say no more. There's no arguing with my father about the original Sean Murphy. He has his own ideas, and no one will tell him otherwise.

"The second question you asked," Lauren says, "was about my father."

"Yes," I say. "Do you know who he was?"

"I do," she says, "though I never met him."

"Mom..." Jack says.

"It's all right, honey. Let's just get this over with." Lauren picks up her teacup but doesn't take a sip. "I never met my father, but I do have my original birth certificate from when I was born. Before my mother had my name changed."

"How did she do that?" Dad asks.

"If I knew, I'd tell you. My mother has resources and can get almost anything done. She's a brilliant woman. An IQ around a hundred and sixty, along with no ethics and no regard for the law. So yeah, she gets things done." Lauren rises. "I'll get the birth certificate. I'll be right back."

Once she leaves, I feel Jack staring at me.

"What?" I ask him.

"It's just..." His gaze seems to fall on my mouth. "We do have some similar features. My hair's darker."

"It is. But your mother's hair is brown."

"True. I don't know how all that works." He clears his throat. "I'd like to take a DNA test, if you're okay with that."

"Sure," I say. "Dad?"

"Yeah, of course. It will at least be able to tell us if we're related. You're clearly not my uncle's son, and like Brendan said, Sean Murphy *is* a pretty common name."

"I just don't have any family other than my mom and grandmother, and we don't have any relationship with her. You seem like nice guys. It'd be cool to have some relatives."

I turn to my dad, relieved that he's calmer now. "We'd know, though, if there were another Sean Murphy in our immediate family, Dad."

"True. But he could still be a distant relative. If you want the test, Jack, I'll be happy to submit my blood."

"Me too," I agree.

Lauren whisks back into the room holding a paper. "Here—"

The door knocker.

"Excuse me," she says, still holding the birth certificate.

"This is tough on her," Jack says. "I hope her other son doesn't show up—"

Lauren returns from the foyer, and with her is...

Pat Lamone.

Who doesn't look much like Jack. His hair is mousy brown,

and his eyes are bluish-gray. There's a slight resemblance to Lauren, specifically the nose and lips, but his coloring clearly came from his father—one of three rapists.

Jesus. He has no idea.

Jack rises. "Who's this?"

"Apparently, Jack," Lauren says, "this is your brother."

Lauren's face has gone white, and she trembles. Jack takes her arm and leads her back to the couch. She sits, but Jack stays standing, glaring at Lamone.

"Jack, this isn't his fault," Lauren says softly.

Jack turns and regards his mother. Clearly she's his Achilles' heel. But she's also right. It's not Lamone's fault that he's the product of his mother's rape.

As much as Lamone grates on my nerves now that I know what he did to Diana Steel and the Pike sisters, I kind of feel sorry for him in this moment.

"What are you two doing here?" Lamone asks Dad and me.

"Looking for answers," Dad says. "Same as you. Lauren . . . the birth certificate?"

She hands it to Dad, who widens his eyes slightly. He hands it to me.

It's old and faded. Lauren was born fifty-four years ago. She looks good for her age. Mother is listed as Wendy Madigan.

And the father?

William Elijah Steel. Son of George Steel, half brother of Bradford Steel.

I'll be goddamned.

Pat Lamone *is* a Steel.

So is Lauren, and so is Jack. And if Jack is also related to us?

There's our link to the Steels.
And it all begins with Wendy Madigan.
Fuck it all to hell.

CHAPTER THIRTY-NINE

Ava

I pull into the long driveway leading to my parents' ranch house. I didn't call ahead of time. Normally, I would, but I need to see my mother. My father is probably at the winery, but even if he's here, I'm getting my mother alone.

Dad gave me his answers. Now it's Mom's turn.

I walk in without knocking, nearly bowling over the housekeeper.

"Miss Ava. I wasn't expecting you."

"I'm sorry, Michaela," I say. "Is my mother home?"

"She's in the library, I believe."

"And my father?"

"With her."

"Why are they— Oh, never mind. It doesn't matter. I'll find out myself." I whisk past her.

"Can I get you anything?"

"Yeah. Some lunch would be great."

"What—"

"Anything."

I promised Brendan, Brock—and myself—that I'd eat. So I'll eat whatever Michaela makes . . . while I listen to my mother's secrets.

And hope that I don't upchuck it all.

I tear open the door to the library.

"Ava!" Mom looks up from some documents laid out on the wooden table.

Dad sits beside her. "Sweet pea? What are you doing here?"

"I'm ready to hear the rest of our sordid family history," I say. "I've heard Dad's side, Mom. Now I want yours."

"Ava..."

"No excuses. I've been pulling my hair out, starving myself, over all this. I'm done. The tower is falling, and if I'm going to escape the rubble, I need to know the truth."

"The tower?" Dad asks.

"Her tarot card," Mom says.

"Yes. The fucking tower. I'm actually taking a break from the tarot, and do you want to know why?" I don't wait for an answer. "Because I'm tired of the negativity. I'm tired of questioning who I am. I'm just fucking tired, Mom, Dad. So get on with it. I'm descended from not one but two psychopaths. I want to know about my Greek side, Mom. I want to know about Theodore Mathias."

Dad clears his throat. "Ava, I thought long and hard before I told you about my birth mother. I decided it was time. But your mom—"

"It's okay, Ryan." Mom pats his hand. "She deserves to know the truth from both of us."

"Damned right I do, and so does Gina."

"Dad and I have decided not to tell Gina until after graduation. Let her finish her college career, Ava."

I draw in a breath. "All right. Why mess up the awesome foursome?"

"Ava..."

"I get it, Dad. We leave her in the dark for now. But after she graduates..."

"We'll tell her," Mom says.

"Good."

Mom clears her throat. "There's no easy way to start."

"Try the beginning, sweetie," Dad says.

"I've put a lot of it out of my mind," Mom says. "But I suppose it all begins with Gina."

"What's Gina got to do with this?"

"Not your sister," Mom says. "My cousin. Gina Cates."

"Right. You named Gina after her."

"I did. She meant a lot to me."

"I was your firstborn. Why didn't you name me after her?"

Mom sighs. "I thought about it, but it was all too fresh in my mind back then. I didn't want to be reminded of it every single day. By the time your sister came along, we had done a lot of healing, and I wanted to pay homage to my cousin."

I breathe in, confused. And hungry. "What does your cousin Gina have to do with all of this?"

"Gina was a patient of Aunt Melanie's," Mom goes on, "but now that I think about it, it actually began long before Gina. I didn't even know about Gina until I met my birth father. It began with your Grandma Didi."

"When you were born."

"Yes. My father, Theo Mathias, was a terrible man. Of course I didn't know any of this. Not until I was fifteen years old."

"But you lived with Grandma, right? They weren't married."

"No, they weren't. Grandma and I lived modestly, but we were happy. At least I thought we were. Then..." Mom's voice begins to shake. "God, it's all so buried beneath everything horrible."

"Easy, baby," Dad says. "We're not in any hurry."

I'm in a hurry, but I don't say anything. Mom opens her mouth again, but she's interrupted by a knock on the library door.

"Yes?" Dad says.

The door opens and Michaela enters. "I have Miss Ava's lunch."

"Thank you, Michaela." I take the tray from her and set it on the table. Then I close the door.

Funny. How can I be hungry and nauseated at the same time? But I am. I take the cover off the plate. A green salad with vinaigrette and a roast beef sandwich on my own sourdough bread. A plate of fruit and cheese plus a peanut-butter cookie rounds out the meal.

I don't have a sweet tooth by any means, but I grab the cookie first and take a bite. I've got to get something down before my mother continues her story.

"Grandma Didi was beautiful in her day," Mom says wistfully. "Her hair was brown but lighter than mine, fair skin, blue eyes. I look a lot like her."

I remember my grandmother's blue eyes. They were just like Mom's and mine. Though she was old and worn, I always considered her beautiful. She and I understood each other.

"I never looked anything like my father," Mom continues.

"Are you sure he was your father?" I can't help asking.

Mom widens her eyes.

"I mean . . . you know. Because Dad found out the woman he thought was his mother wasn't . . . and all."

"Believe me, Ava, I wish I didn't have to claim him, but

he was my father. He had olive skin from his Mediterranean roots, and his eyes and hair were dark."

I take another bite of the cookie. This one is drier.

A sigh whooshes out of Mom's mouth. "Anyway... my mother died when I was fourteen."

"What?" I drop the cookie back onto the plate.

Perhaps I shouldn't be surprised. Resurrection from the dead seems to happen a lot in this family.

Mom continues, "She didn't, as I found out later, but that's what I was told. I never saw a body. Who would show a fourteen-year-old girl her dead mother's body? She didn't have any family that I knew of or that anyone could find, so the court sent me to the man whose name was on my birth certificate. My father. Theodore Mathias."

I pick up the cookie, break off a piece, and hold it.

"I found out later that my father forced my mother to leave. He convinced her that he could give me a better life. She didn't believe him, but then he threatened both of our lives, and, according to Grandma, he meant it. Knowing what I know about him now, yes, he meant it."

I swallow. It doesn't help the nausea.

"My mother felt she had no choice. She figured the best thing to do was disappear and make me a ward of the state. She thought that would protect me." Mom shakes her head. "I never had the heart to tell her what actually happened. Not everything, anyway."

"You okay, baby?" Dad squeezes Mom's hand.

"I'm fine. I need to get this out as much as Ava needs to hear it."

I don't realize I'm squeezing what's left of the cookie until I see the crumbs on top of my salad. Peanut-butter-cookie salad. Great.

"You're aware of how your father and I met."

I nod.

"If not for my father and his mother, we wouldn't have met, and he and I have had a wonderful life together. We were blessed with you and Gina, and... That's how I've come to think of all of this, Ava. As a blessing in disguise. But when I tell you..."

"When you tell me what?"

"She's strong, Ruby," Dad says. "She can handle it. She handled my story with the strength of a thousand warriors."

I gulp. I'm not sure I do justice to Dad's words, but I nod. "I'm okay, Mom."

Mom nods and then meets my gaze, her blue eyes full of determination. "When I was fifteen, Ava, my father tried to rape me."

CHAPTER FORTY

Brendan

"What is that?" Lamone asks, eyeing the paper in my hand.

"It's . . ." Am I at liberty to say? He certainly has the right to know his heritage, but Lauren and Jack seem like nice people, and we're in their home.

Lauren takes the paper from me and hands it to Pat. "Here. This is your business. If you're wondering, you *are* a Steel. And you are my son. I gave you up after I had you."

Lamone's eyes grow wide. "So it's true. But who is William Steel?"

"As far as we know," Dad says, "he was the half brother of Brad Steel. His father was George Steel, Brad's father."

"Who was his mother?" Lamone asks.

"Not Mackenzie Steel, who was his wife," I say. "And we don't know. William was apparently the result of an extramarital affair between George Steel and another woman. Mackenzie Steel only had one child. She wasn't able to give George more children."

"How do you know all this?" Dad asks me.

"Dale told me the whole story. He asked his dad and his uncle."

"It's . . . nice to meet you," Pat says to Lauren. "I would

have come sooner, but I had a hard time tracking you down."

"My mother went out of her way to make sure you couldn't find me when you were younger. I'm sorry about that."

Pat nods. "Thank you ... you know. For giving me life and all that."

Lauren nods. "I'm sorry I couldn't keep you."

"I understand. I mean, I'm going to try to. But I need to know. Who is my father?"

I look to Dad.

He nods slightly and stands. "Brendan and I should be going." He pulls out his wallet and hands Jack a card. "My cell phone number is on there. Call me when you want Brendan and me to do the DNA tests."

Jack takes the card. "I will. Thanks. Both of you."

Once we're out of the house, I turn to Dad. "My God. I don't like Lamone, but damn. He's about to be told his father could be one of three men—and they're all rapists. No one deserves that."

CHAPTER FORTY-ONE

Ava

God. Those two bites of cookie were a bad idea.

"Ava," Dad says. "Are you okay?"

"How can you ask me that?" I gulp down the bile creeping up my throat as I push the plate of food across the table. "Mom…"

"It's okay," she says.

"Ruby…"

"Ryan, I'm fine. None of that is my life now, but she has to know. That's the only way she'll understand everything."

"But—"

"I don't know any other way to tell the story, Ryan."

And then she begins, and I listen.

And I learn more about my mother than I ever wanted to know.

★ ★ ★

"See you later," I said to my father, who was sitting at the kitchen table with a cup of coffee. I'd left him a plate of dinner that was currently heating in the microwave.

"Where are you off to?" The harsh fluorescent lighting in the kitchen illuminated his features—was he angry, or simply mistrustful?—in an eerie way.

"Just meeting a friend for a milkshake. I'll be home before dark."

I'd had dinner alone. Theo was rarely home for dinner, and I had learned to fend for myself while living with my mother. She had worked three jobs to keep us afloat, and I'd been doing my own cooking since I was eight years old. Real cooking because the processed meals were more expensive than buying actual meat and vegetables. I'd been shopping and cooking for what seemed like most of my life.

Since I was only fifteen, it had *been most of my life.*

I walked toward the door, but his footsteps followed, and he overtook me. He stood against the door. "You're not going anywhere tonight."

I'd only lived with my father for a couple of months. So far, he'd given me an allowance. More money than I'd ever seen. He'd been good to me. He'd helped me get acclimated to my new home, the community, and had helped me make friends in the neighborhood. I was planning to meet one of those friends tonight for a shake.

"Dad." The word fell from my lips in slow motion. It still didn't feel right. The man was still a virtual stranger to me. But he'd been trying. At least up until now. "Dana's expecting me. I won't be late." I reached for the doorknob.

"Not tonight, Ruby." He brushed my hand from the knob.

I looked up at him. His eyes were so dark, almost black. He was a handsome man, olive complexion and dark hair, but something sinister lurked in his gaze tonight.

Something I hadn't seen before.

Maybe I hadn't been looking.

I was in danger.

I turned to run back into the kitchen and toward the back

door, but he grabbed me by the arm and yanked me against his chest. Hard.

"What do you want? Why can't I go meet Dana?"

"Because I need you here tonight."

My heart thumped wildly. "Okay. What do you need?"

He yanked me over to the couch in the living room. "Take off your clothes."

★ ★ ★

"No, Mom. Stop. Please."

"I was wrong. She can't take this, Ruby," Dad soothes, "and neither can you."

"That's where you're wrong, Ryan." My mom inhales, steeling herself. "Have you forgotten how I grew up after that? How I was on my own for three years? Living on the streets and using a fake ID to get work?"

I drop my jaw. Mom lived on the streets? Did her father kick her out? Did—

"Ava has lived a sheltered life," Dad says.

This time anger pulses through me, and I pound my fist on the table, nearly sending the plates flying. "Because *you* sheltered me! You sheltered all of us! You didn't trust us with the truth of our history!"

"Put yourself in our shoes for a moment," Dad says. "Would you want to tell a child of yours—an innocent child— about the horrific past of our family?"

I swallow, regard my father.

His brown eyes are sunken and sad, but then—

I look at my mother.

Her blue eyes are on fire.

"Speak for yourself, Ryan," she chides. "Not everyone agreed it was best to stifle our past. Melanie and I wanted to tell them. Just bits and pieces as they could handle it. But no. You and Marjorie and your brothers wanted to bury it all. You thought it would all magically disappear. Life isn't like that. Life isn't one big Steel party!"

"Ruby, baby…"

Mom chokes back what may be a sob. Or it may just be anger. "I'm all in now. And my daughter is as strong as I was at that age, perhaps even stronger. I went out on my own because I had no choice. Ava had every resource available to her, and she went out and made a life for herself anyway. That's strength, Ryan." She turns to me. "Can you take it, Ava? The rest of my story?"

I see my mother's strength, then. Truly see it. I never doubted it. Always knew, as a cop, she had to be strong. But I never actually saw it in action—not with the defiant look she's giving Dad now.

And I know. I know I'm more like her than I ever realized.

"Yes, Mom. Yes. I can take it. Tell me your story. I want to know where I came from."

"Are you sure? Because I haven't told this story in nearly three decades, and I'm not about to mince words."

I nod, swallowing back the last of my nausea. No more. No more getting sick over the past. It's time to face it, deal with it, and learn from it.

"I'm sure."

★ ★ ★

I jolted backward. "What?"

"You heard me. Take off your clothes. You're beautiful. Let me see that body of yours."

I crossed my arms over my chest. "No. I won't."

I scrambled away, but he caught me again and then dragged me into his bedroom. I wrenched away, but he grabbed me and turned me around to face him.

"Come here. Show Daddy how much you love him." His grasp was firm. "Now take off those clothes."

"I won't!"

"Don't make this harder than it has to be."

"Are you crazy? I'm your daughter!"

"Makes no difference. Let me see that body."

I gathered every ounce of strength and ran toward the door, but again he caught me.

"You asked for it now." He punched me in the cheek, and a dull thud echoed in the room.

For a second, nothing happened, and then the pain hit. I cried out.

"Scream. Go ahead and scream. It's better that way," he said, an evil gleam in his eye.

I made a deal with myself at that moment. I would not scream again, no matter what he did to me.

"You're a slut, just like your slut mother. She wasn't good for anything but a fuck. A one-nighter that went wrong, and now I'm saddled with you."

My heart thrummed wildly as fear overtook me and self-preservation kicked in. "You don't have to be. I'll leave. I'll never bother you again." And I meant those words, for now I knew who and what my father truly was.

"Not yet. Not until I see what you have to offer. You're a pretty thing, with your mother's fair skin. My dark hair. And you don't mind showing off that tight little body in those belly tops and tight jeans you wear. What do you expect?"

"I don't expect my own father to rape me!"

He grabbed me and tossed me onto the bed. "Well, little daughter, rarely in this life do we get what we expect."

Acid bubbled in my stomach and meandered up my throat. I turned my head and retched, but nothing came up.

He punched me again.

"You throw up, and I'll make this worse."

As if in answer, I heaved again and vomited onto his bed.

"Bitch!" He punched me again and then shook me. Then he ripped my shirt off me.

I closed my eyes. Maybe I could escape into my mind. Think of something else.

But instead, without looking, I raised both my legs and pushed outward, kicking.

He flew across the room.

I opened my eyes in time to see him land with an oof.

I got up and ran for the door, but again he caught me, turning me.

I scrunched my eyes closed again and kneed him between his legs, hoping I had the strength I needed to incapacitate him.

"Auugh!" This time he yelled and crumpled to the floor. "Bitch. You fucking little slut!"

Thank God my purse was where I'd left it in the living room. I grabbed it and headed out the door in my bra and jeans, my own vomit coating one side of my body.

I ran as hard as I could with no idea where I was going.

Only that I was never going back to my father, no matter what I had to do.

★ ★ ★

Tears well in my eyes. Strength doesn't mean never hurting. Never crying.

My mother has always meant everything to me, but now? If possible, she means even more.

"What did you do, Mom? Did your father—ugh, my *grandfather*—go after you?"

She shakes her head. "No. He never wanted me in the first place. Not as a daughter, anyway. Once I found out what he was into, I'm damned glad I got away. Others weren't so lucky."

"Others like Dale and Donny? Uncle Talon."

She nods. "To name only a few."

"Oh, God . . . Cousin Gina."

"Yes, Ava, but we'll get to that."

I nod. "Where did you go? You weren't wearing any clothes, and you were . . ."

"Covered in vomit, yes." She closes her eyes. "Some of it I've truly blanked out. I made it to my friend Dana's, where I showered and she gave me some clothes. But her mother was ready to call my father, so I took off. It was summer when I left, and I lived on the streets for a few weeks. It wasn't that difficult. My mom and I had been pretty poor, and I'd been reduced to stealing to eat more than once. So this was nothing new, though I tried to avoid stealing as much as possible. I didn't want to be arrested and sent home. Once fall came, I knew I had to find other arrangements. I was afraid to go to social services, for fear they would send me back to him. So I got a job waiting tables, with the help of a fake ID I got from a guy I met on the streets—"

"How did you get it, if you didn't have any money?" I ask.

Mom looks down.

I don't ask again.

She clears her throat. "That was the only time. Then, within a few weeks, I had scraped together enough to move into this really shitty place on the wrong side of town. But I kept quiet, slid under the radar, and stayed safe for the next three years, until my eighteenth birthday. I went to the police department and filed a complaint against my father. Then I applied to the police academy."

"Wow."

"My happy ending didn't start there, though. I found out I had to be twenty-one and a high-school graduate to be accepted into the police academy. So I needed a new plan. I had worked my way up to night manager at the little diner where I waitressed, so I kept that job, moved into a slightly better place, got my GED, and waited another three years. During that time, the PD never did anything about my father. I contacted them every week for a while. Then I gave up."

"Wow," I say again.

"At that point, I didn't want to leave anything to chance, so I started working out voraciously. I was determined that in three years, I would be accepted at the academy and become the best police officer out there. I would put people like my father away."

"Did you ever put him away?" I ask.

"If only..." she says wistfully. "He was part of an elite group of criminals. They were backed by big money, and they were very good at what they did. They never left a trail. I never had probable cause to even have him arrested, let alone evidence that would stick through a trial and conviction. Not until the end, anyway, and by then it was too late."

"What was the relationship between Grandma Didi and him?"

"It was nonexistent. I didn't even know who he was until my mom left me with him." She clears her throat. "She never told me anything about my father. Always refused to talk about it when I asked. Then, when she disappeared, my birth certificate was pulled, and there was his name and birth date."

"So you never knew the story between them?"

"Nope. According to my father, it was a one-night stand that went wrong. After we were reunited, Grandma Didi still wouldn't talk about it, so I stopped asking."

God, so many questions. The nausea has been replaced with morbid curiosity. How did Grandma Didi resurface? Did my grandfather come after my mother?

But the questions have to wait, because my mother— usually so stoic and strong—bursts into tears.

CHAPTER FORTY-TWO

Brendan

Dad drops me off back at the bar, and I walk to the bakery to check on Ava . . . only to find her gone.

"What do you mean she left?" I demand of Luke. "Ava never leaves the bakery during the day."

"Surprised the hell out of me too," he says. "Brock showed up earlier, and after that, Ava said she was leaving after the lunch rush. When the lunch rush didn't happen, which was odd in itself, she left earlier."

"Unbelievable." I shake my head.

"Right?"

"Have you heard from her?"

"Nope. Maya and I have things under control, though. It'll be smooth sailing the rest of the day. And Maya says she can stay late to do the cleanup if Ava doesn't get back."

"Any idea where she went?"

"She said she needed to talk to her mom."

Ruby. She went home to the ranch. "All right. Thanks, Luke."

I leave the bakery quickly and head back to the bar. Everything's under control there, and I don't have to open until later, so I'm heading to Steel Acres.

Somewhere inside, I know Ava needs me.

And I'm going to be there.

CHAPTER FORTY-THREE

Ava

"Ava," Dad says. "You're going to need to give us a minute."

Mom wipes her eyes and shakes her head. "No, Ryan. Just no. I need to get this out, and she needs to hear it."

"It's in the past, sweetheart. None of it matters."

"It matters to me," I interrupt. "I'm sorry, Mom. So sorry that you've been through so much. This is my history too. Where I come from. The cards—"

"Please, Ava," Dad says. "You said earlier you were taking a break from the tarot."

"I am." I pause. "But I'm rethinking that stance because, frankly, what's happening here—first with my conversation with Dad and now this—only proves what the cards have been telling me this whole time. I'm going to question who I am."

"We've been through this," Dad says. "You haven't changed. You are still *you*."

"I understand that now," I say truthfully, "but this is all happening now for a reason. I need this information."

"Why?" Mom sniffles.

"I don't know the answer to that question," I tell her. "At least not yet. But I'm positive that I need to know. Not to figure out who I am, but to understand *why* I am."

They both look at me as though I have two heads. I don't

blame them. I'm not sure what I mean either. I know only that the cards—and my very existence—have led me to this moment. To find out *why* I am. Why my family is my family . . . and how they came to be the Steels.

I know the Steels—all of them—are good people. At least I want to believe that.

"Tell me," I say to Mom. "Tell me about your cousin Gina."

Mom sighs, sniffling, and blows her nose into a tissue. "I didn't know Gina very well. I only met her when I was taken to live with my father when I was fourteen. She was much younger, the daughter of my father's sister, Erica, and her husband at the time, Rodney Cates."

"How does she fit into all this, then?" I ask.

"This part of the story begins when my father—your grandfather, Theo Mathias—was in high school. It was a private school. Damn, I can't remember the name of it."

"Tejon Prep," Dad says, "in Grand Junction."

"Right. That's it. My father, along with Brad Steel, Wendy Madigan, and several others, including Rodney Cates, were members of something called the future lawmakers club."

My eyes widen. "You're kidding."

Mom shakes her head.

"There's a future lawmakers club at Snow Creek High School. At least there was six years ago when I was there."

"There is?"

"Yeah. It was for people who wanted to go into law enforcement or into law. I wonder if Donny was a member?"

"If he was, we'd know about the club," Mom says.

"Hmm. That's weird." Mental note—ask Donny and Callie about the future lawmakers club.

"It must be something different," Dad says.

"Probably," Mom agrees. "Anyway, the future lawmakers club was apparently not for future lawmakers at all. At least not at the time my father was involved. They were more into business ventures. Making money. And Brad Steel funded them."

Man. So both my grandfathers were members of this business club. Sounds okay on its face, but I know better than to take anything at face value. Something's coming.

"Brad Steel had plenty of money," Mom continues, "but the others didn't. They got greedy, and they wanted more. So they began bending the law."

"The future lawmakers *bent* the law?"

"Yes. The name of the club didn't have anything to do with what the club actually did. At least not by that time."

"They got into drugs," Dad adds. "And by the time our fathers graduated, they were still working together on business deals."

Mom swallows and nods. "Yes. My father and two of the others—Tom Simpson—"

"Simpson?" I ask.

"Yes. He was Uncle Bryce's father. And Larry Wade, who was the half brother of Daphne Steel."

"God. We're related to all of them?"

"In one way or another," Dad says. "Yeah. Is it making a little more sense to you now? Why we chose to bury this part of our family's past?"

I curl my hands into fists. "Don't go there again with me, Dad. Not now. I'm too far in. I have to know everything."

"She's right, Ryan. I thought so all those years ago, and I agree with her now. Melanie and I were right back then. We knew this would come back to haunt us."

"It didn't have to," Dad says.

"How could it not?" Mom raises both her hands. "It's our history. If we don't learn from it, we're doomed to repeat it."

"We would never repeat any of this," Dad says through clenched teeth.

"That's not what I mean, and you know it. But our children deserve to know where they come from. Even if it's not pretty, and it's not."

"I suppose I should buckle up," I say.

"Absolutely," Mom says. "Let me tell you about Gina. But first, I need to tell you about what my father"—she winces—"and his friends Tom and Larry got into."

A feeling of dread enshrouds me.

Already, I know what's coming.

"Their greed got the best of them, turned them. Not that there was much good in them to begin with. I think they all must have had sociopathic tendencies before high school. That's what Aunt Mel says, anyway."

"She should know," I say.

"Right." Mom clears her throat. "They began their business legally. Brad Steel funded them, and they bought up products at wholesale and sold them retail. They specialized in hard-to-find toys for a while, but they soon found if they started bending the law, they could make a lot more money. So they turned to drugs."

I nod. The nausea is still gone. I'm ready for anything now.

"They were smart, and with your Grandfather Steel's money backing them and Wendy Madigan's brain power, they got away with everything." She clears her throat again. "Still, their greed got the best of them, and they found something that was more lucrative than drugs."

"Do I want to know?" I ask.

Though I already know.

"People," Mom says. "They got involved in human trafficking."

"Uncle Talon," I say. "Dale and Donny."

"Were all victims, yes. But that was later."

"So... Gina?"

"Gina became a patient of Aunt Melanie's about a year before Aunt Melanie met Uncle Joe."

"She did?"

"Yes. Aunt Mel and I both encountered the Steel family through sheer circumstance. She was Uncle Talon's therapist, and I was a uniformed officer who spoke to Aunt Melanie after Gina committed suicide."

"Why would she—"

"Let me finish, Ava. Please. This is difficult."

I nod.

"I got away from my father that day, Ava, but Gina didn't." One more throat clear. "Gina was raped repeatedly by my father, beginning at age eight."

I really thought I'd heard it all. That the nausea was gone.

I was wrong.

I swallow. Then swallow again. Slide my hand over my mouth.

"My father and the two others were groomers. They participated in the training of women and children to be sold as human slaves."

"And he—" I slide my hand back over my mouth.

"Once I escaped him, my father turned to Gina. She was never sold into trafficking—at least not at that time—but participating in this brutality made my father and the two others even sicker than they were. They became true psychopaths and abused men, women, and children whenever they wanted. Tom Simpson, Uncle Bryce's father, turned out to be the worst of the three. He lived a double life for many years. He was even the mayor of Snow Creek for a while. Not to discount what my father did. He was evil. Demonic, even. He was the smartest of the three, he went by many aliases, and he was the last one to get caught. Actually, he never got caught. He was killed by Wendy Madigan. But I'm getting ahead of myself."

"Right." I swallow again. "Gina."

"Gina, as an adult, sought psychiatric treatment with Aunt Melanie. Aunt Mel thought they were making progress, but she ended up getting a letter from Gina. It was a suicide letter. Aunt Mel almost gave up being a therapist because she thought she'd missed something."

"What did she miss?"

"She missed that Gina was suicidal."

"But Aunt Mel specializes in childhood trauma."

"Exactly. And she's the best at what she does, so eventuall—"

"Gina didn't commit suicide," I say.

"No, she didn't. She was taken as an adult. Taken and sold into the trafficking ring. I tried so hard to find her." Mom chokes back a sob. "But she had died by the time we broke it up."

"Mom... Oh my God..."

Mom sniffles. "I was devastated, of course. By then I'd met your father, and the two of us had fallen in love. So there was a happy ending. For Dad and me. For Uncle Talon and Aunt Jade. For Uncle Joe and Aunt Mel. For Uncle Bryce and Aunt Marj. And my father and the other two, Tom Simpson and

Larry Wade, were dead by that point as well. And so was—we thought at the time—Wendy Madigan."

"My God, Mom. How? How have you led such a normal life after ... After what he tried to do to you?"

"I wouldn't say I lived a normal life. I lived on the streets, and I was scared to death of men for many years. I didn't wear makeup, didn't wear clothes that showed my body. Nothing that might attract a man. Ask your father. When he met me, I pulled my hair back tight and wore mostly masculine clothing and sensible shoes."

Dad touches her hair. "You were still beautiful."

"I didn't want to be. Not until you, Ryan."

Love passes between them. Pure love.

And that's the beauty that comes from the horrific past. Love. As inane as it sounds, love does conquer all.

"My father was a horrible man," Mom says. "A true psychopath, and I wish I didn't share his genes. I wish I didn't pass them to you and Gina. But in the end—the very end—he saved my life. And he gave my mother back to me."

"What?"

"That day. The day I shot Wendy. We all thought she died. When she shot my father, he told me Gina was dead, but he pushed a piece of paper into my hand. The paper had a name on it. Diamond Thornbush—my mother—and an address.

"We drove to a trailer park on the outskirts of Grand Junction. I was frantic. Would she be there? Was this one last hoax by my father? I had no way of knowing, but we had to check it out. We drove up in Ryan's pickup. The yard was well-kept, and a plastic lawn chair sat outside. The stoop built of rickety wood creaked as I walked up to the door and knocked."

Mom's voice becomes hypnotic, and again, I see the events as she tells them.

★ ★ ★

The door opened, and a woman stood there in capri pants and a worn T-shirt.

A woman I recognized, though her hair was silvery white now, and a few lines marred her pretty face.

"Mom," was all I said.

Her blue eyes—the same color as my own—widened. "I think I'm seeing a ghost."

"It's me. It's Ruby."

"It can't be. He told me you were . . ."

"I'm here."

"Your father forced me to leave. He said he could give you a better life. He said . . . I didn't believe him, but he threatened both of our lives, and he meant it. I figured the best thing for me to do was disappear and make you a ward of the state. I thought they'd protect you. God, I've always regretted that day! How could I give up my baby?" She grabbed me into a hug.

I inhaled. She still smelled the same. Like honeydew melon.

"I'm sorry I didn't look for you. I was told you were dead."

"Sweetie, it's okay. Did they protect you? Did you have a good life?"

I couldn't bear to lie to her. At least not yet. "I've had a good life. And it's about to get better." I motioned to Ryan. "This is my fiancé, Ryan Steel."

"Ms. Thornbush," he said. "It's good to meet you."

"Honey, call me Diamond. Or Didi. Or Mom. Whatever you want."

"Mom sounds good." Ryan smiled that killer smile of his.

★ ★ ★

"That's right," I say. "You called her Mom."

"I didn't have a mother of my own," Dad says. "Daphne wasn't my mother, and Wendy was dead, or so we thought. I never would have called her Mom anyway. Didi was Mom to me until she passed away."

Mom rises. "I have something for you." She leaves and returns a few moments later carrying a satin bag. She opens it and pulls out three delicate gold bangle bracelets. "Grandma Didi gave these to me. She said they were for an old soul like herself, and that I'd know the right moment to give them to you."

I take the bracelets from my mother, caress their beauty. "They were Grandma's?"

"Yes. The only thing of value she owned, and no matter how bad things got, she never sold them."

"So they're real gold, then?"

"They are, but they wouldn't have fed us for long. They aren't that valuable."

I continue to stroke them and then slip them onto my left wrist. "They are to me."

The gold burns against my flesh, but in a good way. Grandma Didi's strength, Mom's strength—my own strength—pulses through me.

Mom and Dad say no more.

Is this the end? Truly the end?

Do I know everything now?

The image of the tower invades my mind. The fire, the falling rubble.

No.

I don't yet know everything.

But I'm stronger. I have the strength of my mother and grandmother and the women who came before them.

And I'll survive.

CHAPTER FORTY-FOUR

Brendan

I ring the doorbell at Ryan and Ruby Steel's house.

Their housekeeper, Michaela, opens the door. "Hello, Brendan."

"Is Ava here?"

"Yes. Won't you come in?"

"Thank you."

"She's in the library with Mr. and Mrs. Steel. I'll let her know you're here."

Michaela disappears down a hallway. I shove my hands into my jeans pockets and wait in the foyer. I can't stop thinking about Lauren Wingdam, her son Jack—who may be a distant cousin of mine—and Pat Lamone and the circumstances of his conception.

Did Lauren tell him? I never thought I'd feel sorry for the guy, but damn . . .

Ryan Steel strides toward me. "Brendan." He holds out his hand.

I shake it firmly. "I came to see Ava. I heard she left the bakery in the middle of the day, and I was worried."

"She's with her mother."

"May I see her?"

"That's up to her. She and Ruby need a few moments, though."

"All right. I'll wait."

Ryan simply nods.

"What's going on?" I finally ask.

"Reality has hit Ava hard the past few days. I gave her some information about my heritage, and Ruby just enlightened her about her own."

"I take it that it's not pretty."

"Far from it. I assume she told you about our conversation?"

I nod. "She did. I suppose I should tell you what I found out this morning." I quickly relay what Dad and I learned during our visit with Lauren Wingdam.

"God..." Ryan rubs his forehead. "I can't... No. My mother wouldn't do that to her own child."

"What do you mean? You don't think that Wendy orchestrated Lauren's rape..."

"One thing my mother was a fanatic about was her children. She protected me at the cost of my brother. And now I have this sister who I've never met. Who apparently isn't just a sister but a cousin as well. My God, Brendan. You must think our family are monsters."

"No. I don't think that."

"How can you not?"

"You're not them, Ryan. You had no choice in who your mother was or who your father was."

"I know. It took me a while to get to that point, but I did. That's a huge reason why we chose to keep all this from Ava, her sister, and her cousins. We wanted to forget. We wanted to have a normal family. But it wasn't in the cards."

"Ava would appreciate that sentiment."

"I'm not talking about the tarot."

"I know you're not, but she'd see it that way."

He smiles weakly. "She would. You know her well."

"I do." I clear my throat. "I'm in love with her, Ryan. I'd like to have a life with her. A family. Children."

"She's still very young."

"She is, and I respect that."

"After what she's learned about her heritage, she may not want children."

"It didn't stop you and Ruby."

He shakes his head. "No, it didn't. We wanted to share our love and our good fortune with children. And we got lucky. Ava and Gina are both wonderful. So smart and talented."

"Yes, they are."

"But Ava..."

"Is her own person, for sure. She and I haven't discussed children. Or even marriage. But she does share my feelings, Ryan."

"I know she does."

"You do?"

"Of course. I'm her father. I see the way her face lights up when you're around, or when she talks about you."

I try not to beam too brightly.

Ryan rakes his fingers through his slightly gray hair. "When you mentioned three rapists, I couldn't help thinking... But my mother wouldn't do that to her own child."

"You're going to have to tell me what you're talking about here. I'm lost."

"It's another dark part of Steel history. My mother—not my mother. After all these years, I still do that. *Daphne's* half brother, Larry Wade, Ruby's father, and Bryce's father worked together for decades in..."

"Human trafficking," I say. "I know."

"Right." He nods. "Anyway, the three of them often... Please don't make me spell it out for you."

"They worked together. I see."

"Yes. They assaulted Daphne when she was a teenager. And Talon. And who knows who else."

My bowels cramp up. God. Just the thought...

"But they couldn't have harmed Lauren. My mother would have never allowed harm to fall on her own child."

"Are you sure about that?"

He nods with confidence. "Yes."

"She was obsessed with your father, though. Right?"

"She was."

"When she couldn't have him, she clearly went to his half brother, who we still know nothing about. Perhaps she didn't feel the same way about William's child as she felt about Brad's child."

"No, I can't imagine—"

"This is a psychopathic woman, Ryan. Not a normal protective mother."

"God." Ryan grimaces. "I have to say it was the first thought that crossed my mind when you told me it was three men. And Pat Lamone is what? Twenty-eight?"

"Twenty-seven, I think. One year younger than Rory Pike."

"The timing works. The three of them were still alive... and still engaging in sickening acts."

Ruby and Ava arrive, both red-nosed with swollen eyes and tear-stained cheeks.

"Brendan, what are you doing here?" Ava asks.

"I was concerned when Luke told me you left the bakery."

"I'm okay." She sniffles and walks into my arms. "I'm glad you're here."

I kiss the top of her pink head. "Me too. What do you need?"

She pulls back, meets my gaze. "I'll be all right. I'm still me."

"You are." I brush my lips across hers, not caring that her parents are watching us. "Nothing will ever change that."

"I have a lot to tell you, but first I need to talk to Donny and Callie."

"What about?"

"Something called the future lawmakers club at Snow Creek High School."

"Doesn't ring a bell with me," I say.

"Me neither, but apparently it was a club that both my grandfathers and my biological grandmother were a part of, and it may still exist. Donny and Callie may remember it since they were both interested in law."

"Okay. I'll take you back to town."

"It's okay. I have my car."

"Why don't we just have Donny come over here?" Ryan says. "I'll give him a call. It's almost dinnertime. You two can stay, and—"

"I can't stay, Ryan. I have to open the bar."

Ava smiles. "I'll stay. You go ahead back to town. I'm okay. I'll see you later tonight."

"Promise?" I trail a finger over her cheek.

"Promise. I'll text you when I get back to my place."

"Okay. I love you."

"I love you too."

CHAPTER FORTY-FIVE

Ava

Donny and Callie are hardly in the door when I pounce.

"I need to know everything you know about the future lawmakers club at Snow Creek High School."

Donny takes Callie's jacket from her and hangs it on the coatrack in the entryway. "Good evening to you too, cuz."

Michaela takes Donny's blazer once he removes it.

"Goodness, Ava," Mom says. "Let them get inside the house first."

I can't help myself. I'm starved for information. I've finally got a lot of the story behind my ancestors, and though it's nausea-inducing, I'm determined to find out everything.

"Don, Callie, what do you want to drink?" Dad asks.

"Just Diet Coke or water for me," Callie says. "Thanks."

"Water's good." Donny follows Mom into the kitchen and then the family room. "Something smells good."

"Michaela made rigatoni." Dad takes his place behind the bar. He pulls a can of Diet Coke out of the refrigerator for Callie and a bottle of water for Donny. Then he pours a glass of one of his reds for himself. "Ava, Ruby? Anything to drink?"

"I'll have some of the Ruby," Mom says, smiling at the mention of her namesake wine.

"Just water for me, thanks." I take a seat next to Donny and

Callie on the leather couch. "So . . . the future lawmakers . . ."

"Sounds like something from the past," Donny says.

"How much do you know?" I ask him.

"I know a lot, unfortunately."

Yes, he does. But I can't go there. The thought of what happened to him and Dale, to Uncle Talon . . .

"I can answer your question," Callie says. "The future lawmakers club didn't exist when Dale and Donny were in high school. But they did when Rory and I were there. It was a newer club, and I went to a meeting."

I drop my jaw and look to Donny.

"Callie and I don't have any secrets," he says.

"So you and she both know . . ."

"About the future lawmakers of the past? Yeah, we do."

"It was called the FLMC for short. I don't know who started the club when I was in school." Callie takes a sip of Diet Coke. "But as I've always been interested in law, I went to a meeting once."

"And . . . ?"

She takes another sip. "There was no discussion about the law or making law at all. It was all about"—air quotes—"*sticking it to the man*."

"What's that mean?" I ask. "I mean, I know what it means. But what did it mean with regard to the club?"

"I don't know," Callie says. "I didn't stick around long enough to find out. Soon after that, the club became invite only."

"Oh?" I lift my eyebrows.

"Yeah, but anyone could get an invite. The FLMC members soon established themselves as troublemakers. They took credit for a lot of the crap that went on at school. When

Rory and I decided to try to figure out who had spiked the punch at the homecoming bonfire her senior year, the FLMC was where I was going to start investigating."

"What did you find?"

"Nothing, because I never got that far. I ended up overhearing Pat Lamone and Jimmy Dawson bragging about it, so I had my answer."

"Do you know anything else about the club?" I ask. "Was Pat Lamone a member?"

"Honestly, I have no idea. I don't even know if the club still exists."

"The question," Donny says, "is whether the reincarnation of the club had anything to do with the club our grandfather belonged to. And I sure hope not."

"I hope not as well," I say, "but with everything else that seems to be reappearing..."

"So Brock told you."

"He did. It made me sick. A lot of things have made me sick lately. It's getting easier to stomach each time I learn something new... which in itself is disturbing."

"I know. I hear you, Ava."

"You know about... Wendy?" I ask.

Donny nods. "Yes."

"So you know I'm not a full-blood Steel."

Donny frowns slightly. "You're more of a full-blood Steel than I am."

"I didn't mean—"

Donny nods, though he doesn't smile. "I know you didn't. Blood doesn't matter. Dale and I were fathered by a man who sold us into slavery for five thousand dollars."

I drop my jaw.

"I guess you don't know everything," Donny says.

"Donny, go easy on her," Callie says. "This is difficult for all of us."

"I know. I'm only saying that blood doesn't matter. Our ancestors don't matter. What matters is who we are. Who we want to be."

I nod, swallowing. "I'm so sorry for everything you and Dale have been through."

"It's ancient history, Ava. It sucked. I won't lie. But it was so long ago, and we've had amazing lives here on the ranch."

"I know. So have I."

"So our true parentage doesn't matter. We've all got major skeletons in the closet."

I take a drink of water. "How can we find out what this FLMC is up to now?"

"I don't even know if they still exist," Callie says. "I graduated eight years ago."

"Our family doesn't have anyone at that school anymore," Donny says.

"True. Maybe it's nothing."

But even as I say the words, I don't believe them. The FLMC, whether they're related to the original or not, are still around.

The question is what they're up to, and whether it's good or bad.

CHAPTER FORTY-SIX

Brendan

The bar is busy for a weeknight, and hours pass before I remember to check my phone. Hmm. No text from Ava yet. I text her quickly and stuff my phone back into my pocket . . . just in time to see Pat Lamone walk into the bar.

Lord.

Did his mother tell him?

It's not my problem, but man . . .

He walks to the bar and takes an empty seat right in front of me.

"What can I get you, Lamone?"

"Answers," he says.

"Look, I'm sorry about your birth mother, and—"

"I can't talk about that." His tone is robotic. "Not yet."

"So she told you."

He nods.

"What can I get you?" I ask again.

"Scotch. Neat."

I pour his drink and slide it in front of him.

He downs it in one gulp and slides it back to me. "Another."

I pour another, set it in front of him. "If you have another after that one, I'm taking your keys."

"No problem. I walked over here."

"You still living at Mrs. Mayer's place?"

He nods, downs the second drink.

I don't want to get into his life any more than I already am, but I'm a bartender. This is what I do.

"Spill it," I say. "Tell me what's on your mind."

"My grandmother," he says.

"Dyane Wingdam. Also known as Wendy Madigan."

"Yeah. I went to see her tonight. At the hospital in Grand Junction."

"I see."

"I wanted answers. I needed answers. Answers my birth mother couldn't give me. Answers about my grandfather. The man who made me a Steel."

"I understand, but how did you expect to get answers from a comatose woman?"

"I don't know, but my trip turned out to be in vain."

Now my curiosity is piqued.

"What's that supposed to mean?"

"It means . . . the very day that I meet my birth mother and learn the circumstances of my birth . . . my grandmother . . ." He stares at his drink, picks it up, swirls the scotch in the glass.

"For God's sake, Lamone, what? What are you trying to say?"

"She's gone. Her hospital bed was empty." He slides the glass toward me once more. "Another."

CONTINUE THE STEEL BROTHERS SAGA

WITH BOOK TWENTY–SEVEN

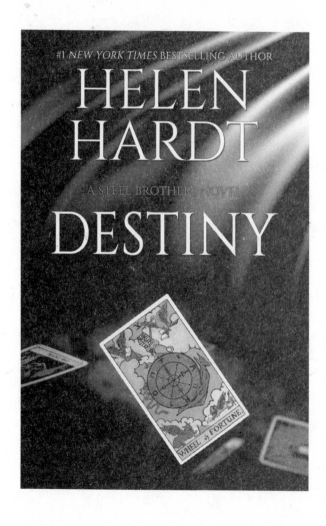

MESSAGE FROM HELEN HARDT

Dear Reader,

Thank you for reading *Fortune*. If you want to find out about my current backlist and future releases, please like my Facebook page and join my mailing list. I often do giveaways. If you're a fan and would like to join my street team to help spread the word about my books, please see the web addresses below. I regularly do awesome giveaways for my street team members.

If you enjoyed the story, please take the time to leave a review on a site like Amazon or Goodreads. I welcome all feedback. I wish you all the best!

Helen

Facebook
Facebook.com/HelenHardt

Newsletter
HelenHardt.com/SignUp

Street Team
Facebook.com/Groups/HardtAndSoul

ALSO BY HELEN HARDT

The Steel Brothers Saga:
Craving
Obsession
Possession
Melt
Burn
Surrender
Shattered
Twisted
Unraveled
Breathless
Ravenous
Insatiable
Fate
Legacy
Descent
Awakened
Cherished
Freed
Spark
Flame
Blaze
Smolder
Flare
Scorch
Chance
Fortune
Destiny
Melody
Harmony
Rhythm

Blood Bond Saga:
Unchained
Unhinged
Undaunted
Unmasked
Undefeated

ACKNOWLEDGMENTS

I loved writing *Fortune*. It was fun to go back in time and remember all chaos from twenty-five years ago in the Steel universe. We answered some questions, and many more will be answered in *Destiny* as Brendan and Ava hit a rough patch and Ryan, Ruby, and the rest of the Steels deal with the fallout of decisions made long ago.

Huge thanks to the always brilliant team at Waterhouse Press: Audrey Bobak, Haley Boudreaux, Jesse Kench, Jon Mac, Amber Maxwell, Michele Hamner Moore, Chrissie Saunders, Scott Saunders, Kurt Vachon, and Meredith Wild.

Thanks also to the women and men of Hardt and Soul. Your endless and unwavering support keeps me going.

To my family and friends, thank you for your encouragement. Special shout out to Dean—aka Mr. Hardt—and to our amazing sons, Eric and Grant. Special thanks to Eric for giving *Fortune* a much-needed edit before I handed it in to Scott at Waterhouse.

Thank you most of all to my readers. Without you, none of this would be possible. I am grateful every day that I'm able to do what I love—write stories for you!

Destiny is coming soon!